50
WORLD'S GREATEST STORIES

50 WORLD'S GREATEST STORIES

Published by
Rupa Publications India Pvt. Ltd 2024
7/16, Ansari Road, Daryaganj
New Delhi 110002

Sales centres:
Bengaluru Chennai
Hyderabad Jaipur Kathmandu
Kolkata Mumbai Prayagraj

Edition copyright © Rupa Publications India Pvt. Ltd 2024

All rights reserved.

No part of this publication may be reproduced, transmitted, or stored in a retrieval system, in any form or by any means, electronic, mechanical, photocopying, recording or otherwise, without the prior permission of the publisher.

P-ISBN: 978-93-6156-560-1
E-ISBN: 978-93-6156-116-0

First impression 2024

10 9 8 7 6 5 4 3 2 1

Printed in India

This book is sold subject to the condition that it shall not, by way of trade or otherwise, be lent, resold, hired out, or otherwise circulated, without the publisher's prior consent, in any form of binding or cover other than that in which it is published.

CONTENTS

1. Queer Quest — 1
   William Mackay

2. Lord Lundy's Snuff-Box — 7
   William Mackay

3. 'One Was Rent and Left to Die' — 13
   William Mackay

4. Res Est Sacra Miser — 19
   William Mackay

5. Mr Grey — 25
   William Mackay

6. The Prodigal's Return — 30
   William Mackay

7. A Philanthropic 'Masher' — 36
   William Mackay

8. A Dishonoured Bill — 41
   William Mackay

9. A Man of Genius — 46
   William Mackay

10. A Dignified Dipsomaniac — 52
    William Mackay

11. The Little Match Girl — 57
    Hans Christian Andersen

12.	The Story of an Hour *Kate Chopin*	61
13.	Regret *Kate Chopin*	65
14.	The Cactus *O. Henry*	70
15.	The Cat *Mary E. Wilkins Freeman*	75
16.	The Lady, or the Tiger? *Frank R. Stockton*	84
17.	The Night Came Slowly *Kate Chopin*	93
18.	The Romance of a Busy Broker *O. Henry*	95
19.	Transients in Arcadia *O. Henry*	100
20.	The Voice of the City *O. Henry*	107
21.	Vanka *Anton Chekhov*	113
22.	A Defenseless Creature *Anton Chekhov*	119
23.	The Death of a Government Clerk *Anton Chekhov*	126
24.	A Pair of Silk Stockings *Kate Chopin*	130

25. The Caline 136
    Kate Chopin

26. A Dead Woman's Secrets 139
    Guy de Maupassant

27. A Family 144
    Guy de Maupassant

28. The Beggar 150
    Guy de Maupassant

29. The Blind Man 157
    Guy de Maupassant

30. The Open Window 162
    Saki

31. The Dreamer 167
    Saki

32. The Wolves of Cernogatz 173
    Saki

33. The Imp of the Perverse 179
    Edgar Allan Poe

34. The Masque of the Red Death 187
    Edgar Allan Poe

35. Jim Baker's Blue-Jay Yarn 195
    Mark Twain

36. Punch, Brothers, Punch! 201
    Mark Twain

37. The Story of the Bad Little Boy 208
    Mark Twain

38. The Story of the Good Little Boy 213
    Mark Twain

39. Teddy Martin's Brief 219
    William Mackay

40. Bluebeard's Cupboard 225
    William Mackay

41. The Devil's Playthings 231
    William Mackay

42. Love and a Diary 239
    William Mackay

43. Miss Brill 246
    Katherine Mansfield

44. The District Doctor 252
    Ivan Turgenev

45. How a Muzhik Fed Two Officials 264
    M.Y. Saltykov

46. The Servant 274
    S.T. Semyonov

47. An Ominous Baby 282
    Stephen Crane

48. A Great Mistake 286
    Stephen Crane

49. An Eloquence of Grief 289
    Stephen Crane

50. A Detail 292
    Stephen Crane

1

QUEER QUEST

William Mackay

In the *Times* newspaper of Monday, 1st July, 18–, there appeared a notice of Mr White's last novel. The notice—for one cannot dignify with the name of review an article which did not exceed a quarter of a column—contained the following sentence:—

> 'Mr White's novels appear to us to lack but one element. Having achieved that one thing needful, Mr White at once and without cavil takes his place in the first rank of modern novelists. In one word, Mr White must learn to study Human Nature from the life. His characters are too often evolved from his inner consciousness, and as beings thus produced are apt to be wanting in backbone, it is not surprising that many of this popular author's works are weak and flabby—shadows without substance—pictures without colour. If Mr White were to give one-half of the time to the study of the men and women by whom he is surrounded, which he gives to the elaboration of plot and the cultivation of style, we do not know that there is any seat in the republic of letters which we would deny him.'

Mr White was a timid gentleman, with thin reddish hair—a very tall forehead and weak eyes. He was also a very well tailored man, and lived in a neatly-appointed villa, in the Hilgrove Road, St John's Wood, N.W. He was married, but had no children. He was by profession a briefless barrister, but he made his name by writing novels. It so happened that the public applauded Mr White from the very first moment that he appealed to them—at least in book form: his tentative efforts in periodicals having fallen very short of creating a *furor*. *His* nonsense, which, it must be confessed, was not of a very rollicking description, suited *their* nonsense. And that was the whole secret of his success. Being a very industrious man, he wrote a great many fictions, and being modest withal, attributed his fame to hard work rather than to any endowment of genius.

When Mr White neglected his grilled bone, his buttered toast, his hot coffee, and his new-laid egg, and seemed spellbound by what appeared in the *Times* newspaper, his wife instinctively knew that there was a notice of her husband's book in that great organ, and she guessed by the twitching of his mouth, and the flushing of his face, that the notice was the reverse of favourable.

'It is quite true. It is quite true,' said Mr White, aloud, but to himself, as he laid the paper down.

'What is quite true?' asked Mrs White, who, while greatly appreciating the pecuniary results of her husband's labour, had but little sympathy with the work itself.

'I am all wrong,' he replied, grimly.

'Good gracious! What is the matter with you?'

'I am wanting in backbone,' he explained, gloomily—'criminally deficient in backbone.'

'Why, John, you must be mad,' said the wife of his bosom. And, indeed, there was a seeming irrelevancy in his remarks, which favoured his helpmate's theory. But John knew quite well what *he* was about.

'Tell Edward to fetch my coat and hat,' he said, having trifled with his breakfast instead of eating it like a Briton; 'and lend me your scissors.'

The dutiful young woman handed her lord and master the scissors, with which he proceeded to cut out the *Times* review—the which, when carefully abstracted, he placed in his pocket-book. But before Edward came with his coat and hat, Mrs White, with natural and justifiable curiosity asked,—

'Where are you going so early, John?'

'I am going,' said John, quoting from the article, 'I am going among the men and women by whom I am surrounded. I am going to study human character from the life.'

Mrs White shrugged her little shoulders, elevated her little eyebrows, kissed her husband, and when she heard the hall-door close behind him, she said very quietly, as though she were making an observation which did not affect her even remotely,—

'He doesn't seem to study *me* very much.'

John White's great crony was Anthony Lomax, of Paper Buildings. And John White took a ticket to the Temple Station, being determined to consult his old friend on this new revelation which the great *Times* newspaper had opened up to him. He was fortunate in finding Mr Lomax at home, devouring a frugal meal of brandy and soda, preparatory to appearing before Vice-Chancellor Bacon in the celebrated case of Breeks v. Woolfer.

'You see,' said John White, with characteristic modesty, 'you see I never thought of achieving a first rank. My books take well and I make money—thank heaven. But this fellow in the newspaper absolutely says that I am possessed of genius!'

'And haven't *I* always said it?' asked Tony, with an offended air; 'haven't we all always said it?'

'Yes; but you are friends, don't you know?'

'Not a bit. Do I ever tell Jones that he has genius? Do I ever tell Sandford that he has genius—although he *is* a Fellow of Merton? Did I ever tell Barlow that his works would set the Thames on fire? Never! Friendship in my case never interferes with strict impartiality.'

This pleased Mr White. He absolutely blushed with pleasure. A kind word from Lomax was more real satisfaction to him than a page of praise from the *Sultry Review*—which is not, perhaps, rating the eulogy of Mr Lomax very highly.

'And are they right about the—the want of backbone?' he inquired, nervously, 'and the necessity to study character from the life?'

'As right as nine-pence, my boy. Doctors analyse dead bodies, and pull live ones about. Artists draw, I am told, from the nude. Actors imitate particular individuals. Yes, I think the *Times* rascal is absolutely right.'

'Then I shall commence and study from the life at once. But where now,' he asked plaintively, 'where would you advise me to commence? You don't know of any very likely place for the acquirement of the backbone?'

'Well, my boy, there's Breeks and Woolfer; if you'll step over to the Vice-Chancellor's Court—it's quite full of character.'

But the novelist only shuddered at the mention of the case, and saying gently that he thought he would take his own course, bade his friend 'Good-bye,' and departed much disturbed in his mind at the magnitude and amount of the task the censor of Printing-house Square had set for him.

Three months and a couple of weeks had passed away. It was

now the 15th of October, 18–, and Tony Lomax once more sat in his chambers. He had been away for his holidays, and had just returned, brown and invigorated, and ready to grapple with and subdue that insatiable monster, 'Breeks and Woolfer.' He was sitting with his legs stretched well under his table, his coat was off notwithstanding the chilliness of the weather, and his white shirt-sleeves were rolled up to his elbows. He looked the picture of rude health and high animal spirits.

A feeble knock on the panel of his door. A loud and cheery 'Come in' from Tony. The door opened, and Mr White entered, glanced nervously round, and gliding up to Lomax, said in a whisper,—

'Are we alone?'

Lomax could hardly believe his eyes. The dapper little friend of his youth had grown prematurely old. His thin red hair was no longer neatly arranged. His weak eyes had a wild and nervous shifting. His hands moved convulsively. His lips were dry, and his throat—to judge from his voice—parched.

'What in heaven's name—!' exclaimed Lomax, starting from his seat.

'Hush,' said the other, in extreme agitation, 'don't speak so loudly. *They might hear you.*'

'Who might hear me?'

'The human characters—from the life—don't you know. I have plenty of backbone now—too much, Tony. It's very awful!'

Lomax saw how it was, attempted to calm him, and induced him to take a seat, and to release his hat from his trembling fingers. Then he said, with something of a tremor in his voice,—

'Now, old man, tell us all about it.'

John White looked nervously about the room, again asked whether they were quite alone, and commenced, in a husky whisper, to tell his narrative, with awful rapidity.

'It was all right at first, Tony, and I made some capital notes, but in a few days I tired. All the human characters seemed so much alike when studied in the life. So brutally alike. It pained me. The monotony of it made me giddy. But then the worst came, Tony. Whenever I went out to study a character—from the life—the character began to study me. I tried to brave it and bear up against it, because you know, Tony, the *Times* said I had genius and only wanted backbone. But just fancy to yourself setting out to study murderers and thieves, and all sorts and conditions of unmentionable men, and the murderers and thieves and unmentionables—from the life—turning round and studying you! What do you think of that? Study *you*—d'ye hear?—from the life! Ay, and follow you, too—to your club, to your home:—to your very bed!'

The trembling hands searched for the hat. Mr White had jumped from his chair, and uttered a wild shriek, that sounded like '*Here they are—from the life*,' and had fled out on to the pavement of Paper Buildings.

Poor White died at Hanwell just two years ago—and Lomax married his widow. She, poor creature, finds in her new husband a practical person, whom she can understand, and seems all the happier for the change.

2

LORD LUNDY'S SNUFF-BOX

William Mackay

'Not another farthing, Tom. Not another farthing.'

'But my dear father—'

'But me no buts, Tom, as the man says in the playbook. You have an ample allowance. I never object to a hundred or two in advance to pay your club subscriptions, or for any other legitimate purpose. But extravagance like yours means vice, and vice I never *will* encourage.'

Lord Lundy shook his grey head at his son, heaved a sigh, felt in the left-hand pocket of his vest, missed something, heaved another sigh, and became absorbed in the Report with which he had been engrossed when his son entered the library.

'I only want a paltry two hundred,' pleaded Tom, not by any means willing to give up without a struggle.

His father once more looked up from his statistics, and without altering his tone replied,—

'Harkye, Tom. I have said my say. You know the position which I hold as the patron of religious and philanthropic societies. You are aware of the repute which I bear. With your proceedings, and those of your associates, rumour is busy. Such rumours reflect upon me. Common decency should suggest to you that I am the last person in the world to whom you should apply for fresh means wherewith to procure fresh indulgence.'

'Indeed, sir—'

'Enough, Tom. I am busy. Good-morning.'

It was useless to argue further. The Hon. Tom Foote, with downcast countenance, withdrew; reflected that he must once more have recourse to his friends, Shadrach, Mesech, and Abednego in Throgmorton Street; and inwardly apostrophized his stern parent as Old Father Adamant.

When Tom left the library Lord Lundy rang the bell. When the menial entered his lordship was still feeling in the left-hand pocket of his vest.

'Oh, James,' he said, 'tell my man to look for the snuff-box I usually carry. Must have dropped it somewhere.'

James bowed and departed on his mission.

Meanwhile Tom, descending into Grosvenor Square, hailed a passing hansom; but when the driver pulled up by the kerb he was undecided in what direction to drive.

'Shall I go to the Raleigh and consult Bruiser, or shall I go direct to old Abednego, or shall I see Dot and explain matters?' This to himself. Then, suddenly making up his mind to see Dot, he gave his cabman an address in the vicinity of the Regent's Park, and abandoned himself to his fate.

To his great delight, and, indeed, surprise, he found Dot in the very best of tempers. Her little villa was surrounded by a wall which protected it from the vulgar stare of the passer-by, and Tom found her in her breakfast-room arranging flowers and humming an air out of *Diana*, a burlesque which she was at that time engaged in illustrating at the Mausoleum Theatre. She was arrayed in a morning-gown of light-blue, trimmed with some fluffy stuff strangely suggestive of powder-puffs. She received her guest with considerable warmth; asked her 'poor old boy' why he looked so 'glum,' and when in reply he admitted that he had been unable to obtain the trifling sum which she had requested, burst out laughing, and said,—

'Don't look so solemn, Dolly,'—'twas her pet name for him. 'I shall be able to do without it for the present. A wealthy connection of mine has just died leaving me sufficient for all immediate wants. And now what's the news?'

Tom having mentally blessed the rich and opportune relative, and having regretted aloud that any person should have deprived him of the coveted opportunity of playing the part of relieving officer, declared that there was no news.

He then began to look about the room. This is a habit which most men have in visiting rooms where others, perchance, may be received—others that they know not of. There is a suspicion of the very furniture. A jealousy of articles left behind. Great Heavens! what heart-burnings have been caused by the discovery of a strange cigar-case or a ring with an unfamiliar monogram.

Tom, strolling up to the mantel-piece while chatting to Dot, or listening to her artless prattle, perceived, nestling between the ormolu timepiece and a vase of early primroses, a snuff-box. He took it up and involuntarily ejaculated,—

'Halloa!'

Dot looked up, and observing the object of his curiosity, exclaimed,—

'Oh, put that down, it—it's nothing.'

'Nothing?' said Tom. 'It's a snuff-box. Come, where did you get it?'

Dot pouted. She must not be cross-examined. It was an insult to her. Did Dolly doubt her?

But Dolly was in perfect temper. He declared himself as devoid of doubt as a minor prophet, and having calmed the rising emotions of the lady, said, with the greatest *sang-froid*,—

'Lend me the snuff-box till to-morrow at this hour, and I'll bring you the two hundred. Yes, and a fifty into the bargain.'

'Only a loan, mind,' stipulated the girl, who, like most of her charming sex, had a mind irrevocably fixed on the main chance.

'Of course—only a loan,' replied the elated Tom; 'd'ye think I'm going to turn snuff-taker?'

Whether Tom's logic or the hope of Tom's money mollified Miss Dot, it is certain that when, an hour after, he left Laburnum Villa, Regent's Park, N.W., he had the snuff-box in his pocket.

It was from Lady Lundy that his lordship had imbibed his religion and his philanthropy. She was, indeed, a marvellous woman, and had been known on at least one occasion to take the chair from which indisposition had driven her husband. If ever a nobleman could have been said to be hen-pecked, that devoted aristocrat was Lord Lundy. And Tom, although more audacious in his expressions of defiance, also stood in considerable awe of his mother. When on the evening of the day during which all the events of this unvarnished tale arrived, Tom sat down to dinner, both his father and his mother were surprised at the flow of his animal spirits, the redundancy of his anecdotes, and the impudent way in which he relegated to some future occasion all discussion concerning Outcast London, or the heathen living in dark places of the earth.

Being a Christian household, certain Christian customs were observed in the Lundy establishment; so when Lady Lundy left the room her husband and her son remained to discuss a glass of claret.

'You seem in excellent spirits to-night, my boy,' said the father. And the remark was not uncalled for; because when last father and son had met, the latter was extremely downcast.

'Pretty well, thank you,' replied the youth.

'And to what may I attribute this change?'

'I've taken your advice, sir, and have commenced to do something useful. I have gone into trade.'

'God bless my soul! *Trade*!'

'Yes. I'm dealing in articles—if I may call them so—of *virtue*.'

'You're joking.'

'Never more serious, I assure you. To prove it I will sell you something.'

'What?'

'A snuff-box.'

The philanthropist laughed.

'And so it is you who have been hiding my favourite box. Hand it over this minute, you rascal.'

But Tom shook his head.

'No; this can't be *yours*. This is a snuff-box with a history. It belonged, my dear father, to a great philanthropist; and it was discovered in a breakfast-room in the Regent's Park.'

At this Tom exhibited the pretty receptacle, saying,—

'How much do you say for this highly authenticated heirloom?'

'The two hundred you asked for this morning, Tom,' replied the father, with more coolness than might reasonably been expected under the circumstances.

'Not enough,' said the son.

'Three hundred—five hundred!' gasped the philanthropist.

'Say a thousand,' insinuated Tom.

'I'll be d—d if I do!' replied the philanthropist, with the utmost decision.

'Then,' said Tom, rising, 'I'll take it to her ladyship, and see what she'll give me for it—and for its story.'

'Tom, sit down, I command you. Not a word of this. The money is yours.'

How Tom managed with Dot about retaining the snuff-box history does not say. But it has been noticed with considerable alarm that Tom has now a greater influence over Lord Lundy than ever was obtained even by her ladyship.

3

'ONE WAS RENT AND LEFT TO DIE'

William Mackay

After the traveller passes the City of Oxford the Thames greatly changes its aspect. Locks are deserted by their keepers. One has to open these waterways for oneself, and there is usually a difficulty in finding the bolts rust-eaten and honey-combed into a very corrugated species of small-pox. For traffic has ceased a great way below, and the gentle dwellers by the banks are a dull and slow race of men given greatly to the consumption of beer. You may proceed to great distances without seeing a human being. It is a narrow Thames hereabouts and a shallow. Yet it is infinitely pleasant in the early spring, when the birds sing against each other in what to us appear songs of unaffected gladness, but which are really cries of baffled envy—of angry jealousy. For even the note of the nightingale is now relegated by the advance of knowledge to a place among our shattered illusions.

Innocent lambs, sweetly unconscious of the rapidly growing mint, bleat feebly at the unexpected apparition of a boat containing a human being in flannels, and the great kine slaking their thirst gaze with meek contemptuous eyes at the intruder. How cool the rushes show standing by the water's edge, unheeding as yet the earlier efforts of a sun rehearsing for his summer effects. And above all, the deep cerulean with its white clouds, motionless as those of the painted canvas in the theatre—seeming more intensely white as the black wings of the rook pass beneath with lazy sweep.

Twenty miles above Oxford—more than twenty or less than twenty, for I do not wish the place identified—is the village of—. It is situated about a mile and a half from the banks of the Thames, and is a place which was at one time of some consideration, but now is half asleep. It has done its business and retired. Some wealthy men live in the place and its vicinity. The labourers look fat on a wage of a shilling or so a day, and once a year there is a fair, which is greatly deplored by the godly as calculated to undermine the morals of the simple villagers, whom to my own knowledge stand in need of no such temptation, being by nature somewhat prone to forget that part of the moral law which inculcates advice regarding the regulation of a man's desires.

The prettiest girl in—was Jessie Bracebridge. She had long golden hair rigidly suppressed under her garden hat, and soft blue eyes and a figure lithe but rounded. Her dress was plain to a fault. For she was the only daughter of William Bracebridge, cobbler and Methodist local preacher, a pious enthusiast of great original power and extraordinary will; but a pious enthusiast whose notions of Duty if carried out to their fullest by mankind generally, would render the world a very uncomfortable place to live in. In the year 1741 the Rev. John Wesley had visited—, and, as appears from his 'Journal,' being greatly scandalized by the fact that the Vicar hunted three days a week in the season, and that every second name inserted in the registry of birth was that of an illegitimate infant, established a conventicle in the village and set apart a local or lay preacher to look after his converts until such time as he could send a regularly ordained minister to supply their spiritual wants. The lay preacher was named Bracebridge, and the Bracebridge whose name appears in this unvarnished tale was grandson of the friend of John Wesley. Bracebridge was indeed in a sort of Apostolical Succession.

In the glorious spring weather of 18–, Jessie Bracebridge had wandered down to the river and stood among the reeds looking across the great expanse of meadow beyond the other shore, and wishing that her mother were alive again, and wondering if people might be really good and relatively happy without being so strict and stern as her father, or so instant as he was in season and out of season. Perhaps, too, she was indulging in day dreams of the great world outside, for she was in her seventeenth year, and had read of the wonders of cities, and, notwithstanding her father's denunciation of the wickedness in them, longed perhaps to see and judge for herself. Suddenly her thoughts were diverted. A lamb more silly than its companions—if indeed one lamb can be more silly than another—had approached too near the edge of the stream, and the bank giving way under its small weight it fell into the stream and wakened the echoes with piteous bleating. At that catastrophe Jessie shrieked aloud, regarding the quadruped's as a life only less precious than that of a human being.

A skiff came round the bend of the stream, and its occupant was soon pulling toward the shrieking maiden. In her distress she pointed to the drowning lamb, and he, not without difficulty, rescued the woolly unfortunate, and then returned to receive the thanks which he considered were his due—for although we are all agreed that virtue is its own reward, few of us are satisfied with that intangible recompense. He was a frank-looking, bronzed, and brown-haired English youth, and she blushed as, with the candid impulse of his nature, he expressed his sorrow for her distress and his unfeigned delight that he had been in a position to render a service which had given her pleasure.

It was a short interview but it was a fatal one. She had looked and loved. He had looked and loved. They met again. And again. And for the first time in her life she had a secret from the father whom she feared.

But ah! for her what unthought of bliss in these meetings. How she listened as her lover, her hero, talked of the world of wealth and fashion—of the grand mansions of London, of the historic colleges of Oxford. He sang to her songs of the world, and even taught her, who heretofore regarded as morally wrong anything in the way of a musical exercise not contained in the compilation of John and Charles Wesley, to warble such ditties. Of these it gave him a dreamy pleasure to hear her sing to him a composition—which commenced or ended—for I forget which—with the words—

> 'We threw two leaflets you and I,
>   To the river as it wandered on,
> One was rent and left to die,
>   The other floated onward all alone.'

An ominous quatrain.

Tom was the name of this sweet-voiced young lover. And Tom was the son of an eminent judge, who has since exchanged the ermine for a crown of glory. Tom was at that time a student of Magdalen College, Oxford. And Jessie, as you know, was the daughter of a Methodist cobbler. Yet they loved all the spring till he went away to the Continent and forgot all about that pleasant spooning.

∞

On the following spring Judge—, his revered parent, went the Oxford Circuit. One day after the Court had risen, he called at his son's chambers in Magdalen College. There was an affectionate greeting between father and son, and the latter, whom as we have seen, was a most impulsive and kind-hearted young fellow, saw that his father was not looking well.

'You look ill,' he said, in his sweet musical tones. 'The pestilential atmosphere of those infernal courts.'

'No. I have been engaged in trying a very sad case.'

Tom smiled incredulously.

'The idea of a judge of your experience affected by anything that transpires in a Court of Justice.'

'And yet so it is.'

'The story must be an exceptionally terrible one.'

'No. It is only exceptionally sad. I will tell it to you briefly. A young woman was charged with the murder of her infant. The young woman was unmarried. So far the story is unfortunately an ordinary one. She refused to make any defence or divulge anything with regard to the parentage of the child. A plea of not guilty was entered, and I assigned counsel to defend her. But the facts were too strong. The legal guilt of the unfortunate, and, I may say, very beautiful victim was clearly established by the witnesses for the Crown. But one witness appeared for the defence, and he volunteered his evidence. He was a tall, gaunt man, with a highly intelligent face. He was dressed in broadcloth. He entered the box, and said, in slow tones—the tones of a man suffering an unutterable agony—"My lord, I wish to speak to the character of my daughter." He had no sooner spoken the words than the prisoner uttered a shriek, which, to my dying day, I shall remember. She shrieked the word "Father," and fell to the floor of the dock. There was great confusion in court for some minutes. A medical man was sent for. When he arrived he pronounced the prisoner dead. The prosecuting counsel rose and announced the fact to the court.

The father still stood in the witness-box. His face was ghastly pale, his hands clenched before him, his eyes were cast towards the roof of the building and looked bright, as though he could see through that obstacle to something above. Amid a dead silence, in deep and infinitely pathetic tones he repeated the words, "The Lord gave and the Lord hath taken away, blessed be the name of the Lord." I'm not ashamed to tell you that tears fell on my note-book from these old eyes of mine.'

'And the man's name?' asked Tom, casually.

'William Bracebridge, of—.'

For one moment a deadly paleness spread over the face of the son. But in an instant he regained his self-possession, and with his characteristic, frank, engaging manner, said,—

'Dear old dad, no wonder the scene upset you. It is, indeed, a sad story. Try a Laranaga, and let us talk of something else.'

4

RES EST SACRA MISER

William Mackay

'You refuse absolutely to give up the papers. You decline to comply with the order of the Court. Then, sir, I shall commit you for contempt. In prison you will have leisure in which to reflect on the enormity of your conduct.'

'But, my lord—'

'Not another word, sir. Your duty is to respect the Court, not to argue with it. Officer, remove your prisoner!'

And William Sadd was hurried away, placed in a fly, driven off to Marston Castle, and handed over to the safe custody of the governor of that establishment. The gates of Marston Castle never closed on a prisoner more innocent of offence.

William Sadd was an inventor. His name will be chiefly known to the public in connection with a patent corkscrew, but he had devised many other useful implements from which he derived a comfortable income; for Sadd was a Scotchman, and had carefully protected his rights against all persons piratically inclined. He was born near Glasgow, where he remained for some five-and-twenty years. Then, like many of his countrymen, he came to England, and settled in the town of—, a manufacturing community in the North.

He was a sanguine, good-tempered little man, and had

married a sanguine and good-tempered little wife, who bore him three sanguine and good-tempered little boys. He had at one time possessed a chum—another Scotch inventor. This man of genius—McAllister by name—had died, leaving certain papers to his friend as he lay on his death-bed. These documents, chiefly relating to uncompleted inventions, he confided to his friend with a last injunction that he should under no circumstances surrender them, but complete and patent them for the benefit of mankind and of his own pocket. Sadd gave the promise readily enough, feeling that nothing was more unlikely than that the papers would be inquired after. Much to his surprise, however, McAllister's executors, having by some means heard of the existence of the documents, applied for them as essential evidence in a case then in hand. Sadd replied that they were not essential nor even relevant. His assertion, however, availed him nothing. Finally, the judge made an order for their production. Sadd calmly, but determinedly, refused to comply with the mandate, and was thereupon ordered to be confined in Marston Castle.

Although William Sadd felt acutely that it was an inconvenient thing to be separated from his family even for one night, he was sustained by the thought that he had done his duty, that he was the victim of a misconception on the part of the learned judge, and that his solicitor would, no doubt, set things right in the morning. When, about an hour after his introduction to the debtors and first-class misdemeanants occupying a common room in the Castle, his solicitor visited him, he became quite indignant with that luminary for suggesting that he should give up the papers. He urged the man of law to have His Lordship informed by the mouth of eminent counsel that the documents had no earthly bearing on the case.

'The whole thing's jest re-deeckless,' said the prisoner,

absolutely smiling at the absurdity of the judge's order.

His solicitor only shook his head and went away.

Among the other prisoners William Sadd became instantly popular. He had the latest news from the outer world, and as he was going to rejoin it on the morrow, he essayed to execute all kinds of commissions for this brotherhood of misfortune. His cheery conversation had aroused the drooping spirits of those around him, when suddenly one and all became depressed again. William, following the eyes of the other victims, glanced towards the door, and, seeing a clergyman enter, instinctively rose to his feet. His example was not followed by any of the others, who turned sulkily away from beholding the ecclesiastic.

The new arrival was the Rev. Joseph Thorns, Chaplain of Marston Castle, and was familiarly alluded to by his congregation as 'Holy Jo.' He was a man of small stature, and was afflicted with a deformity between the shoulders, the knowledge of which had permanently soured a temper not originally angelic. He strode up to the latest arrival, who bowed respectfully, and pulling out a note-book, asked brusquely,—

'Your name?'

The prisoner told him: but with the air of a man who regarded the formality of taking it down in a book as an operation quite superfluous, he being merely a lodger for the night.

'For what have you been committed?'

'Well, ye ken,' replied Mr Sadd, 'it's jest a bit mistake. I've been neglacted by my soleecitor.'

'I see,' said the Chaplain. 'Contempt of Court,' and he wrote that down opposite the inventor's name. 'What religion?'

'A'm a member of the Auld Kirk,' replied the contemptuous prisoner.

'I should have thought that even in the Auld Kirk,' said the clergyman, 'they would have taught you to obey the law. Here is a book for you,' and he handed him a copy of the hymn-book used in the chapel, turned sharply round, and left the long, bare apartment, now looking longer and more bare than ever in the eyes of the latest inmate. Sadd soon, however, recovered his accustomed spirits, and eventually became sufficiently composed to look through the hymnal. As he by no means relished the chaplain's sneer at the Church of his fathers, he observed somewhat maliciously to his companions, holding up the book of sacred songs,—

'Comparrit wi' the Psawlms of David, they're a wheen blithers,' an observation which was heartily applauded by the other misdemeanants as indirectly reflecting on the parson.

The next day Mrs Sadd appeared upon the scene, conveying a basket of delicacies not included in the prison fare, and conveying also the information that it would take some days before the judge was in a temper to be addressed on the subject of Sadd's contempt. When three days had passed, and the judge was tackled by an eminent Queen's Counsel, he absolutely refused to reconsider his sentence.

'Let the prisoner surrender the documents, and then the Court will consider whether or not he has purged the contempt.'

Thus my lord on the Bench.

But Sadd was firm, and through his solicitor petitioned the Home Secretary. The Home Secretary, having taken three weeks to consider the matter, refused to interfere with the order of the judge.

Then the spirits of the sanguine inventor fell suddenly to zero. Nor were they manifestly revived by the daily visits of his wife, for she, poor woman, with tears in her eyes, begged and prayed her recalcitrant husband to give up the documents. But even his love for her did not induce him to forget his duty to the dead.

Sadd was committed to Marston Castle in the early part of November. And before a month had passed over his head he had become the most melancholy and morose of those resorting to the common room. The others had some hope of release. It seemed that he must remain there for ever, unless he relinquished the sacred papers. His cheeks became sunken, his shoulders bent, and his hair prematurely grey. He sat apart from his fellows and mumbled continually to himself.

It was during the first week in December that the others thought he had gone mad. His 'little woman,' as he fondly called her, did not pay her customary visits. His solicitor looked in and informed him that Mrs Sadd was dangerously ill in bed, and urgently pleaded this as an additional reason for complying with the order of the Court. Duty to the dead, love for the living—these conflicting emotions tore his heart. In an agony of spirit he motioned his solicitor to withdraw. Then he burst out crying like a child, and never again opened his lips to mortal man.

On Christmas Day there was service in the jail chapel. Mr Thorns preached an excellent sermon from the text—'The law is good if a man use it lawfully.' This exemplary cleric dwelt with great severity on the evil that is in the world, and particularly on the evil which brought men into jails. He then proceeded to inform his attentive congregation of a fact which one would have thought was painfully obvious to them—that punishment did not fall only on the wrong doer, but also upon those who were near and dear to him. 'Picture to yourselves,' went on the minister of the Gospel, 'picture your wives on this holy anniversary, seated in silence and sadness, surrounded by their weeping children. Think of their untold agony as these innocent children—inheritors of a parent's brand—put the tormenting question, "Where's father?" Picture—'

It all happened in a moment; a prisoner had burst from the benches occupied by the first-class misdemeanants; had scaled the pulpit like a wild cat; had caught the chaplain by the throat; had suddenly released his grasp; and, with a groan which those who heard it will never forget, had fallen back on to the stone pavement in front of the pulpit—dead.

When the body was searched the precious documents were found stitched beneath his waistcoat. They disclosed an unfinished scheme of the late Mr McAllister's for so dealing with horsehair as to render the wigs of judges not only awful to the multitude, but comfortable to the wearer.

5

MR GREY

William Mackay

For five and twenty years, and on every day during term time, Reginald Grey took his place on the seats devoted to the Junior Bar in one of the Courts allotted to Vice-Chancellors. He did not live to attend before Vice-Chancellors in the spick-and-span mausoleum, that goes by the name of the Royal Courts of Justice. When he was at the Bar, the Vice-Chancellors sat in dingy buildings in Lincoln's Inn Fields—the same, indeed, which have been so fully described in *Bleak House*.

To the reporters, barristers, general public, and to successive Vice-Chancellors, Reginald was as well known as 'the Fields' themselves. He was a modest, self-contained man, and he never held a brief. But he must have known a wonderful deal of law, for he never missed a case, and he listened to every argument and suggestion as though Coke *in propriâ personâ* were lecturing him upon Littleton. Even when lunch time came Reginald did not hurry out of Court with the chattering, surging crowd of litigants and lawyers' clerks. He sat quietly in the position which he had taken up, and when the Court was quite empty, drew a penny bun from his pocket, which he devoured, gazing absently up at the roof of the Court. When the Court resumed its duties, he brushed the crumbs from his trousers, and when the Vice-Chancellor entered, he rose with the rest of the Bar and bowed to his lordship with every dignity.

Wigs, gowns, and bands are, as articles of attire, subject to the very same law of decay which affects a great-coat or a suit of sables, and the years had not spared the robes which denoted Mr Grey's professional status. His wig was discoloured by dust, smoke, and other accidents. Whole wisps of horsehair stuck out here and there, and one of the little tails which depend behind had fallen bodily away—had perhaps been eaten away by rats. His bands were most disreputable specimens of man-millinery; for indeed he was his own laundress, and washed those symbolic rags in his own basin, drying them before his fire in his chambers in Gray's Inn. His stuff gown was a frayed and ragged garment; no ragman would have advanced sixpence on it. For five and twenty years had it—but there! it is about the man himself I would speak. There is something to my mind so pathetic in the sight of these forensic shreds and patches, that I cannot bear to dwell on their dilapidation.

There was only one man in Court who took the slightest notice of Mr Grey: and he was a tall, florid, bustling, and—as he once had a case of mine, I take the liberty of adding—impudent gentleman, with an impressively loud and boisterous manner. When he saw Grey even in his scarecrow days he would sometimes throw him a hearty 'How d'ye do, Grey?'—but sometimes, I imagine, he pretended not to see him. This counsel learned in the law was none other than Mr Stanley Overton. Grey took a great interest in him, following him from court to court, and listening to him with rapt attention as he bullied his opponents and even the Court; for a more vulgar, bullying, swaggering man than Overton while he was at the Bar I never encountered. He toned down greatly after his elevation.

As Grey grew from month to month more worn and

shabby, so did Overton become more sleek and resplendent. When once a man commences in earnest there is no stopping him. The proverb which tells us about the facility of the descent to Avernus is only half a truth. The ascent to the stars is equally easy, and is achieved every day both by the brave man and the bully. It is as easy as the descent, and is a very great deal more comfortable.

Some people were surprised when Overton was made a Vice-Chancellor. In fact, the surprise was very general. But it was not shared by Grey. That devoted man thought it the most natural thing in the world. He would not again have to follow this luminary in its erratic circuit from court to court. His idol was now enthroned. The worship would in future be offered in one temple, and not in two or three.

On the morning when Overton took his seat as Vice-Chancellor, Mr Grey took *his* place in the back benches. And when the newly-made judge entered, flushed with victory and imposing in brand-new wig and robes, the whole Bar rose with great rustling of stuff and silk. Grey rose too; and a solicitor's clerk who sat next him saw his face turn ashen white, while two great tears rolled down his emaciated cheeks; and when he sat down he leaned his head on the ledge in front of him, covered his eyes with his poor thin hand and sighed.

At four o'clock that evening, when the Court rose to go, Grey remained in that position till everyone had left. An usher found him, and touched him on the elbow. He started, looked about him on the emptiness in a dazed sort of way, and, without saying a word, walked quietly off, the usher observing to his plump assistant that Mr Reginald Grey was 'a rum old file.'

Mr Grey's chambers were very, very high up in one of the gaunt sets in Gray's Inn. Indeed, they were at the top of the building—mere garrets. When he arrived at them he found his laundress arranging the tea things—he seldom dined—and there was a decided odour of the savoury kipper about the apartment.

'Ah! Mrs Tracy,' he said, assuming a thin affectation of gaiety, 'this has been a great day for the Inn—a great day.'

'Indeed, sir,' assented that slipshod female.

'Yes, they've made a Vice-Chancellor of my old friend, Stanley Overton.'

'Oh, indeed, sir. Which I'm sure, I'm 'appy to 'ear it, an' 'appy to 'ear as he's a friend of *yours*, Mr Grey.'

'A very old friend indeed, Mrs Tracy. Why, we were boys together. We were at school together. We were at college together. And we were both called to the Bar the same day.'

'Law!' exclaimed Mrs Tracy.

Indeed, what *could* she say? Mr Grey had always been a remarkably reserved, reticent man—a 'little queer,' the good lady thought—and, beyond what was necessary in the way of speech, quite silent and inscrutable.

'Yes, indeed, ma'am,' went on the poor barrister, 'and I'll tell you something that will surprise you even more. We were both in love with the same lady.'

This indeed *did* surprise the draggle-tailed bed-maker, and she looked her astonishment.

'It's quite true; and the strange thing is that she preferred me, or at least she told me so. And when I left my home in Devonshire I was engaged to her.'

Mrs Tracy did not now think that the gentleman was a 'little queer'—she was convinced that he was stark staring mad. She looked apprehensively at the poor thin knife that lay on the table. Reticent! Why, the man was as garrulous and confidential as a village gossip.

He continued:

'You see, Overton was always a more pushing man, and a cleverer man too; and after we were called he borrowed a hundred pounds from me and went down to Devonshire. Some wicked stories got circulated about my doings in London, in consequence of which my sweetheart ceased to care for me, and Overton, who was always a plucky fellow, ran away with her and married her.'

His voice trembled as he narrated that episode; but he returned to the affectation of gaiety, and said,—

'Yes, Mrs Tracy, and she's now Lady Overton; and of course I'm very glad of it, for her sake.'

'Of course, sir,' acquiesces Mrs Tracy.

'And the funny thing is,' he added, with the most pitiable attempt at hilarity, 'he never paid me back that hundred pounds—ha, ha, ha!'

It was a mockery of laughter, the cachinnation of a ghost.

'And to-night, Mrs Tracy,' he said, 'I am going home.'

'To Devonshire, sir?'

'I *said* home,' he answered; 'but you will come as usual in the morning, and see that all is right. You can go, Mrs Tracy. Good-bye.'

And to the utter astonishment of the poor woman, he shook hands with her, and, I fear, retained her hand for a moment, and there was the suspicion of moisture in his eyes.

The next morning, when Mrs Tracy came to see that all was right, she found Mr Reginald Grey stretched lifeless on the hearthrug. A revolver lay beside him, and there was a bullet through his forehead. In his left hand was an open locket, containing a little wisp of straw-coloured hair.

6

THE PRODIGAL'S RETURN

William Mackay

'Leave my house!' shouted the Rev. Stanley Blewton to his son. Two women—they were the Prodigal's mother and sister—wept and pleaded. But the man of God was inexorable.

'Silence!' he exclaimed. 'And'—turning to his son—'never cross this threshold again.'

'Father!' cried the boy.

'Thief!' retorted the reverend gentleman.

The face of his progeny burnt red, his eyes flashed, and he clenched his fists. The women meanwhile redoubled their sobs.

'But, hold,' added Mr Blewton, as his son turned to go. 'You shall be treated beyond your deserts. Here are ten pounds. Use them discreetly. They are the last you will ever have from me.'

'Keep your money, sir,' answered Master Henry Blewton—he was but seventeen years of age, and inherited the hot temper of his parent, 'Mother, good-bye. Maude, God bless you. I am innocent.'

He kissed his mother and sister. The flush of resentment had died from his face. He turned to his father, and extending his hand, said,—

'Wish me good-bye, sir. Time will set me right.'

But an ominous sneer played about the thin lips of the clergyman. He pointed to the door, and his last words to his son were,—

'I will have no parley with one who has brought dishonour on my name. Go!'

Henry Blewton cast one longing look at his mother and sister, and then walked straight into the hall, took his hat off the peg, and, as the door closed on him, Mrs Blewton screamed in her agony, and fell into a faint that looked like death.

The Rev. Stanley Blewton was a man with a sense of honour pushed to its extremest point. He had no forgiveness for the sinner who brought discredit on an honest name. Like all good Christians, he was bound, I presume, to accept the story of the thief on the cross. But as long as there remained another text in the Bible he would never select that particular scripture as the text of a discourse. His only son had through his influence obtained a good appointment in a clerical insurance office, in which the reverend gentleman was a shareholder. He had been accused by his superiors of peculation. His father's position, backing his remonstrances, kept the case from coming into the police court. The matter was 'squared,' as the slang term has it. A public scandal was averted. But certain persons at least would know the secret. The Blewton name was smirched. This his reverence would never forgive.

Henry walked with a rapid pace down Brixton Hill, for on that reputable eminence his father's house was situated; passed through Kennington, along the Westminster Bridge Road, crossed the bridge, passed under the shadow of the clock tower, and went up to a recruiting sergeant who stood at the corner of Parliament Street.

During that walk the circumstances of Henry Blewton underwent many important changes. To begin with, he had changed his name, his age, and his occupation. He enlisted, passed the doctor with credit, and blossomed eventually into Private Nott of a valiant regiment of the line.

From that moment all trace of Henry Blewton became lost to his friends and relatives, and for years they mourned for him as people mourn for the dead. His concluding prophecy, delivered with such meaning to his father, came true. Time set him right. He had not been a year in the army before the real delinquent was discovered; and, as the genuine sinner had no influential acquaintances on the directorate of the company, his case was remitted to the Old Bailey for the consideration of a judge and jury. He was found guilty, and sentenced to a term of imprisonment. Thus was the character of Henry Blewton vindicated.

Useless, alas! now were the regrets and repentances of his reverend father. Vain were the efforts of the private detectives whom he engaged. The advertisements that he caused to be inserted in the papers brought no response, and, after five years of fruitless labour and unavailing self-reproach, his family came to the conclusion that he was dead. He had perished from hunger, perhaps, or had hurried himself into the presence of his Maker, goaded to distraction by the paternal taunts. The reflection that his innocence had been established ameliorated to some little extent the pangs of mother and sister. But the very thought which gave them consolation added to the poignancy of the father's feelings. He mourned in secret, and cried with the man of yore,—

'Would to God I had died for him! My son, my son!'

At the very point where Brixton Rise merges into Brixton Hill there is an avenue. It is a very well-kept avenue, and a stately row of young trees runs along each side of it. A notice-board informs the passers-by that there is 'No Thoroughfare,' and that this trimly-kept approach is 'Private.' On some fine days honest people are beguiled by the spectacle of half-a-dozen men with cropped hair and unbecoming uniform repairing the roadway. These operators are directed by another person. He is also in uniform, and carries side arms and a musket—for the avenue leads to Brixton Gaol, and the sullen road-menders are inmates of that suburban retreat. It is perhaps within the knowledge of the reader that military prisoners are now received in the Brixton seminary; if not, the reader must take it from me that it is so.

One wild November morning the gates of Brixton Gaol opened and let loose a prisoner who had been confined for an assault on his superior officer, that gallant captain having contributed somewhat to the offence by dubbing the man a thief. He was a fine, soldierly-looking young fellow of two-and-twenty, though he looked much more. When he came to the end of the avenue he found the chaplain waiting there, notwithstanding the inclemency of the weather.

'Good-morning,' said the chaplain—a kind-hearted Devonshire parson, who took more than the usual perfunctory interest in his patients, as he was wont to call them.

'Good-morning, sir,' replied the soldier, respectfully, and with an accent of surprise.

'You have no money, I suppose?'

'Not a soul, your reverence,' replied the man.

'Then,' said the chaplain, 'here are two shillings. They will at least keep you for a day or two. Seek work and keep honest. God bless you.'

'Heaven reward you!' replied the man, writhing under the kindness of the clergyman. The visitant to the outer world did not move, however. He looked up and down the hill, as if hesitating in what direction he should go.

'That,' said the parson, pointing down the hill, 'that is the way to London'—saying which he turned up the avenue, and so re-entered the precincts of the gaol. But the man did not take the direction indicated by his benefactor. There was something in the atmosphere of Brixton which seemed to agree with him. He found its attractions more considerable than do most visitors to the noted locality. He wandered in an aimless way up and down by-streets. But the police—always solicitous about the welfare of discharged prisoners—kept their eyes on him. He had an uncomfortable feeling that he was being watched. And he repeated with something of bitter irony in his tone the parting admonition of the chaplain.

'"Seek work and keep honest!" No easy matter, Mr Parson, with these sleuth-hounds on the trail.'

Towards evening he entered a small beer-house in the Cornwall Road, a thoroughfare not far removed from the gaol. Here he refreshed himself with bread and cheese and beer. Here also he found company who did not object to his society, for it is a comforting reflection that there are more wicked people outside gaols than in them. And among these excellent fellows he spent the time, until at the hour of twelve the landlord was obliged to turn his customers into the bleak and blustrous night.

The man bade good-bye to his companions, and sought the high road. He proceeded up the hill with his back turned on London. When he came to the substantial house of the Rev. Stanley Blewton he stopped, looked up and down the road to see that he was not followed, and then passed into the clergyman's front garden, creeping forward under the shadow of the bushes.

At one o'clock in the morning the reverend occupant of the house was wakened by a noise below; he listened, warned his wife to keep quiet, drew on his trousers, took his revolver, and crept downstairs in his naked feet. Yes, the thief had entered the library. Mr Blewton was, as we have seen, a person of some determination. He opened the library door and said,—

'Speak, or I'll fire.'

'It is—' But the voice was not allowed to proceed. The sound indicated the position of the robber. The minister fired two barrels in the direction of the voice, and heard a body fall with a groan of—

'Oh—father—you—have—killed—me!'

Then there was silence. Then another groan, and the fall of another man. When the servants came with a light they found the dead body of the father stretched by the dead body of the son.

7

A PHILANTHROPIC 'MASHER'

William Mackay

An elderly man with a pleasant expression, iron-grey hair, and faultlessly dressed may occasionally be seen walking along the shady side of St James's Street in the early afternoon. He gazes a good deal under the bonnets of the pretty women. But there is a demure and half-respectful expression in his glance which withers any rising feeling of resentment. His age and his unmistakably sympathetic half-smile give him an immunity which would not be extended to younger and bolder men. He is known to society as the Hon. Archibald Flodden.

Flodden is a member of three excellent clubs. His name is on some extremely desirable visiting lists. He goes to church when in town every Sunday morning. His conduct in public is most exemplary. And yet, somehow, Flodden has no men friends. He has money, and therefore can always command the society of a select circle of parasites. But men who ought to be in his own set—or of whose set he ought to be—do not care for his company. Nor do the female leaders of society give him great countenance. He is not, perhaps, regarded exactly as a *mauvais sujet*. But it is generally admitted that there is something queer about Flodden.

This sentiment was not, of course, inspired originally by

the fact that after two years of domestic infelicity his wife left him, taking her infant daughter with her. Society naturally took the man's part. The wife placed herself outside the pale, and Flodden never asked her to re-enter it. He took the matter philosophically, gave up his house in Sloane Square, took chambers in the Albany, refused all communication with his wife, and led the life of a sedate and philanthropic bachelor. For eighteen years he has led this blameless and almost idyllic life, and yet there exists in society an undefined distrust of him which is utterly unaccountable.

But though the great ladies of society, guided by an infallible instinct, do not regard the Hon. Archie Flodden with favour, there are certain other desirable persons who worship him as the very *beau ideal* knight. These are ladies of the middle-class, the wives of professional men, or the gushing ornaments of suburban Bohemia. Their experience of gentlemen is, perhaps, limited. They may be excused, therefore, in mistaking Flodden's tinsel of politeness for the gold of real gallantry.

It is quite surprising the number of interesting young persons of the emotional and impressionable kind who have acquired a sincere, romantic, but quite Platonic, regard for Mr Flodden. Happy chance has in the majority of instances procured the introduction; and, as a rule, the male relatives of the ladies are quite unaware of the discreet intimacy existing between Flodden and their women-folk. Indeed, these male relatives are all mere brutes, and it is part of Flodden's edifying mission to sympathize with these dear creatures, to express distress that their sweetness should be wasted on such clods of earth, and generally to insinuate comparisons between himself and the lawful husband, which are infinitely detrimental to the latter.

This hoary-headed squire of dames has the pleasantest possible little five o'clock teas at his chambers in the Albany, and sometimes as many as eight, or even nine, of his young friends will join him at that simple repast. Lord Roach ('Cock' Roach he used to be called in his regiment), who lives in the next set, seeing the ladies file out at half-past six or so, has put it about that Flodden keeps a dancing academy. But, though there is occasionally a little piano playing, there has never been a dance; indeed, the entertainment is chiefly conversational. Mr Flodden never used a rude or an improper expression. He has, however, a wonderful knack of leading the conversation into doubtful topics. The chaste annals of the Divorce Court afforded him much agreeable food for comment. He would argue with some of his impressionable admirers as to the possibility of a purely Platonic affection, and at times he would scribble off an epigram in choice French on some living beauty, notorious for the number of her amours. These trifles, written in a formal but trembling hand, have found themselves in the private albums of many an honest house in the suburbs. The ladies who were the objects of his disinterested regard invariably alluded to him as 'a dear, kind creature,' the 'most gentlemanly person,' 'so sympathetic,' and the rest. The more gushing, recklessly declared him to be a 'duck.' Dean Swift, remembering his own definition of the phrase, would have called him 'a nice man.'

One hot afternoon in the July of last year, Mr Flodden sat in his luxurious chambers surrounded by half-a-dozen of his female admirers, descanting on the superiority of French art as illustrated by the examples which adorned his walls. Having exhausted this topic, he proceeded to one more calculated to stimulate the curiosity of his guests.

'I have got a little surprise for you, my dear ladies: a fresh addition to our charmed, and may I say charming, circle.'

Six fragile cups descended from twelve ruby lips, and twelve eyes opened wide with curiosity.

'Such a charming creature—so young, so beautiful, so romantic, and so unfortunate.' Six long-drawn sighs.

'Husband a cruel brute; absolutely beats her.'

Twelve eyes cast in mute appeal to the heaven that exists above Albany ceilings. Then the still, small voice of a sympathetic inquirer—

'And where did you meet this—this—paragon?'

'A secret, my dear madam, an absolute and positive secret. She was on her way to give lessons—she sings divinely—in order to maintain her keeper in tobacco and beer. Faugh!'

Six more long-drawn sighs.

'If she keep her appointment she will be here directly. She is a shy, reserved little creature, but should, I think, in such genial society thaw somewhat. Yes, she really must thaw.'

In five minutes Flodden's man—a highly-respectable person, well versed in his master's little ways—announced Mrs Bird. This was the lady who had so greatly fascinated the philanthropist, thereby driving six sympathetic souls into paroxysms of jealousy.

It must be admitted that anything less reserved or shy than Mrs Bird had never before been presented to six neglected matrons. Mrs Bird was stylishly dressed, greatly made up, and exhibited the undefinable *cachet* of the professional. She called Mr Flodden 'old chappie,' shook hands, unintroduced, with the assembled tea-drinkers, hoped they were quite jolly, and then asked the master of the establishment for a brandy and soda. That worthy man of the world had turned red and white and even blue. He was completely thunder-struck. It was evident he must stop the compromising flow of her conversation. The modest woman of his rambles had suddenly become transformed into a something too terrible for contemplation. A brilliant idea. He would ask her to sing. Mrs Bird was a woman of a most obliging disposition. She sat down at the piano and dashed off a showy prelude and commenced her song. You remember the effect of Captain Shandon's tipsy ditty upon the good Colonel Newcome; an effect somewhat similar was now produced on the neglected wives. Mrs Bird warbled out with unctuous accent one of the most notorious ballads of a Parisian *café chantant*. The matrons rose for shawls, and the songstress, apprehending their intention, jumped from the piano and burst into an uncontrollable fit of laughter. Flodden looked humiliated beyond measure; there was not a pennyweight of philanthropy left in him.

'This is awful!' he exclaimed; 'in heaven's name who and what are you?'

'I am your daughter Gwendolyn,' she hissed.

At that moment voices were heard from without—Flodden's man shouting, 'You sha'n't go in,' and another voice consigning Flodden's man to Hades. Then the door was thrust open, and a cad in loud check trousers, a green-coloured Newmarket coat, a white hat and innumerable rings, stood bowing to the assembled company. He eventually fixed a somewhat bloodshot eye on the philanthropist and said,—

'Now, then, my festive fossil, when next you go a followin' other men's wives, you see as they ain't your own daughters! I'm the Great O'Daniel, the star comique. Gwen's my wife, an' you're my pa-in-lor. Here's a horder; give us a turn and bring your lady friends with you. My new song, "The Elderly Masher," is no end of a go. Come along, Gwen. Good-bye, par. Ladies, bong joor!'

So saying he tucked Gwendolyn under his arm, bowed, and left the apartment. The other guests retired in solemn silence, wiser, and, let us hope better, women.

And that was Mr Flodden's last five o'clock tea at the Albany.

8

A DISHONOURED BILL

William Mackay

The bill itself, considering the prospects of the acceptor, was not for a very alarming amount. He was heir to a baronetcy and £50,000 per annum. The bill was for 'a monkey'—or, in more intelligible phraseology than that usually adopted by the acceptor himself, for the sum of five hundred pounds sterling. The extraordinary circumstance about the bill was that the acceptor, Harry Jermyn, paid Abednego, of Throgmorton Street, interest at the rate of sixty per cent per annum for the accommodation, and that in addition he had to take part of the proceeds in the shape of a park hack, which he found difficulty in selling to a cab proprietor for a five-pound note. The consideration deducted from the bill in respect of this animal was fifty pounds.

Harry Jermyn was a mauvais sujet; that is to say, he was a young gentleman kept by his father on a short allowance. He gambled a little, went to all the races, was a member of the Raleigh and other social centres of a similar kind, and evinced a considerable interest in the drama—that is to say, at theatres where the sacred lamp was kept burning. In fact, he resembled hundreds of other young men of our acquaintance; and probably he would not have been called a mauvais sujet were it not that the old baronet restricted him to means inadequate to supply his simple desires.

Mr Abednego was not a mauvais sujet. He was a most respectable man; had a house in Mayfair, another in Richmond, and a mansion in Scotland which he modestly called his shooting box. He occasionally entertained live lords, who borrowed his money and sneered at him behind his back. He had contrived to obtain a seat on a county bench, and was a Colonel of Volunteers in the same happy county, by reason of which he was known to society at large as Colonel Abednego.

When Harry Jermyn's bill fell due he rushed down in a hansom to Abednego's office in Throgmorton Street, and was—after an ominous delay—admitted to the sanctum of the great Abednego himself. That potentate did not rise, but nodded quickly to his visitor, with a short, and by no means encouraging, 'Mornin'.'

Harry was a man with a fine flow of animal spirits, and was not to be dashed by the studied coolness of his reception.

'I say, old chappie,' he replied, with the greatest good humour, 'what's the matter? Feel a little chippy this morning? or lost a point or two at sixpenny whist last night—eh?'

'Mr Jermyn, this is the City,' said the money-lender. 'What is your business?'

'Well, the fact is, old boy,' answered Jermyn, sitting on the edge of the table opposite the financier, 'that damn bill of mine falls due to-morrow.'

'Well?'

'And of course you'll renew?'

'Of course I'll do nothing of the kind,' answered Abednego, rising and taking out his watch.

Harry's jaw fell considerably. His former experience of this exemplary man had not prepared him for this. It had only prepared him for the incurring of fresh interest and the possession of park hacks anything *but* fresh.

'But look here, old man, I *must* have the coin, don't you know?'

Young Jermyn considered this sort of argument unanswerable. His host resumed his seat, and looking the young man in the face, said,—

'Well, I found her expensive myself. I'm not surprised that *you* do.'

Harry jumped from his seat on the table, and exclaimed, 'What in Hades do you mean?'

'I mean Baby Somerville of the Frivolity.'

'You scoundrel!' shouted the borrower, 'she is my wife. I have married her.'

'You lie,' quietly answered Mr Abednego.

Of course a blow followed. When Abednego had pulled himself together, and wiped the blood from his face, he said, in tones now quivering with rage,—

'You young scoundrel, you shall suffer for this!'

That was the end of the interview. Jermyn withdrew at once, wrathful and defeated, and next day the bill for 'a monkey' was dishonoured.

Now, strange as it may appear, Harry Jermyn had really married Baby Somerville of the Frivolity, a shapely, vain, and heartless woman, incapable of an affection, except perhaps for some brute of a chorus man. There was a period in her career, however, when she was considered chic by a certain number of men about town. Jermyn unfortunately allowed his passion to take an honourable direction. He wanted to have her all to himself; and she, knowing him to be heir to a baronetcy, without any conventional coyness consented to be his wife. But at the time of his marriage, and until he heard it on the day before his bill was dishonoured, he had no suspicion that Abednego had been among the admirers of his wife; and when he taxed her with it, she denied the fact with such accent of sincerity that he clasped her to his heart and called her by a hundred endearing names. He was, you see, an indubitable mauvais sujet.

Mr and Mrs Jermyn were spending the early days of their married life on the upper Thames, where, to her credit be it said, the lady affected a pretty interest in waving corn, and floating lily leaves, and shrilling larks, and other beauties which, I am told, abound in the neighbourhood of that incomparable stream; and, on the Sunday following the unpleasant interview with the magnate of Throgmorton Street, Mr Jermyn was sculling his young bride in the skiff which he had purchased for her, and called after her name.

It was a glorious July day, and the river was crowded with craft of every description.

The lock at—was open and half full when they reached it. Jermyn took his skiff gently in, and held on to the side of a launch, the deck of which was crowded with laughing women and men in gorgeous array. In the cabin a lunch was laid, and cases of champagne reposed pleasantly in the stern. Jermyn cursed his indiscretion a moment after, when he discovered that a number of the sirens on deck were members of the Frivolity chorus. But the worst was to come. Abednego, flashing with diamonds, exquisitely raddled as to his cheeks, stood at the tiller, and addressing Mrs Jermyn, said, with an air of easy familiarity,—

'Hallo, Baby, how are you gettin' on, eh?'

That was bad enough, but when Harry turned sharply round on his wife, he saw her big eyes turned longingly on the resplendent Hebrew, and her smile cast boldly on his painted countenance. At that moment the devil entered into Jermyn's soul as surely as ever it took possession of the Gadarene swine. His lips turned blue, his face was livid; but he made no other sign. His was the last boat to leave the lock. He rowed steadily on, and never spoke to the woman he had loved so well and so unwisely.

Mr Abednego had enjoyed a real good time on board the launch, and on his way down stopped at the famous riparian village of—. Here also Jermyn landed some time after. He sent his wife home by train, and put up at the same hotel as that occupied by his opulent rival.

No one ever knew how it happened. Close to the village there is a lock, and by the lock is what is called a hook—a horseshoe of water running round from a point above it, and, after making a vast circuit, emerging at a point below. For the most part this hook is shallow, but in places it is deep as the wells described by Herodotus. At six o'clock on the following morning, Abednego, who was fond of the water, repaired to a remote part of the hook. Five minutes after Harry Jermyn also proceeded to the bathing place. He must, however, have selected a spot out of sight of the 'Colonel,' for that gentleman was unfortunately drowned without Jermyn's even having seen him. A certain mark was discovered round Abednego's throat, but the coroner very sagely informed the jury that with that they had nothing to do—it might be a mark of long-standing. Mr Jermyn volunteered evidence as to having seen nobody in the vicinity of the hook. Verdict in accordance with such evidence as was produced—'Accidental death.'

Six months afterwards the famous case of Jermyn v. Jermyn, Smith, Jones, and Another was heard, which, as the public will recollect, resulted in a verdict for the husband, who is now a prematurely aged and curiously reticent man—the inheritor of a baronetcy and fifty thousand pounds a year.

9

A MAN OF GENIUS

William Mackay

Felix Carter was always on the look out for unappreciated genius, the which, when discovered, he would clothe, feed, and house until the time came—as it invariably did come—when he found out that the gold was tinsel. He never for one moment suspected that he himself was the happy possessor of that divine endowment which he so reverenced in others. And yet his friends all swore that if any man ever were gifted with genius, Felix Carter was that individual. He was a sort of artistic Admirable Crichton. He painted exquisite pictures. He had written three novels. Plays of his had been produced with success. And he played the violin like a very Paganini. Acquaintances spoke of him as being eccentric. But every man is accounted eccentric whose talents cover a wide area and whose heart is abnormally large.

Play writing, novel spinning, and violin practice Felix regarded as recreations. His real profession was that of an artist. And his big bachelor establishment in a North Western suburb of London will be remembered as the scene of some brilliant receptions, at not a few of which Carter's latest Man of Genius would put in an appearance, to the great surprise of guests, who very properly refused to see any merit whatever in his utterances. Sometimes three or four undesirable pensioners would be quartered on the establishment. And although Carter's friends deplored the circumstance, not one of them dare remonstrate. He was the victim of perpetual disappointment in his protégés, but would resent any interference with his practical philanthropy.

One of Carter's Men of Genius lived with him and on him for a period of more than six months. It was amusing always to hear his enthusiasm over this big, blotchy-faced loafer. He bored all his friends by a description of his first meeting him, of his desire to see him again, and of the happy coincidence of their second encounter. Carter was greatly given to prowling about unknown London for the purpose of picking up 'effects.' He knew the opium-smoking quarter. He had been in a thieves' kitchen, and he knew his way to the most disreputable common lodging-houses in the metropolis. He occasionally dropped in at the 'White Elephant,' a public-house situated in a slum off Fleet Street, where every night in the week a discussion took place on the events of the day. This discussion was carried on in a hall at the back of the 'White Elephant,' and was mainly contributed to by subsidized speakers whose feats of oratory were intended to encourage the ambitious vestryman who smoked his pipe there, or the occasional young barrister who dropped in upon his way to or from the Temple. But the audience generally was made up of solicitors' clerks, solicitors who had been struck off the Rolls, with here and there a fiery disciple of Bradlaugh from the unsavoury fastnesses of Clerkenwell. It was in this resort that Carter first saw and admired Joseph Addison, the large and very loathsome person who eventually shared his home.

'I tell you,' he would say, 'Joseph is the most wonderful chap. By Jove, sir, you should have heard the way he pegged into those Radicals. He made them squirm. I wish old Gladstone had been there to hear him, upon my soul I do.'

Unfortunately it happened that late one night Felix encountered his paragon lying asleep under a bench in St James's Park. It is more than probable that the creature was drunk after a day of successful sponging. But his admirer only saw a man full of gifts and faculties suffering from cold and hunger.

'By Gad, old boy,' he said in describing the scene, 'I could have cried to see a man, who could talk Sir William Harcourt's head off, perishing for want of a penny roll.'

So Addison was treated as reverently as if he had been his great namesake, was made free of Carter's house, was introduced to his studio friends, and was generally rendered a great deal more comfortable than he deserved to be. His appearance was sadly against him. His eyes were shifty and blood-shot; his bushy black whiskers were never submitted to the torture of the comb; his finger nails were invariably dirty, and his expression was that of effrontery struggling with awkwardness. His clothes of seedy black vainly endeavouring to conceal an unwashed shirt seemed as if they had been persistently slept in, and his eyeglass depending from a white string completed the picture of a rakish adventurer.

It is true that these deficiences of attire were gradually ameliorated, and Joseph Addison appeared in the linen and jackets of our friend, to which, however, this hopeless and abominable ale-house ornament managed to impart a debauched and dissipated air. Of this Carter saw nothing. Nor did he consider it extraordinary that the unsightly incubus should drink his brandy at eleven o'clock in the morning, or that he should smoke his Latakia out of his favourite pipes. All these little familiarities he set down as being so many eccentricities of genius.

'What's a bottle of brandy to me if it makes Joseph talk! I tell you I have heard that man emit epigrams by the hour. He's a little shy before strangers. But you should hear him when we're alone. By the lord Harry, Rochfoucauld isn't in it with him.'

And so Felix Carter, a man of taste, refinement, culture, and genius, worshipped this idol of mud, this tavern sponge, this bar-soiled, gin-soddened impostor. So Titania was enamoured of an ass.

Although it was perfectly true that Joseph Addison never ventured on any epigrams before Carter's friends, he committed some of them to writing, for the benefit of posterity. These wonderful sentiments Addison's hand had traced with charcoal on the white-washed walls of the studio, and Carter would point them out with genuine enthusiasm as though they were

—jewels five words long
That on the stretched forefinger of all time
Sparkle for ever.

Respect and love for Carter induced his associates to affect a great belief in the value of these jewels of thought scrawled on the walls in the most vulgar hand imaginable. That there may be no doubt as to the literary and philosophical value of the gems, I will reproduce them here. On one wall—just where Carter could see it as he painted, was inscribed the legend—

God Loves the Worker.

Opposite the entrance to the studio appeared in characters of greater magnitude the intimation—

Labour is Prayer.

While above the mantel-piece, between two beautiful 'studies' from the nude, ran the inscription—

Labor Omnia Vincit.

As the Latinity of this recondite quotation was impeccable, I presume that Mr Addison had extracted it from Bartlett's Dictionary of Quotations.

Had it not been for the large heart and simple faith of the artist, one would have been inclined to see nothing in the unholy alliance but its ludicrous side. But knowing how firm was the faith of the victim in his new discovery, there was a dash of pathos in it which checked laughter.

Many attempts were made to expose the fraud. Secret meetings of the admirers of Carter met in adjoining studios. All sorts of conspiracies were set on foot. Most ingenious devices were proposed and unanimously adopted. But they were unavailing. All were frustrated by the unsuspicious nature of Carter, or by the low cunning of the beer-swilling brute who was living in easy idleness on his money. It is generally believed that at this period certain of the younger and more enthusiastic followers of Carter had set on foot a plot for the extermination of Addison, and that his early assassination was by some deemed feasible and desirable.

'I will tell you what it is,' said Carter on one occasion to the most plain-spoken of his friends, 'I've found out why all you fellows fail to see that Addison is a Man of Genius.'

'And what may the reason be?' asked Plain Speaker.

'You're all jealous of his ability—that's what it is.'

'Bah!'

'It's all very well to say "Bah,"' said Carter, waxing enthusiastic as he invariably did on this theme, 'but it's impossible to explain your dislike on any other theory. Joseph is worth a dozen of the fellows who make money by literature in these days. I have written books myself, and ought to know something about it. You'll find him out one of these days.'

'And so will you,' was Plain Speaker's response.

Herein Plain Speaker indulged in unconscious prophecy. That which friendly conspirators could not bring about was contrived by the omnipotent finger of Fate.

Felix Carter went to the Isle of Wight to execute a commission for an invalid magnate in that pleasant settlement, and as he was anxious that a trustworthy and gentlemanly person should take charge of his house during his absence, he left his friend and protégé, Joseph Addison, in that responsible position. The artist had been about a week at work when he came upon the following gratifying item in one of the London papers:—

'POLICE INTELLIGENCE.

'BOW STREET. A THIEF.—*Joseph Addison* alias *Ward*, alias *Peters*, 40, was charged before Mr Flowers with stealing from the waiting-room of the Charing Cross Station a black bag containing jewellery, the property of M. Laurent of Paris. On the prisoner were found a gold watch, an opera-glass, a silver fruit-knife, and a valuable cigar-case. These articles bear the initials "F.C." The prisoner was remanded for further inquiries.'

'My initials!' sighed Carter.

'Our friend will now get plenty of that labour which he affects to love,' said Plain Speaker.

10

A DIGNIFIED DIPSOMANIAC

William Mackay

'A most remarkable man, sir,' said the Secretary of the Teetotal Union to the President.

'But don't he strike you as being a trifle—a trifle soiled, eh?' asked the President, glancing down at his own immaculate shirt-cuffs.

'N—no,' replied the Secretary, hesitatingly. 'He's a most dignified man—most dignified. An' in his dress shoot most impressive.'

'But really, now, Mr Bottle, I thought, d'ye know, that he rather smelt of beer. Just a little, eh?' suggested the President.

'Beer!' echoed the Secretary, in a tone of mingled astonishment and indignation. 'Beer! Why, sir, he's one of the most ardent spirits engaged in the teetotal cause. He has been one of us for upwards of ten years or more.'

'And before that, eh?'

'He was on the Press.'

'Hum!' observed the President.

'But he's quite reformed *now*,' answered the Secretary, to the objection implied in the President's monosyllable.

'And you say he is really eloquent?'

'Remarkably so—*very*, remarkably so. In fact, I may say a puffick J.B. Gough.'

'Has he written in favour of the cause?'

'Largely, sir. His tracks is well known.'

'Then send him in again.'

The subject of this conversation—which took place in the Committee Room of the Teetotal Union, in Aldersgate Street, City—stood in an outer chamber, gravely contemplative. All that Mr Bottle, the Secretary, had urged in favour of his dignified demeanour, was quite justified by his appearance. But the reflections of Alderman Lamb, the President, were also to a great extent borne out by what little of him was visible to the naked eye. Indeed, the remarkable man was a trifle more than soiled. He was very dirty. He might be described as an old-young man. He had curly grey hair, thin and rather distinguished features, a small nervous hand, an imperturbable solemnity of expression, and a dignity of pose worthy the immortal Mr Turveydrop.

At the bidding of the Secretary, he re-entered the sanctum of the President, to whom he bowed low and impressively. He sat in the chair offered to him, and looked at Mr Lamb as though he would have said to that worthy Alderman and Spectacle Maker, 'Will you have your case disposed of now, or do you wish it sent to the Assizes?'

'Our Mr Bottle,' began the President, as Mr Browley, the remarkable man, bowed condescendingly to that functionary, 'our Mr Bottle suggests that you should temporarily fill the place of one of our regular lecturers. A lecture is announced for to-morrow night at the Temperance Hall, New Cut The remuneration is small—two pounds, in fact. Will you accept the offer?'

'Sir,' replied Mr Browley, in solemn tones, 'you honour me. I accept.'

'*I*,' went on the Alderman, 'will be in the chair.'

'You overwhelm me with honours,' replied Mr Browley, with another obeisance.

'And may I ask,' said the President, 'the title of your lecture?'

'With pleasure, sir. Indeed, you have a right to know. I call it an Oration. It is entitled, "The Demon Drink."'

'Capital, capital,' said the Alderman, rubbing his hands as if relishing the idea of being made personally acquainted with the Demon in question; 'and you won't forget the hour—eight o'clock at the Temperance Hall. Good-bye, Mr Browley; glad to have made your acquaintance.'

But Mr Browley made no motion of withdrawal. With a slight movement of the right hand he signalled that he was about to speak.

'Excuse me,' he said, 'but there is a slight preliminary. I have made it a rule in dealing with religious and philanthropic societies always to extort a small sum in advance as a pledge of good faith. I am not in any want of money, nor do I doubt your ability and willingness to pay it. But I have made it a rule, and I invariably insist on compliance with it. If you will pay me half a sovereign—not necessarily for publication, but as a guarantee of good faith—I will accept that amount.'

'Certainly, my dear sir. Mr Bottle, pray let the gentleman have ten shillings, or a sovereign if he wants it.'

'I said *half* a sovereign,' said the lecturer, impressively.

That sum was handed to him by Mr Bottle, who took his receipt, and Mr Browley appeared once more in the outer air.

For a remarkable man with a great interest in the temperance cause, it must be admitted that his first two visits were somewhat singular in their nature. His first visit was to a pawnbroker's, where he redeemed a dress suit pledged for three shillings, and his next visit was to a public-house, where he called for a pint of bitter and Burton—in a pewter.

'That's both meat and drink,' he murmured, as he licked his lips. It was evident that the remarkable man spoke from conviction, for he hardly passed a tavern on his way from town to the remoter slums of Islington without eating and drinking after the same fashion—with this slight variation, that at the last half-dozen houses of call he substituted for the beer that decoction which Mr Eccles alludes to as 'cool, refreshing gin.'

He reeled at last into his own street, and staggered into the one room occupied by himself and his wife. He threw the bundle of dress clothes on the bed.

'Maggie! get me that "Demon Drink." I'm going to deliver the "Demon" to-morrow. D'ye hear?'

'But, John, remember what the doctor said at the hospital. All excitement is so bad for you.'

'Damn the doctors. Produce the "Demon," d'ye hear?'

And so alternately damning the doctors and demanding the Demon, he sank on the bed and snored the snore of the drunk. She knelt by his side and wept, and—God help her!—prayed. She remembered him, you see, when he returned from College with his University honours thick upon him, and before the Demon had got him—tight.

There was a great audience the next night at the New Cut Hall, and Mr Browley, in his dress clothes, looked somewhat more presentable than on the previous day. His wife had managed to procure linen, and the worthy Alderman in the chair was quite pleased and encouraged by the improved appearance of the lecturer; though it is true he once whispered to Mr Bottle that he thought he detected a very strong smell of drink in the room.

Mr Browley was in due course presented to the large and highly expectant audience. And it must be admitted that rarely had an audience the opportunity of listening to an oration of such force and vigour. The whole figure of the lecturer seemed to change, his face glowed, the assumption of *hauteur* left him as he assailed the drink Demon and portrayed his victims. Now a torrent of applause followed some well-aimed hit at the vendors of drink, and now some pathetic anecdote drew tears from the eyes of his auditors. The Alderman was enchanted, and applauded vociferously; now agreeing with his secretary, that Mr Browley was indeed a very remarkable man.

Presently the lecturer proceeded to deal with the awful disease which turns the habitual drunkard into a dangerous maniac. He described the progress and effect of *delirium tremens*. His eyes now flashed wildly as he portrayed to the affrighted audience devils from the pit of hell; and goblin forms and pursuing shapes of beast and reptile. His body swayed to and fro: he spoke in gasps; his mouth seemed parched and hot. Now his eye-balls appeared to shoot from his head, and his arms were moved in front of him as if to ward off the creatures of his fancies. The effect was electrical. The audience rose at him, and followed his effort with long-continued applause.

In the middle of it all the lecturer's face appeared to grow livid, his eyes fixed, and his limbs stiff. He placed his left hand to his temple, and with his stretched forefinger pointed in front of him. Then he moaned as a wild animal moans in pain, and fell backward on the platform. A wild shriek burst from the back of the hall as his wife rushed forward, jumped upon the platform, and threw herself on the prostrate body.

A doctor arrived in due course.

'Drunk?' inquired Mr Bottle, when he had examined him.

'No. Dead!' answered the physician.

11

THE LITTLE MATCH GIRL

Hans Christian Andersen

Most terribly cold it was; it snowed, and was nearly quite dark, and evening—the last evening of the year. In this cold and darkness there went along the street a poor little girl, bareheaded, and with naked feet. When she left home she had slippers on, it is true; but what was the good of that? They were very large slippers, which her mother had hitherto worn; so large were they; and the poor little thing lost them as she scuffled away across the street, because of two carriages that rolled by dreadfully fast.

One slipper was nowhere to be found; the other had been laid hold of by an urchin, and off he ran with it; he thought it would do capitally for a cradle when he some day or other should have children himself. So the little maiden walked on with her tiny naked feet, that were quite red and blue from cold. She carried a quantity of matches in an old apron, and she held a bundle of them in her hand. Nobody had bought anything of her the whole livelong day; no one had given her a single farthing.

She crept along trembling with cold and hunger—a very picture of sorrow, the poor little thing!

The flakes of snow covered her long fair hair, which fell

in beautiful curls around her neck; but of that, of course, she never once now thought. From all the windows the candles were gleaming, and it smelt so deliciously of roast goose, for you know it was New Year's Eve; yes, of that she thought.

In a corner formed by two houses, of which one advanced more than the other, she seated herself down and cowered together. Her little feet she had drawn close up to her, but she grew colder and colder, and to go home she did not venture, for she had not sold any matches and could not bring a farthing of money: from her father she would certainly get blows, and at home it was cold too, for above her she had only the roof, through which the wind whistled, even though the largest cracks were stopped up with straw and rags.

Her little hands were almost numbed with cold. Oh! a match might afford her a world of comfort, if she only dared take a single one out of the bundle, draw it against the wall, and warm her fingers by it. She drew one out. 'Rischt!' how it blazed, how it burnt! It was a warm, bright flame, like a candle, as she held her hands over it: it was a wonderful light. It seemed really to the little maiden as though she were sitting before a large iron stove, with burnished brass feet and a brass ornament at top. The fire burned with such blessed influence; it warmed so delightfully. The little girl had already stretched out her feet to warm them too; but—the small flame went out, the stove vanished: she had only the remains of the burnt-out match in her hand.

She rubbed another against the wall: it burned brightly, and where the light fell on the wall, there the wall became transparent like a veil, so that she could see into the room. On the table was spread a snow-white tablecloth; upon it was a splendid porcelain service, and the roast goose was steaming famously with its stuffing of apple and dried plums. And what was still more capital to behold was, the goose hopped down from the dish, reeled about on the floor with knife and fork in its breast, till it came up to the poor little girl; when—the match went out and nothing but the thick, cold, damp wall was left behind. She lighted another match. Now there she was sitting under the most magnificent Christmas tree: it was still larger, and more decorated than the one which she had seen through the glass door in the rich merchant's house.

Thousands of lights were burning on the green branches, and gaily-coloured pictures, such as she had seen in the shop-windows, looked down upon her. The little maiden stretched out her hands towards them when—the match went out. The lights of the Christmas tree rose higher and higher, she saw them now as stars in heaven; one fell down and formed a long trail of fire.

'Someone is just dead!' said the little girl; for her old grandmother, the only person who had loved her, and who was now no more, had told her, that when a star falls, a soul ascends to God.

She drew another match against the wall: it was again light, and in the lustre there stood the old grandmother, so bright and radiant, so mild, and with such an expression of love.

'Grandmother!' cried the little one. 'Oh, take me with you! You go away when the match burns out; you vanish like the warm stove, like the delicious roast goose, and like the magnificent Christmas tree!' And she rubbed the whole bundle of matches quickly against the wall, for she wanted to be quite sure of keeping her grandmother near her. And the matches gave such a brilliant light that it was brighter than at noon-day: never formerly had the grandmother been so beautiful and so tall. She took the little maiden, on her arm, and both flew in brightness and in joy so high, so very high, and then above was neither cold, nor hunger, nor anxiety—they were with God.

But in the corner, at the cold hour of dawn, sat the poor girl, with rosy cheeks and with a smiling mouth, leaning against the wall—frozen to death on the last evening of the old year. Stiff and stark sat the child there with her matches, of which one bundle had been burnt. 'She wanted to warm herself,' people said. No one had the slightest suspicion of what beautiful things she had seen; no one even dreamed of the splendour in which, with her grandmother she had entered on the joys of a new year.

12

THE STORY OF AN HOUR

Kate Chopin

Knowing that Mrs Mallard was afflicted with a heart trouble, great care was taken to break to her as gently as possible the news of her husband's death.

It was her sister Josephine who told her, in broken sentences; veiled hints that revealed in half concealing. Her husband's friend Richards was there, too, near her. It was he who had been in the newspaper office when intelligence of the railroad disaster was received, with Brently Mallard's name leading the list of 'killed.' He had only taken the time to assure himself of its truth by a second telegram, and had hastened to forestall any less careful, less tender friend in bearing the sad message.

She did not hear the story as many women have heard the same, with a paralysed inability to accept its significance. She wept at once, with sudden, wild abandonment, in her sister's arms. When the storm of grief had spent itself she went away to her room alone. She would have no one follow her.

There stood, facing the open window, a comfortable, roomy armchair. Into this she sank, pressed down by a physical exhaustion that haunted her body and seemed to reach into her soul.

She could see in the open square before her house the

tops of trees that were all aquiver with the new spring life. The delicious breath of rain was in the air. In the street below a peddler was crying his wares. The notes of a distant song which someone was singing reached her faintly, and countless sparrows were twittering in the eaves.

There were patches of blue sky showing here and there through the clouds that had met and piled one above the other in the west facing her window.

She sat with her head thrown back upon the cushion of the chair, quite motionless, except when a sob came up into her throat and shook her, as a child who has cried itself to sleep continues to sob in its dreams.

She was young, with a fair, calm face, whose lines bespoke repression and even a certain strength. But now there was a dull stare in her eyes, whose gaze was fixed away off yonder on one of those patches of blue sky. It was not a glance of reflection, but rather indicated a suspension of intelligent thought.

There was something coming to her and she was waiting for it, fearfully. What was it? She did not know; it was too subtle and elusive to name. But she felt it, creeping out of the sky, reaching toward her through the sounds, the scents, the colour that filled the air.

Now her bosom rose and fell tumultuously. She was beginning to recognize this thing that was approaching to possess her, and she was striving to beat it back with her will— as powerless as her two white slender hands would have been. When she abandoned herself a little whispered word escaped her slightly parted lips. She said it over and over under the breath: 'free, free, free!' The vacant stare and the look of terror that had followed it went from her eyes. They stayed keen and bright. Her pulses beat fast, and the coursing blood warmed and relaxed every inch of her body.

She did not stop to ask if it were or were not a monstrous joy that held her. A clear and exalted perception enabled her to dismiss the suggestion as trivial. She knew that she would weep again when she saw the kind, tender hands folded in death; the face that had never looked save with love upon her, fixed and grey and dead. But she saw beyond that bitter moment a long procession of years to come that would belong to her absolutely. And she opened and spread her arms out to them in welcome.

There would be no one to live for during those coming years; she would live for herself. There would be no powerful will bending hers in that blind persistence with which men and women believe they have a right to impose a private will upon a fellow-creature. A kind intention or a cruel intention made the act seem no less a crime as she looked upon it in that brief moment of illumination.

And yet she had loved him—sometimes. Often she had not. What did it matter! What could love, the unsolved mystery, count for in the face of this possession of self-assertion which she suddenly recognized as the strongest impulse of her being!

'Free! Body and soul free!' she kept whispering.

Josephine was kneeling before the closed door with her lips to the keyhole, imploring for admission. 'Louise, open the door! I beg; open the door—you will make yourself ill. What are you doing, Louise? For heaven's sake open the door.'

'Go away. I am not making myself ill.' No; she was drinking in a very elixir of life through that open window.

Her fancy was running riot along those days ahead of her. Spring days, and summer days, and all sorts of days that would be her own. She breathed a quick prayer that life might be long. It was only yesterday she had thought with a shudder that life might be long.

She arose at length and opened the door to her sister's

importunities. There was a feverish triumph in her eyes, and she carried herself unwittingly like a goddess of Victory. She clasped her sister's waist, and together they descended the stairs. Richards stood waiting for them at the bottom.

Someone was opening the front door with a latchkey. It was Brently Mallard who entered, a little travel-stained, composedly carrying his grip-sack and umbrella. He had been far from the scene of the accident, and did not even know there had been one. He stood amazed at Josephine's piercing cry; at Richards' quick motion to screen him from the view of his wife.

When the doctors came they said she had died of heart disease—of the joy that kills.

13

REGRET

Kate Chopin

Mamzelle Aurélie possessed a good strong figure, ruddy cheeks, hair that was changing from brown to gray, and a determined eye. She wore a man's hat about the farm, and an old blue army overcoat when it was cold, and sometimes top-boots.

Mamzelle Aurélie had never thought of marrying. She had never been in love. At the age of twenty she had received a proposal, which she had promptly declined, and at the age of fifty she had not yet lived to regret it.

So she was quite alone in the world, except for her dog Ponto, and the negroes who lived in her cabins and worked her crops, and the fowls, a few cows, a couple of mules, her gun (with which she shot chicken-hawks), and her religion.

One morning Mamzelle Aurélie stood upon her gallery, contemplating, with arms akimbo, a small band of very small children who, to all intents and purposes, might have fallen from the clouds, so unexpected and bewildering was their coming, and so unwelcome. They were the children of her nearest neighbor, Odile, who was not such a near neighbor, after all.

The young woman had appeared but five minutes before,

accompanied by these four children. In her arms she carried little Elodie; she dragged Ti Nomme by an unwilling hand; while Marcéline and Marcélette followed with irresolute steps.

Her face was red and disfigured from tears and excitement. She had been summoned to a neighboring parish by the dangerous illness of her mother; her husband was away in Texas—it seemed to her a million miles away; and Valsin was waiting with the mule-cart to drive her to the station.

'It's no question, Mamzelle Aurélie; you jus' got to keep those youngsters fo' me tell I come back. Dieu sait, I wouldn' botha you with 'em if it was any otha way to do! Make 'em mine you, Mamzelle Aurélie; don' spare 'em. Me, there, I'm half crazy between the chil'ren, an' Léon not home, an' maybe not even to fine po' maman alive encore!'—a harrowing possibility which drove Odile to take a final hasty and convulsive leave of her disconsolate family.

She left them crowded into the narrow strip of shade on the porch of the long, low house; the white sunlight was beating in on the white old boards; some chickens were scratching in the grass at the foot of the steps, and one had boldly mounted, and was stepping heavily, solemnly, and aimlessly across the gallery. There was a pleasant odour of pinks in the air, and the sound of negroes' laughter was coming across the flowering cotton-field.

Mamzelle Aurélie stood contemplating the children. She looked with a critical eye upon Marcéline, who had been left staggering beneath the weight of the chubby Elodie. She surveyed with the same calculating air Marcélette mingling her silent tears with the audible grief and rebellion of Ti Nomme. During those few contemplative moments she was collecting herself, determining upon a line of action which should be identical with a line of duty. She began by feeding them.

If Mamzelle Aurélie's responsibilities might have begun and

ended there, they could easily have been dismissed; for her larder was amply provided against an emergency of this nature. But little children are not little pigs: they require and demand attentions which were wholly unexpected by Mamzelle Aurélie, and which she was ill prepared to give.

She was, indeed, very inapt in her management of Odile's children during the first few days. How could she know that Marcélette always wept when spoken to in a loud and commanding tone of voice? It was a peculiarity of Marcélette's. She became acquainted with Ti Nomme's passion for flowers only when he had plucked all the choicest gardenias and pinks for the apparent purpose of critically studying their botanical construction.

"T ain't enough to tell 'im, Mamzelle Aurélie,' Marcéline instructed her; 'you got to tie 'im in a chair. It's w'at maman all time do w'en he's bad: she tie 'im in a chair.' The chair in which Mamzelle Aurélie tied Ti Nomme was roomy and comfortable, and he seized the opportunity to take a nap in it, the afternoon being warm.

At night, when she ordered them one and all to bed as she would have shooed the chickens into the hen-house, they stayed uncomprehending before her. What about the little white nightgowns that had to be taken from the pillow-slip in which they were brought over, and shaken by some strong hand till they snapped like ox-whips? What about the tub of water which had to be brought and set in the middle of the floor, in which the little tired, dusty, sun-browned feet had every one to be washed sweet and clean? And it made Marcéline and Marcélette laugh merrily—the idea that Mamzelle Aurélie should for a moment have believed that Ti Nomme could fall asleep without being told the story of *Croque-mitaine* or *Loup-garou*, or both; or that Elodie could fall asleep at all without being rocked and sung to.

'I tell you, Aunt Ruby,' Mamzelle Aurélie informed her cook in confidence; 'me, I'd rather manage a dozen plantation' than fo' chil'ren. It's terrassent! Bonté! Don't talk to me about chil'ren!'

"T ain' ispected sich as you would know airy thing 'bout 'em, Mamzelle Aurélie. I see dat plainly yistiddy w'en I spy dat li'le chile playin' wid yo' baskit o' keys. You don' know dat makes chillun grow up hard-headed, to play wid keys? Des like it make 'em teeth hard to look in a lookin'-glass. Them's the things you got to know in the raisin' an' manigement o' chillun.'

Mamzelle Aurélie certainly did not pretend or aspire to such subtle and far-reaching knowledge on the subject as Aunt Ruby possessed, who had 'raised five an' bared (buried) six' in her day. She was glad enough to learn a few little mother-tricks to serve the moment's need.

Ti Nomme's sticky fingers compelled her to unearth white aprons that she had not worn for years, and she had to accustom herself to his moist kisses—the expressions of an affectionate and exuberant nature. She got down her sewing-basket, which she seldom used, from the top shelf of the armoire, and placed it within the ready and easy reach which torn slips and buttonless waists demanded. It took her some days to become accustomed to the laughing, the crying, the chattering that echoed through the house and around it all day long. And it was not the first or the second night that she could sleep comfortably with little Elodie's hot, plump body pressed close against her, and the little one's warm breath beating her cheek like the fanning of a bird's wing.

But at the end of two weeks Mamzelle Aurélie had grown quite used to these things, and she no longer complained.

It was also at the end of two weeks that Mamzelle Aurélie, one evening, looking away toward the crib where the cattle were being fed, saw Valsin's blue cart turning the bend of the road. Odile sat beside the mulatto, upright and alert. As they drew near, the young woman's beaming face indicated that her home-coming was a happy one.

But this coming, unannounced and unexpected, threw Mamzelle Aurélie into a flutter that was almost agitation. The children had to be gathered. Where was Ti Nomme? Yonder in the shed, putting an edge on his knife at the grindstone. And Marcéline and Marcélette? Cutting and fashioning doll-rags in the corner of the gallery. As for Elodie, she was safe enough in Mamzelle Aurélie's arms; and she had screamed with delight at sight of the familiar blue cart which was bringing her mother back to her.

The excitement was all over, and they were gone. How still it was when they were gone! Mamzelle Aurélie stood upon the gallery, looking and listening. She could no longer see the cart; the red sunset and the blue-gray twilight had together flung a purple mist across the fields and road that hid it from her view. She could no longer hear the wheezing and creaking of its wheels. But she could still faintly hear the shrill, glad voices of the children.

She turned into the house. There was much work awaiting her, for the children had left a sad disorder behind them; but she did not at once set about the task of righting it. Mamzelle Aurélie seated herself beside the table. She gave one slow glance through the room, into which the evening shadows were creeping and deepening around her solitary figure. She let her head fall down upon her bended arm, and began to cry. Oh, but she cried! Not softly, as women often do. She cried like a man, with sobs that seemed to tear her very soul. She did not notice Ponto licking her hand.

14

THE CACTUS

O. Henry

The most notable thing about Time is that it is so purely relative. A large amount of reminiscence is, by common consent, conceded to the drowning man; and it is not past belief that one may review an entire courtship while removing one's gloves.

That is what Trysdale was doing, standing by a table in his bachelor apartments. On the table stood a singular-looking green plant in a red earthen jar. The plant was one of the species of cacti, and was provided with long, tentacular leaves that perpetually swayed with the slightest breeze with a peculiar beckoning motion.

Trysdale's friend, the brother of the bride, stood at a sideboard complaining at being allowed to drink alone. Both men were in evening dress. White favours like stars upon their coats shone through the gloom of the apartment.

As he slowly unbuttoned his gloves, there passed through Trysdale's mind a swift, scarifying retrospect of the last few hours. It seemed that in his nostrils was still the scent of the flowers that had been banked in odorous masses about the church, and in his ears the lowpitched hum of a thousand well-bred voices, the rustle of crisp garments, and, most insistently recurring, the drawling words of the minister irrevocably binding her to another.

From this last hopeless point of view he still strove, as if it had become a habit of his mind, to reach some conjecture as to why and how he had lost her. Shaken rudely by the uncompromising fact, he had suddenly found himself confronted by a thing he had never before faced—his own innermost, unmitigated, arid unbedecked self. He saw all the garbs of pretence and egoism that he had worn now turn to rags of folly. He shuddered at the thought that to others, before now, the garments of his soul must have appeared sorry and threadbare. Vanity and conceit? These were the joints in his armor. And how free from either she had always been—But why—

As she had slowly moved up the aisle toward the altar he had felt an unworthy, sullen exultation that had served to support him. He had told himself that her paleness was from thoughts of another than the man to whom she was about to give herself. But even that poor consolation had been wrenched from him. For, when he saw that swift, limpid, upward look that she gave the man when he took her hand, he knew himself to be forgotten. Once that same look had been raised to him, and he had gauged its meaning. Indeed, his conceit had crumbled; its last prop was gone. Why had it ended thus? There had been no quarrel between them, nothing—

For the thousandth time he remarshalled in his mind the events of those last few days before the tide had so suddenly turned.

She had always insisted upon placing him upon a pedestal, and he had accepted her homage with royal grandeur. It had been a very sweet incense that she had burned before him; so modest (he told himself); so childlike and worshipful, and (he would once have sworn) so sincere. She had invested him with an almost supernatural number of high attributes and excellencies and talents, and he had absorbed the oblation as a desert drinks the rain that can coax from it no promise of blossom or fruit.

As Trysdale grimly wrenched apart the seam of his last glove, the crowning instance of his fatuous and tardily mourned egoism came vividly back to him. The scene was the night when he had asked her to come up on his pedestal with him and share his greatness. He could not, now, for the pain of it, allow his mind to dwell upon the memory of her convincing beauty that night—the careless wave of her hair, the tenderness and virginal charm of her looks and words. But they had been enough, and they had brought him to speak. During their conversation she had said:

'And Captain Carruthers tells me that you speak the Spanish language like a native. Why have you hidden this accomplishment from me? Is there anything you do not know?'

Now, Carruthers was an idiot. No doubt he (Trysdale) had been guilty (he sometimes did such things) of airing at the club some old, canting Castilian proverb dug from the hotchpotch at the back of dictionaries. Carruthers, who was one of his incontinent admirers, was the very man to have magnified this exhibition of doubtful erudition.

But, alas! the incense of her admiration had been so sweet and flattering. He allowed the imputation to pass without denial. Without protest, he allowed her to twine about his brow this spurious bay of Spanish scholarship. He let it grace his conquering head, and, among its soft convolutions, he did not feel the prick of the thorn that was to pierce him later.

How glad, how shy, how tremulous she was! How she fluttered like a snared bird when he laid his mightiness at her feet! He could have sworn, and he could swear now, that unmistakable consent was in her eyes, but, coyly, she would give him no direct answer. 'I will send you my answer to-morrow,' she said; and he, the indulgent, confident victor, smilingly granted the delay. The next day he waited, impatient, in his rooms for the word. At noon her groom came to the door and left the strange cactus in the red earthen jar. There was no note, no message, merely a tag upon the plant bearing a barbarous foreign or botanical name. He waited until night, but her answer did not come. His large pride and hurt vanity kept him from seeking her. Two evenings later they met at a dinner. Their greetings were conventional, but she looked at him, breathless, wondering, eager. He was courteous, adamant, waiting her explanation. With womanly swiftness she took her cue from his manner, and turned to snow and ice. Thus, and wider from this on, they had drifted apart. Where was his fault? Who had been to blame? Humbled now, he sought the answer amid the ruins of his self-conceit. If—

The voice of the other man in the room, querulously intruding upon his thoughts, aroused him.

'I say, Trysdale, what the deuce is the matter with you? You look unhappy as if you yourself had been married instead of having acted merely as an accomplice. Look at me, another accessory, come two thousand miles on a garlicky, cockroachy banana steamer all the way from South America to connive at the sacrifice—please to observe how lightly my guilt rests upon my shoulders. Only little sister I had, too, and now she's gone. Come now! take something to ease your conscience.'

'I don't drink just now, thanks,' said Trysdale.

'Your brandy,' resumed the other, coming over and joining him, 'is abominable. Run down to see me some time at Punta Redonda, and try some of our stuff that old Garcia smuggles in. It's worth the, trip. Hallo! here's an old acquaintance. Wherever did you rake up this cactus, Trysdale?'

'A present,' said Trysdale, 'from a friend. Know the species?'

'Very well. It's a tropical concern. See hundreds of 'em around Punta every day. Here's the name on this tag tied to it. Know any Spanish, Trysdale?'

'No,' said Trysdale, with the bitter wraith of a smile—'Is it Spanish?'

'Yes. The natives imagine the leaves are reaching out and beckoning to you. They call it by this name—Ventomarme. Name means in English, "Come and take me."'

15

THE CAT

Mary E. Wilkins Freeman

The snow was falling, and the Cat's fur was stiffly pointed with it, but he was imperturbable. He sat crouched, ready for the death-spring, as he had sat for hours. It was night—but that made no difference—all times were as one to the Cat when he was in wait for prey. Then, too, he was under no constraint of human will, for he was living alone that winter. Nowhere in the world was any voice calling him; on no hearth was there a waiting dish. He was quite free except for his own desires, which tyrannized over him when unsatisfied as now. The Cat was very hungry—almost famished, in fact. For days the weather had been very bitter, and all the feebler wild things which were his prey by inheritance, the born serfs to his family, had kept, for the most part, in their burrows and nests, and the Cat's long hunt had availed him nothing. But he waited with the inconceivable patience and persistency of his race; besides, he was certain. The Cat was a creature of absolute convictions, and his faith in his deductions never wavered. The rabbit had gone in there between those low-hung pine boughs. Now her little doorway had before it a shaggy curtain of snow, but in there she was. The Cat had seen her enter, so like a swift grey shadow that even his sharp and practised eyes had glanced back for the substance following, and then she was gone. So he sat down and waited, and he waited still in the white night, listening angrily to the north wind starting in the upper heights of the mountains with distant screams, then swelling into an awful crescendo of rage, and swooping down with furious white wings of snow like a flock of fierce eagles into the valleys and ravines. The Cat was on the side of a mountain, on a wooded terrace. Above him a few feet away towered the rock ascent as steep as the wall of a cathedral. The Cat had never climbed it—trees were the ladders to his heights of life. He had often looked with wonder at the rock, and miauled bitterly and resentfully as man does in the face of a forbidding Providence. At his left was the sheer precipice. Behind him, with a short stretch of woody growth between, was the frozen perpendicular wall of a mountain stream. Before him was the way to his home. When the rabbit came out she was trapped; her little cloven feet could not scale such unbroken steeps. So the Cat waited. The place in which he was looked like a maelstrom of the wood. The tangle of trees and bushes clinging to the mountain-side with a stern clutch of roots, the prostrate trunks and branches, the vines embracing everything with strong knots and coils of growth, had a curious effect, as of things which had whirled for ages in a current of raging water, only it was not water, but wind, which had disposed everything in circling lines of yielding to its fiercest points of onset. And now over all this whirl of wood and rock and dead trunks and branches and vines descended the snow. It blew down like smoke over the rock-crest above; it stood in a gyrating column like some death-wraith of nature, on the level, then it broke over the edge of the precipice, and the Cat cowered before the fierce backward set of it. It was as if ice needles pricked his skin through his beautiful thick fur, but he never faltered and never once cried. He had nothing to gain from crying, and everything to lose; the rabbit would hear him cry and know he was waiting.

It grew darker and darker, with a strange white smother, instead of the natural blackness of night. It was a night of storm and death superadded to the night of nature. The mountains were all hidden, wrapped about, overawed, and tumultuously overborne by it, but in the midst of it waited, quite unconquered, this little, unswerving, living patience and power under a little coat of grey fur.

A fiercer blast swept over the rock, spun on one mighty foot of whirlwind athwart the level, then was over the precipice.

Then the Cat saw two eyes luminous with terror, frantic with the impulse of flight, he saw a little, quivering, dilating nose, he saw two pointing ears, and he kept still, with every one of his fine nerves and muscles strained like wires. Then the rabbit was out—there was one long line of incarnate flight and terror—and the Cat had her.

Then the Cat went home, trailing his prey through the snow.

The Cat lived in the house which his master had built, as rudely as a child's block-house, but staunchly enough. The snow was heavy on the low slant of its roof, but it would not settle under it. The two windows and the door were made fast, but the Cat knew a way in. Up a pine-tree behind the house he scuttled, though it was hard work with his heavy rabbit, and was in his little window under the eaves, then down through the trap to the room below, and on his master's bed with a spring and a great cry of triumph, rabbit and all. But his master was not there; he had been gone since early fall and it was now February. He would not return until spring, for he was an old man, and the cruel cold of the mountains clutched at his vitals like a panther, and he had gone to the village to winter.

The Cat had known for a long time that his master was gone, but his reasoning was always sequential and circuitous; always for him what had been would be, and the more easily for his marvellous waiting powers so he always came home expecting to find his master.

When he saw that he was still gone, he dragged the rabbit off the rude couch which was the bed to the floor, put one little paw on the carcass to keep it steady, and began gnawing with head to one side to bring his strongest teeth to bear.

It was darker in the house than it had been in the wood, and the cold was as deadly, though not so fierce. If the Cat had not received his fur coat unquestioningly of Providence, he would have been thankful that he had it. It was a mottled grey, white on the face and breast, and thick as fur could grow.

The wind drove the snow on the windows with such force that it rattled like sleet, and the house trembled a little. Then all at once the Cat heard a noise, and stopped gnawing his rabbit and listened, his shining green eyes fixed upon a window. Then he heard a hoarse shout, a halloo of despair and entreaty; but he knew it was not his master come home, and he waited, one paw still on the rabbit. Then the halloo came again, and then the Cat answered. He said all that was essential quite plainly to his own comprehension. There was in his cry of response inquiry, information, warning, terror and finally, the offer of comradeship; but the man outside did not hear him, because of the howling of the storm.

Then there was a great battering pound at the door, then another, and another. The Cat dragged his rabbit under the bed. The blows came thicker and faster. It was a weak arm which gave them, but it was nerved by desperation. Finally the lock yielded, and the stranger came in. Then the Cat, peering from under the bed, blinked with a sudden light, and his green eyes narrowed. The stranger struck a match and looked about. The Cat saw a face wild and blue with hunger and cold, and a man who looked poorer and older than his poor old master, who was an outcast among men for his poverty and lowly mystery of antecedents; and he heard a muttered, unintelligible voicing of distress from the harsh piteous mouth. There was in it both profanity and prayer, but the Cat knew nothing of that.

The stranger braced the door which he had forced, got some wood from the stock in the corner, and kindled a fire in the old stove as quickly as his half-frozen hands would allow. He shook so pitiably as he worked that the Cat under the bed felt the tremor of it. Then the man, who was small and feeble and marked with the scars of suffering which he had pulled down upon his own head, sat down in one of the old chairs and crouched over the fire as if it were the one love and desire of his soul, holding out his yellow hands like yellow claws, and he groaned. The Cat came out from under the bed and leaped up on his lap with the rabbit. The man gave a great shout and start of terror, and sprang, and the Cat slid clawing to the floor, and the rabbit fell inertly, and the man leaned, gasping with fright, and ghastly, against the wall. The Cat grabbed the rabbit by the slack of its neck and dragged it to the man's feet. Then he raised his shrill, insistent cry, he arched his back high, his tail was a splendid waving plume. He rubbed against the man's feet, which were bursting out of their torn shoes.

The man pushed the Cat away, gently enough, and began searching about the little cabin. He even climbed painfully the ladder to the loft, lit a match, and peered up in the darkness with straining eyes. He feared lest there might be a man, since there was a cat. His experience with men had not been pleasant, and neither had the experience of men been pleasant with him. He was an old wandering Ishmael among his kind; he had stumbled upon the house of a brother, and the brother was not at home, and he was glad.

He returned to the Cat, and stooped stiffly and stroked his back, which the animal arched like the spring of a bow.

Then he took up the rabbit and looked at it eagerly by the firelight. His jaws worked. He could almost have devoured it raw. He fumbled—the Cat close at his heels—around some rude shelves and a table, and found, with a grunt of self-gratulation, a lamp with oil in it. That he lighted; then he found a frying-pan and a knife, and skinned the rabbit, and prepared it for cooking, the Cat always at his feet.

When the odour of the cooking flesh filled the cabin, both the man and the Cat looked wolfish. The man turned the rabbit with one hand and stooped to pat the Cat with the other. The Cat thought him a fine man. He loved him with all his heart, though he had known him such a short time, and though the man had a face both pitiful and sharply set at variance with the best of things.

It was a face with the grimy grizzle of age upon it, with fever hollows in the cheeks, and the memories of wrong in the dim eyes, but the Cat accepted the man unquestioningly and loved him. When the rabbit was half cooked, neither the man nor the Cat could wait any longer. The man took it from the fire, divided it exactly in halves, gave the Cat one, and took the other himself. Then they ate.

Then the man blew out the light, called the Cat to him, got on the bed, drew up the ragged coverings, and fell asleep with the Cat in his bosom.

The man was the Cat's guest all the rest of the winter, and winter is long in the mountains. The rightful owner of the little hut did not return until May. All that time the Cat toiled hard, and he grew rather thin himself, for he shared everything except mice with his guest; and sometimes game was wary, and the fruit of patience of days was very little for two. The man was ill and weak, however, and unable to eat much, which was fortunate, since he could not hunt for himself. All day long he lay on the bed, or else sat crouched over the fire. It was a good thing that fire-wood was ready at hand for the picking up, not a stone's-throw from the door, for that he had to attend to himself.

The Cat foraged tirelessly. Sometimes he was gone for days together, and at first the man used to be terrified, thinking he would never return; then he would hear the familiar cry at the door, and stumble to his feet and let him in. Then the two would dine together, sharing equally; then the Cat would rest and purr, and finally sleep in the man's arms.

Towards spring the game grew plentiful; more wild little quarry were tempted out of their homes, in search of love as well as food. One day the Cat had luck—a rabbit, a partridge, and a mouse. He could not carry them all at once, but finally he had them together at the house door. Then he cried, but no one answered. All the mountain streams were loosened, and the air was full of the gurgle of many waters, occasionally pierced by a bird-whistle. The trees rustled with a new sound to the spring wind; there was a flush of rose and gold-green on the breasting surface of a distant mountain seen through an opening in the wood. The tips of the bushes were swollen and glistening red, and now and then there was a flower; but the Cat had nothing to do with flowers. He stood beside his booty at the house door, and cried and cried with his insistent triumph and complaint and pleading, but no one came to let him in. Then the cat left his little treasures at the door, and went around to the back of the house to the pine-tree, and was up the trunk with a wild scramble, and in through his little window, and down through the trap to the room, and the man was gone.

The Cat cried again—that cry of the animal for human companionship which is one of the sad notes of the world; he looked in all the corners; he sprang to the chair at the window and looked out; but no one came. The man was gone and he never came again.

The Cat ate his mouse out on the turf beside the house; the rabbit and the partridge he carried painfully into the house, but the man did not come to share them. Finally, in the course of a day or two, he ate them up himself; then he slept a long time on the bed, and when he waked the man was not there.

Then the Cat went forth to his hunting-grounds again, and came home at night with a plump bird, reasoning with his tireless persistency in expectancy that the man would be there; and there was a light in the window, and when he cried his old master opened the door and let him in.

His master had strong comradeship with the Cat, but not affection. He never patted him like that gentler outcast, but he had a pride in him and an anxiety for his welfare, though he had left him alone all winter without scruple. He feared lest some misfortune might have come to the Cat, though he was so large of his kind, and a mighty hunter. Therefore, when he saw him at the door in all the glory of his glossy winter coat, his white breast and face shining like snow in the sun, his own face lit up with welcome, and the Cat embraced his feet with his sinuous body vibrant with rejoicing purrs.

The Cat had his bird to himself, for his master had his own supper already cooking on the stove. After supper the Cat's master took his pipe, and sought a small store of tobacco which he had left in his hut over winter. He had thought often of it; that and the Cat seemed something to come home to in the spring. But the tobacco was gone; not a dust left. The man swore a little in a grim monotone, which made the profanity lose its customary effect. He had been, and was, a hard drinker; he had knocked about the world until the marks of its sharp corners were on his very soul, which was thereby calloused, until his very sensibility to loss was dulled. He was a very old man.

He searched for the tobacco with a sort of dull combativeness of persistency; then he stared with stupid wonder around the room. Suddenly many features struck him as being changed. Another stove-lid was broken; an old piece of carpet was tacked up over a window to keep out the cold; his fire-wood was gone. He looked and there was no oil left in his can. He looked at the coverings on his bed; he took them up, and again he made that strange remonstrant noise in his throat. Then he looked again for his tobacco.

Finally he gave it up. He sat down beside the fire, for May in the mountains is cold; he held his empty pipe in his mouth, his rough forehead knitted, and he and the Cat looked at each other across that impassable barrier of silence which has been set between man and beast from the creation of the world.

16

THE LADY, OR THE TIGER?

Frank R. Stockton

In the very olden time, there lived a semi-barbaric king, whose ideas, though somewhat polished and sharpened by the progressiveness of distant Latin neighbors, were still large, florid, and untrammelled, as became the half of him which was barbaric. He was a man of exuberant fancy, and, withal, of an authority so irresistible that, at his will, he turned his varied fancies into facts. He was greatly given to self-communing; and, when he and himself agreed upon anything, the thing was done. When every member of his domestic and political systems moved smoothly in its appointed course, his nature was bland and genial; but whenever there was a little hitch, and some of his orbs got out of their orbits, he was blander and more genial still, for nothing pleased him so much as to make the crooked straight, and crush down uneven places.

Among the borrowed notions by which his barbarism had become semified was that of the public arena, in which, by exhibitions of manly and beastly valour, the minds of his subjects were refined and cultured.

But even here the exuberant and barbaric fancy asserted itself. The arena of the king was built, not to give the people an opportunity of hearing the rhapsodies of dying gladiators, nor to enable them to view the inevitable conclusion of a conflict between religious opinions and hungry jaws, but for purposes far better adapted to widen and develop the mental energies of the people. This vast amphitheatre, with its encircling galleries, its mysterious vaults and its unseen passages, was an agent of poetic justice, in which crime was punished. Or virtue rewarded, by the decrees of an impartial and incorruptible chance.

When a subject was accused of a crime of sufficient importance to interest the king, public notice was given that on an appointed day the fate of tile accused person would be decided in the king's arena, a structure which well deserved its name; for, although its form and plan were borrowed from afar, its purpose emanated solely from the brain of this man, who, every barleycorn a king, knew no tradition to which he owed more allegiance than pleased his fancy, and who ingrafted on every adopted form of human thought and action the rich growth of his barbaric idealism.

When all the people had assembled in the galleries, and the king, surrounded by his court, sat high up on his throne of royal state on one side of the arena, he gave a signal, a door beneath him opened, and the accused subject stepped out into the amphitheatre. Directly opposite him, on the other side of the enclosed space, were two doors, exactly alike and side by side. It was the duty and the privilege of the person on trial, to walk directly to these doors and open one of them. He could open either door he pleased: he was subject to no guidance or influence but that of the aforementioned impartial and incorruptible chance. If he opened the one, there came out of it a hungry tiger, the fiercest and most cruel that could be procured, which immediately sprang upon him, and tore him to pieces, as a punishment for his guilt. The moment that the case of the criminal was thus decided, doleful iron bells were clanged, great wails went up from the hired mourners posted on the outer rim of the arena, and the vast audience, with bowed heads and downcast hearts, wended slowly their homeward way, mourning greatly that one so young and fair, or so old and respected, should have merited so dire a fate.

But, if the accused person opened the other door, there came forth from it a lady, the most suitable to his years and station that his majesty could select among his fair subjects; and to this lady he was immediately married, as a reward of his innocence. It mattered not that he might already possess a wife and family, or that his affections might be engaged upon an object of his own selection: the king allowed no such subordinate arrangements to interfere with his great scheme of retribution and reward. The exercises, as in the other instance, took place immediately, and in the arena. Another door opened beneath the king, and a priest, followed by a band of choristers, and dancing maidens blowing joyous airs on golden horns and treading an epithalamic measure, advanced to where the pair stood side by side; and the wedding was promptly and cheerily solemnized. Then the gay brass bells rang forth their merry peals, the people shouted glad hurrahs, and the innocent man, preceded by children strewing flowers on his path, led his bride to his home.

This was the king's semi-barbaric method of administering justice. Its perfect fairness is obvious. The criminal could not know out of which door would come the lady: he opened either he pleased, without having the slightest idea whether, in the next instant, he was to be devoured or married. On some occasions the tiger came out of one door, and on some out of the other. The decisions of this tribunal were not only fair, they were positively determinate: the accused person was instantly punished if he found himself guilty; and, if innocent, he was rewarded on the spot, whether he liked it or not. There was no escape from the judgments or the king's arena.

The institution was a very popular one. When the people gathered together on one of the great trial days, they never knew whether they were to witness a bloody slaughter or a hilarious wedding. This element of uncertainty lent an interest to the occasion which it could not otherwise have attained. Thus, the masses were entertained and pleased, and the thinking part of the community could bring no charge of unfairness against this plan; for did not the accused person have the whole matter in his own hands?

This semi-barbaric king had a daughter as blooming as his most florid fancies, and with a soul as fervent and imperious as his own. As is usual in such cases, she was the apple of his eye, and was loved by him above all humanity. Among his courtiers was a young man of that fineness of blood and lowness of station common to the conventional heroes of romance who love royal maidens. This royal maiden was well satisfied with her lover, for he was handsome and brave to a degree unsurpassed in all this kingdom; and she loved him with an ardour that had enough of barbarism in it to make it exceedingly warm and strong. This love affair moved on happily for many months, until one day the king happened to discover its existence. He did not hesitate nor waver in regard to his duty in the premises. The youth was immediately cast into prison, and a day was appointed for his trial in the king's arena. This, of course, was an especially important occasion; and his majesty, as well as all the people, was greatly interested in the workings and development of this trial.

Never before had such a case occurred; never before had a subject dared to love the daughter of a king. In after-years such things became commonplace enough; but then they were, in no slight degree, novel and startling.

The tiger-cages of the kingdom were searched for the most savage and relentless beasts, from which the fiercest monster might be selected for the arena; and the ranks of maiden youth and beauty throughout the land were carefully surveyed by competent judges, in order that he, young man, might have a fitting bride in case fate did not determine for him a different destiny. Of course, everybody knew that the deed with which the accused was charged had been done. He had loved the princess, and neither he, she, nor any one else thought of denying the fact; but the king would not think of allowing any fact of this kind to interfere with the workings of the tribunal, in which he took such great delight and satisfaction. No matter how the affair turned out, the youth would be disposed of; and the king would take an aesthetic pleasure in watching the course of events, which would determine whether or not the young man had done wrong in allowing himself to love the princess.

The appointed day arrived. From far and near the people gathered, and thronged the great galleries of the arena; and crowds, unable to gain admittance, massed themselves against its outside walls. The king and his court were in their places, opposite the twin doors, those fateful portals, so terrible in their similarity.

All was ready. The signal was given. A door beneath the royal party opened, and the lover of the princess walked into the arena. Tall, beautiful, fair, his appearance was greeted with a low hum of admiration and anxiety. Half the audience had not known so grand a youth had lived among them. No wonder the princess loved him! What a terrible thing for him to be there!

As the youth advanced into the arena, he turned, as the custom was, to bow to the king: but he did not think at all of that royal personage; his eyes were fixed upon the princess, who sat to the right of her father. Had it not been for the moiety of barbarism in her nature, it is probable that lady would not have been there; but her intense and fervid soul would not allow her to be absent on an occasion in which she was so terribly interested. From the moment that the decree had gone forth, that her lover should decide his fate in the king's arena, she had thought of nothing, night or day, but this great event and the various subjects connected with it. Possessed of more power, influence, and force of character than any one who had ever before been interested in such a case, she had done what no other person had done,—she had possessed herself of the secret of the doors. She knew in which of the two rooms, that lay behind those doors, stood the cage of the tiger, with its open front, and in which waited the lady. Through these thick doors, heavily curtained with skins on the inside, it was impossible that any noise or suggestion should come from within to the person who should approach to raise the latch of one of them; but gold, and the power of a woman's will, had brought the secret to the princess.

And not only did she know in which room stood the lady ready to emerge, all blushing and radiant, should her door be opened, but she knew who the lady was. It was one of tile fairest and loveliest of the damsels of the court who had been selected as the reward of the accused youth, should he be proved innocent of the crime of aspiring to one so far above him; and the princess hated her. Often had she seen, or imagined that she had seen, this fair creature throwing glances of admiration upon the person of her lover, and sometimes she thought these glances were perceived and even returned. Now and then she had seen them talking together; it was but for a moment or two, but much can be said in a brief space; it may have been on most unimportant topics, but how could she know that? The girl was lovely, but she had dared to raise her eyes to the loved one of the princess; and, with all the intensity of the savage blood transmitted to her through long lines of wholly barbaric ancestors, she hated the woman who blushed and trembled behind that silent door.

When her lover turned and looked at her, and his eye met hers as she sat there paler and whiter than any one in the vast ocean of anxious faces about her, he saw, by that power of quick perception which is given to those whose souls are one, that she knew behind which door crouched the tiger, and behind which stood the lady. He had expected her to know it. He understood her nature, and his soul was assured that she would never rest until she had made plain to herself this thing, hidden to all other lookers-on, even to the king. The only hope for the youth in which there was any element of certainty was based upon the success of the princess in discovering this mystery; and the moment he looked upon her, he saw she had succeeded, as in his soul he knew she would succeed.

Then it was that his quick and anxious glance asked the question: 'Which?' It was as plain to her as if he shouted it from where he stood. There was not an instant to be lost. The question was asked in a flash; it must be answered in another.

Her right arm lay on the cushioned parapet before her. She raised her hand, and made a slight, quick movement toward the right. No one but her lover saw her. Every eye but his was fixed on the man in the arena.

He turned, and, with a firm and rapid step he walked across the empty space. Every heart stopped beating, every breath was held, every eye was fixed immovably upon that man. Without the slightest hesitation, he went to the door on the right, and opened it.

Now, the point of the story is this: Did the tiger come out of that door, or did the lady?

The more we reflect upon this question, the harder it is to answer. It involves a study of the human heart which leads us through devious mazes of passion, out of which it is difficult to find our way. Think of it, fair reader, not as if the decision of the question depended upon yourself, but upon that hot-blooded, semi-barbaric princess, her soul at a white heat beneath the combined fires of despair and jealousy. She had lost him, but who should have him?

How often, in her waking hours and in her dreams, had she started in wild horror, and covered her face with her hands, as she thought of her lover opening the door on the other side of which waited the cruel fangs of the tiger!

But how much oftener had she seen him at the other door! How in her grievous reveries had she gnashed her teeth, and torn her hair, when she saw his start of rapturous delight as he opened the door of the lady! How her soul had burned in agony when she had seen him rush to meet that woman, with her flushing cheek and sparkling eye of triumph; when she had seen him lead her forth, his whole frame kindled with the joy of recovered life; when she had heard the glad shouts from the multitude, and the wild ringing of the happy bells; when she had seen the priest, with his joyous followers, advance to the couple, and make them man and wife before her very eyes; and when she had seen them walk away together upon their path of flowers, followed by the tremendous shouts of the hilarious multitude, in which her one despairing shriek was lost and drowned!

Would it not be better for him to die at once, and go to wait for her in the blessed regions of semi-barbaric futurity?

And yet, that awful tiger, those shrieks, that blood!

Her decision had been indicated in an instant, but it had been made after days and nights of anguished deliberation. She had known she would be asked, she had decided what she would answer, and, without the slightest hesitation, she had moved her hand to the right.

The question of her decision is one not to be lightly considered, and it is not for me to presume to set myself up as the one person able to answer it. And so I leave it with all of you: Which came out of the opened door—the lady, or the tiger?

17

THE NIGHT CAME SLOWLY

Kate Chopin

I am losing my interest in human beings; in the significance of their lives and their actions. Some one has said it is better to study one man than ten books. I want neither books nor men; they make me suffer. Can one of them talk to me like the night—the Summer night? Like the stars or the caressing wind?

The night came slowly, softly, as I lay out there under the maple tree. It came creeping, creeping stealthily out of the valley, thinking I did not notice. And the outlines of trees and foliage nearby blended in one black mass and the night came stealing out from them, too, and from the east and west, until the only light was in the sky, filtering through the maple leaves and a star looking down through every cranny.

The night is solemn and it means mystery.

Human shapes flitted by like intangible things. Some stole up like little mice to peep at me. I did not mind. My whole being was abandoned to the soothing and penetrating charm of the night.

The katydids began their slumber song: they are at it yet. How wise they are. They do not chatter like people. They tell me only: 'sleep, sleep, sleep.' The wind rippled the maple leaves like little warm love thrills.

Why do fools cumber the Earth! It was a man's voice that broke the necromancer's spell. A man came to-day with his 'Bible Class.' He is detestable with his red cheeks and bold eyes and coarse manner and speech. What does he know of Christ? Shall I ask a young fool who was born yesterday and will die tomorrow to tell me things of Christ? I would rather ask the stars: they have seen him.

18

THE ROMANCE OF A BUSY BROKER

O. Henry

Pitcher, confidential clerk in the office of Harvey Maxwell, broker, allowed a look of mild interest and surprise to visit his usually expressionless countenance when his employer briskly entered at half past nine in company with his young lady stenographer. With a snappy 'Good-morning, Pitcher,' Maxwell dashed at his desk as though he were intending to leap over it, and then plunged into the great heap of letters and telegrams waiting there for him.

The young lady had been Maxwell's stenographer for a year. She was beautiful in a way that was decidedly unstenographic. She forewent the pomp of the alluring pompadour. She wore no chains, bracelets or lockets. She had not the air of being about to accept an invitation to luncheon. Her dress was grey and plain, but it fitted her figure with fidelity and discretion. In her neat black turban hat was the gold-green wing of a macaw. On this morning she was softly and shyly radiant. Her eyes were dreamily bright, her cheeks genuine peachblow, her expression a happy one, tinged with reminiscence.

Pitcher, still mildly curious, noticed a difference in her ways this morning. Instead of going straight into the adjoining room, where her desk was, she lingered, slightly irresolute, in the outer office. Once she moved over by Maxwell's desk, near enough for him to be aware of her presence.

The machine sitting at that desk was no longer a man; it was a busy New York broker, moved by buzzing wheels and uncoiling springs.

'Well—what is it? Anything?' asked Maxwell sharply. His opened mail lay like a bank of stage snow on his crowded desk. His keen grey eye, impersonal and brusque, flashed upon her half impatiently.

'Nothing,' answered the stenographer, moving away with a little smile.

'Mr Pitcher,' she said to the confidential clerk, did Mr Maxwell say anything yesterday about engaging another stenographer?'

'He did,' answered Pitcher. 'He told me to get another one. I notified the agency yesterday afternoon to send over a few samples this morning. It's 9.45 o'clock, and not a single picture hat or piece of pineapple chewing gum has showed up yet.'

'I will do the work as usual, then,' said the young lady, 'until some one comes to fill the place.' And she went to her desk at once and hung the black turban hat with the gold-green macaw wing in its accustomed place.

He who has been denied the spectacle of a busy Manhattan broker during a rush of business is handicapped for the profession of anthropology. The poet sings of the 'crowded hour of glorious life.' The broker's hour is not only crowded, but the minutes and seconds are hanging to all the straps and packing both front and rear platforms.

And this day was Harvey Maxwell's busy day. The ticker began to reel out jerkily its fitful coils of tape, the desk telephone had a chronic attack of buzzing. Men began to throng into the office and call at him over the railing, jovially, sharply, viciously, excitedly. Messenger boys ran in and out with messages and telegrams. The clerks in the office jumped about like sailors during a storm. Even Pitcher's face relaxed into something resembling animation.

On the Exchange there were hurricanes and landslides and snowstorms and glaciers and volcanoes, and those elemental disturbances were reproduced in miniature in the broker's offices. Maxwell shoved his chair against the wall and transacted business after the manner of a toe dancer. He jumped from ticker to 'phone, from desk to door with the trained agility of a harlequin.

In the midst of this growing and important stress the broker became suddenly aware of a high-rolled fringe of golden hair under a nodding canopy of velvet and ostrich tips, an imitation sealskin sacque and a string of beads as large as hickory nuts, ending near the floor with a silver heart. There was a self-possessed young lady connected with these accessories; and Pitcher was there to construe her.

'Lady from the Stenographer's Agency to see about the position,' said Pitcher.

Maxwell turned half around, with his hands full of papers and ticker tape.

'What position?' he asked, with a frown.

'Position of stenographer,' said Pitcher. 'You told me yesterday to call them up and have one sent over this morning.'

'You are losing your mind, Pitcher,' said Maxwell. 'Why should I have given you any such instructions? Miss Leslie has given perfect satisfaction during the year she has been here. The place is hers as long as she chooses to retain it. There's no place open here, madam. Countermand that order with the agency, Pitcher, and don't bring any more of 'em in here.'

The silver heart left the office, swinging and banging itself independently against the office furniture as it indignantly departed. Pitcher seized a moment to remark to the bookkeeper that the 'old man' seemed to get more absent-minded and forgetful every day of the world.

The rush and pace of business grew fiercer and faster. On the floor they were pounding half a dozen stocks in which Maxwell's customers were heavy investors. Orders to buy and sell were coming and going as swift as the flight of swallows. Some of his own holdings were imperilled, and the man was working like some high-geared, delicate, strong machine—strung to full tension, going at full speed, accurate, never hesitating, with the proper word and decision and act ready and prompt as clockwork. Stocks and bonds, loans and mortgages, margins and securities—here was a world of finance, and there was no room in it for the human world or the world of nature.

When the luncheon hour drew near there came a slight lull in the uproar.

Maxwell stood by his desk with his hands full of telegrams and memoranda, with a fountain pen over his right ear and his hair hanging in disorderly strings over his forehead. His window was open, for the beloved janitress Spring had turned on a little warmth through the waking registers of the earth.

And through the window came a wandering—perhaps a lost—odour—a delicate, sweet odour of lilac that fixed the broker for a moment immovable. For this odour belonged to Miss Leslie; it was her own, and hers only.

The odour brought her vividly, almost tangibly before him. The world of finance dwindled suddenly to a speck. And she was in the next room—twenty steps away.

'By George, I'll do it now,' said Maxwell, half aloud. 'I'll ask her now. I wonder I didn't do it long ago.'

He dashed into the inner office with the haste of a short

trying to cover. He charged upon the desk of the stenographer.

She looked up at him with a smile. A soft pink crept over her cheek, and her eyes were kind and frank. Maxwell leaned one elbow on her desk. He still clutched fluttering papers with both hands and the pen was above his ear.

'Miss Leslie,' he began hurriedly, 'I have but a moment to spare. I want to say something in that moment. Will you he my wife? I haven't had time to make love to you in the ordinary way, but I really do love you. Talk quick, please—those fellows are clubbing the stuffing out of Union Pacific.'

'Oh, what are you talking about?' exclaimed the young lady. She rose to her feet and gazed upon him, round-eyed.

'Don't you understand?' said Maxwell, restively. 'I want you to marry me. I love you, Miss Leslie. I wanted to tell you, and I snatched a minute when things had slackened up a bit. They're calling me for the 'phone now. Tell 'em to wait a minute, Pitcher. Won't you, Miss Leslie?'

The stenographer acted very queerly. At first she seemed overcome with amazement; then tears flowed from her wondering eyes; and then she smiled sunnily through them, and one of her arms slid tenderly about the broker's neck.

'I know now,' she said, softly. 'It's this old business that has driven everything else out of your head for the time. I was frightened at first. Don't you remember, Harvey? We were married last evening at 8 o'clock in the Little Church Around the Corner.'

19

TRANSIENTS IN ARCADIA

O. Henry

There is a hotel on Broadway that has escaped discovery by the summer-resort promoters. It is deep and wide and cool. Its rooms are finished in dark oak of a low temperature. Homemade breezes and deep-green shrubbery give it the delights without the inconveniences of the Adirondacks. One can mount its broad staircases or glide dreamily upward in its aerial elevators, attended by guides in brass buttons, with a serene joy that Alpine climbers have never attained. There is a chef in its kitchen who will prepare for you brook trout better than the White Mountains ever served, sea food that would turn Old Point Comfort—'by Gad, sah!'—green with envy, and Maine venison that would melt the official heart of a game warden.

A few have found out this oasis in the July desert of Manhattan. During that month you will see the hotel's reduced array of guests scattered luxuriously about in the cool twilight of its lofty dining-room, gazing at one another across the snowy waste of unoccupied tables, silently congratulatory.

Superfluous, watchful, pneumatically moving waiters hover near, supplying every want before it is expressed. The temperature is perpetual April. The ceiling is painted in water colours to counterfeit a summer sky across which delicate clouds drift and do not vanish as those of nature do to our regret.

The pleasing, distant roar of Broadway is transformed in the imagination of the happy guests to the noise of a waterfall filling the woods with its restful sound. At every strange footstep the guests turn an anxious ear, fearful lest their retreat be discovered and invaded by the restless pleasure-seekers who are forever hounding nature to her deepest lairs.

Thus in the depopulated caravansary the little band of connoisseurs jealously bide themselves during the heated season, enjoying to the uttermost the delights of mountain and seashore that art and skill have gathered and served to them.

In this July came to the hotel one whose card that she sent to the clerk for her name to be registered read 'Mme Héloise D'Arcy Beaumont.'

Madame Beaumont was a guest such as the Hotel Lotus loved. She possessed the fine air of the elite, tempered and sweetened by a cordial graciousness that made the hotel employees her slaves. Bell-boys fought for the honour of answering her ring; the clerks, but for the question of ownership, would have deeded to her the hotel and its contents; the other guests regarded her as the final touch of feminine exclusiveness and beauty that rendered the entourage perfect.

This super-excellent guest rarely left the hotel. Her habits were consonant with the customs of the discriminating patrons of the Hotel Lotus. To enjoy that delectable hostelry one must forego the city as though it were leagues away. By night a brief excursion to the nearby roofs is in order; but during the torrid day one remains in the umbrageous fastnesses of the Lotus as a trout hangs poised in the pellucid sanctuaries of his favorite pool.

Though alone in the Hotel Lotus, Madame Beaumont preserved the state of a queen whose loneliness was of position only. She breakfasted at ten, a cool, sweet, leisurely, delicate being who glowed softly in the dimness like a jasmine flower in the dusk.

But at dinner was Madame's glory at its height. She wore a gown as beautiful and immaterial as the mist from an unseen cataract in a mountain gorge. The nomenclature of this gown is beyond the guess of the scribe. Always pale-red roses reposed against its lace-garnished front. It was a gown that the head-waiter viewed with respect and met at the door. You thought of Paris when you saw it, and maybe of mysterious countesses, and certainly of Versailles and rapiers and Mrs Fiske and rouge-et-noir. There was an untraceable rumour in the Hotel Lotus that Madame was a cosmopolite, and that she was pulling with her slender white bands certain strings between the nations in the favor of Russia. Being a citizeness of the world's smoothest roads it was small wonder that she was quick to recognize in the refined purlieus of the Hotel Lotus the most desirable spot in America for a restful sojourn during the heat of midsummer.

On the third day of Madame Beaumont's residence in the hotel a young man entered and registered himself as a guest. His clothing—to speak of his points in approved order—was quietly in the mode; his features good and regular; his expression that of a poised and sophisticated man of the world. He informed the clerk that he would remain three or four days, inquired concerning the sailing of European steamships, and sank into the blissful inanition of the nonpareil hotel with the contented air of a traveller in his favorite inn.

The young man—not to question the veracity of the register—was Harold Farrington. He drifted into the exclusive and calm current of life in the Lotus so tactfully and silently that not a ripple alarmed his fellow-seekers after rest. He ate in the Lotus and of its patronym, and was lulled into blissful peace with the other fortunate mariners. In one day he acquired his table and his waiter and the fear lest the panting chasers after repose that kept Broadway warm should pounce upon and destroy this contiguous but covert haven.

After dinner on the next day after the arrival of Harold Farrington Madame Beaumont dropped her handkerchief in passing out. Mr Farrington recovered and returned it without the effusiveness of a seeker after acquaintance.

Perhaps there was a mystic freemasonry between the discriminating guests of the Lotus. Perhaps they were drawn one to another by the fact of their common good fortune in discovering the acme of summer resorts in a Broadway hotel. Words delicate in courtesy and tentative in departure from formality passed between the two. And, as if in the expedient atmosphere of a real summer resort, an acquaintance grew, flowered and fructified on the spot as does the mystic plant of the conjuror. For a few moments they stood on a balcony upon which the corridor ended, and tossed the feathery ball of conversation.

'One tires of the old resorts,' said Madame Beaumont, with a faint but sweet smile. 'What is the use to fly to the mountains or the seashore to escape noise and dust when the very people that make both follow us there?'

'Even on the ocean,' remarked Farrington, sadly, 'the Philistines be upon you. The most exclusive steamers are getting to be scarcely more than ferry boats. Heaven help us when the summer resorter discovers that the Lotus is further away from Broadway than Thousand Islands or Mackinac.'

'I hope our secret will be safe for a week, anyhow,' said Madame, with a sigh and a smile. 'I do not know where I would go if they should descend upon the dear Lotus. I know of but one place so delightful in summer, and that is the castle of Count Polinski, in the Ural Mountains.'

'I hear that Baden-Baden and Cannes are almost deserted this season,' said Farrington. 'Year by year the old resorts fall in disrepute. Perhaps many others, like ourselves, are seeking out the quiet nooks that are overlooked by the majority.'

'I promise myself three days more of this delicious rest,' said Madame Beaumont. 'On Monday the *Cedric* sails.'

Harold Farrington's eyes proclaimed his regret. 'I too must leave on Monday,' he said, 'but I do not go abroad.'

Madame Beaumont shrugged one round shoulder in a foreign gesture.

'One cannot bide here forever, charming though it may be. The château has been in preparation for me longer than a month. Those house parties that one must give—what a nuisance! But I shall never forget my week in the Hotel Lotus.'

'Nor shall I,' said Farrington in a low voice, 'and I shall never *forgive* the *Cedric*.'

On Sunday evening, three days afterward, the two sat at a little table on the same balcony. A discreet waiter brought ices and small glasses of claret cup.

Madame Beaumont wore the same beautiful evening gown that she had worn each day at dinner. She seemed thoughtful. Near her hand on the table lay a small chatelaine purse. After she had eaten her ice she opened the purse and took out a one-dollar bill.

'Mr Farrington,' she said, with the smile that had won the Hotel Lotus, 'I want to tell you something. I'm going to leave before breakfast in the morning, because I've got to go back to my work. I'm behind the hosiery counter at Casey's Mammoth Store, and my vacation's up at eight o'clock tomorrow. That paper-dollar is the last cent I'll see till I draw my eight dollars salary next Saturday night. You're a real gentleman, and you've been good to me, and I wanted to tell you before I went.

'I've been saving up out of my wages for a year just for this vacation. I wanted to spend one week like a lady if I never do another one. I wanted to get up when I please instead of having to crawl out at seven every morning; and I wanted to live on the best and be waited on and ring bells for things just like rich folks do. Now I've done it, and I've had the happiest time I ever expect to have in my life. I'm going back to my work and my little hall bedroom satisfied for another year. I wanted to tell you about it, Mr Farrington, because I—I thought you kind of liked me, and I—I liked you. But, oh, I couldn't help deceiving you up till now, for it was all just like a fairy tale to me. So I talked about Europe and the things I've read about in other countries, and made you think I was a great lady.

'This dress I've got on—it's the only one I have that's fit to wear—I bought from O'Dowd & Levinsky on the installment plan.

'Seventy-five dollars is the price, and it was made to measure. I paid $10 down, and they're to collect $1 a week till it's paid for. That'll be about all I have to say, Mr Farrington, except that my name is Mamie Siviter instead of Madame Beaumont, and I thank you for your attentions. This dollar will pay the installment due on the dress to-morrow. I guess I'll go up to my room now.'

Harold Farrington listened to the recital of the Lotus's loveliest guest with an impassive countenance. When she had concluded he drew a small book like a checkbook from his coat pocket. He wrote upon a blank form in this with a stub of pencil, tore out the leaf, tossed it over to his companion and took up the paper dollar.

'I've got to go to work, too, in the morning,' he said, 'and I might as well begin now. There's a receipt for the dollar instalment. I've been a collector for O'Dowd & Levinsky for three years. Funny, ain't it, that you and me both had the same idea about spending our vacation? I've always wanted to put up at a swell hotel, and I saved up out of my twenty per, and did it. Say, Mame, how about a trip to Coney Saturday night on the boat—what?'

The face of the pseudo Madame Héloise D'Arcy Beaumont beamed.

'Oh, you bet I'll go, Mr Farrington. The store closes at twelve on Saturdays. I guess Coney'll be all right even if we did spend a week with the swells.'

Below the balcony the sweltering city growled and buzzed in the July night. Inside the Hotel Lotus the tempered, cool shadows reigned, and the solicitous waiter single-footed near the low windows, ready at a nod to serve Madame and her escort.

At the door of the elevator Farrington took his leave, and Madame Beaumont made her last ascent. But before they reached the noiseless cage he said: 'Just forget that "Harold Farrington," will you?—McManus is the name—James McManus. Some call me Jimmy.'

'Good-night, Jimmy,' said Madame.

20

THE VOICE OF THE CITY

O. Henry

Twenty-five years ago the school children used to chant their lessons. The manner of their delivery was a singsong recitative between the utterance of an Episcopal minister and the drone of a tired sawmill. I mean no disrespect. We must have lumber and sawdust.

I remember one beautiful and instructive little lyric that emanated from the physiology class. The most striking line of it was this:

'The shin-bone is the long-est bone in the hu-man bod-y.'

What an inestimable boon it would have been if all the corporeal and spiritual facts pertaining to man had thus been tunefully and logically inculcated in our youthful minds! But what we gained in anatomy, music and philosophy was meagre.

The other day I became confused. I needed a ray of light. I turned back to those school days for aid. But in all the nasal harmonies we whined forth from those bard benches I could not recall one that treated of the voice of agglomerated mankind.

In other words, of the composite vocal message of massed humanity.

In other words, of the Voice of a Big City.

Now, the individual voice is not lacking. We can understand

the song of the poet, the ripple of the brook, the meaning of the man who wants $5 until next Monday, the inscriptions on the tombs of the Pharaohs, the language of flowers, the 'step lively' of the conductor, and the prelude of the milk cans at 4 a.m. Certain large-eared ones even assert that they are wise to the vibrations of the tympanum produced by concussion of the air emanating from Mr H. James. But who can comprehend the meaning of the voice of the city?

I went out for to see.

First, I asked Aurelia. She wore white Swiss and a bat with flowers on it, and ribbons and ends of things fluttered here and there.

'Tell me,' I said, stammeringly, for I have no voice of my own, 'what does this big—er—enormous—er—whopping city say? It must have a voice of some kind. Does it ever speak to you? How do you interpret its meaning? It is a tremendous mass, but it must have a key.' 'Like a Saratoga trunk?' asked Aurelia.

'No,' said I. 'Please do not refer to the lid. I have a fancy that every city has a voice. Each one has something to say to the one who can hear it. What does the big one say to you? '

'All cities,' said Aurelia, judicially, 'say the same thing. When they get through saying it there is an echo from Philadelphia. So, they are unanimous.'

'Here are 4,000,000 people,' said I, scholastically, 'compressed upon an island, which is mostly lamb surrounded by Wall Street water. The conjunction of so many units into so small a space must result in an identity—or, or rather a homogeneity that finds its oral expression through a common channel. It is, as you might say, a consensus of translation, concentrating in a crystallized, general idea which reveals itself in what may be termed the Voice of the City. Can you tell me what it is?'

Aurelia smiled wonderfully. She sat on the high stoop. A spray of insolent ivy bobbed against her right ear. A ray of impudent moonlight flickered upon her nose. But I was adamant, nickel-plated.

'I must go and find out,' I said, 'what is the Voice of this city. Other cities have voices. It is an assignment. I must have it. New York,' I continued, in a rising tone, 'had better not hand me a cigar and say: "Old man, I can't talk for publication." No other city acts in that way. Chicago says, unhesitatingly, "I will;" I Philadelphia says, "I should;" New Orleans says, "I used to;" Louisville says, "Don't care if I do;" St Louis says, "Excuse me;" Pittsburg says, "Smoke up." Now, New York—'

Aurelia smiled.

'Very well,' said I, 'I must go elsewhere and find out.'

I went into a palace, tile-floored, cherub-ceilinged and square with the cop. I put my foot on the brass rail and said to Billy Magnus, the best bartender in the diocese:

'Billy, you've lived in New York a long time—what kind of a song-and-dance does this old town give you? What I mean is, doesn't the gab of it seem to kind of bunch up and slide over the bar to you in a sort of amalgamated tip that hits off the burg in a kind of an epigram with a dash of bitters and a slice of—'

'Excuse me a minute,' said Billy, 'somebody's punching the button at the side door.'

He went away; came back with an empty tin bucket; again vanished with it full; returned and said to me:

'That was Mame. She rings twice. She likes a glass of beer for supper. Her and the kid. If you ever saw that little skeesicks of mine brace up in his high chair and take his beer and—but, say, what was yours? I get kind of excited when I bear them two rings—was it the baseball score or gin fizz you asked for?'

'Ginger ale,' I answered.

I walked up to Broadway. I saw a cop on the corner. The cops take kids up, women across and men in. I went up to him.

If I'm not exceeding the spiel limit,' I said, 'let me ask you. You see New York during its vocative hours. It is the function of you and your brother cops to preserve the acoustics of the city. There must be a civic voice that is intelligible to you. At night during your lonely rounds you must have heard it. What is the epitome of its turmoil and shouting? What does the city say to you?

'Friend,' said the policeman, spinning his club, 'it don't say nothing. I get my orders from the man higher up. Say, I guess you're all right. Stand here for a few minutes and keep an eye open for the roundsman.'

The cop melted into the darkness of the side street. In ten minutes be had returned.

'Married last Tuesday,' he said, half gruffly. 'You know how they are. She comes to that corner at nine every night for a— comes to say "hello!" I generally manage to be there. Say, what was it you asked me a bit ago—what's doing in the city? Oh, there's a roof-garden or two just opened, twelve blocks up.'

I crossed a crow's-foot of street-car tracks, and skirted the edge of an umbrageous park. An artificial Diana, gilded, heroic, poised, wind-ruled, on the tower, shimmered in the clear light of her namesake in the sky. Along came my poet, hurrying, hatted, haired, emitting dactyls, spondees and dactylis. I seized him.

'Bill,' said I (in the magazine he is Cleon), 'give me a lift. I am on an assignment to find out the Voice of the city. You see, it's a special order. Ordinarily a symposium comprising the views of Henry Clews, John L. Sullivan, Edwin Markham, May Irwin and Charles Schwab would be about all. But this is a different matter. We want a broad, poetic, mystic vocalization of the city's soul and meaning. You are the very chap to give me a hint. Some years ago a man got at the Niagara Falls and gave us its pitch. The note was about two feet below the lowest G on the piano. Now, you can't put New York into a note unless it's better indorsed than that. But give me an idea of what it would say if it should speak. It is bound to be a mighty and far-reaching utterance. To arrive at it we must take the tremendous crash of the chords of the day's traffic, the laughter and music of the night, the solemn tones of Dr Parkhurst, the rag-time, the weeping, the stealthy bum of cab-wheels, the shout of the press agent, the tinkle of fountains on the roof gardens, the hullabaloo of the strawberry vender and the covers of *Everybody's Magazine*, the whispers of the lovers in the parks—all these sounds, must go into your Voice—not combined, but mixed, and of the mixture an essence made; and of the essence an extract—an audible extract, of which one drop shall form the thing we seek.'

'Do you remember,' asked the poet, with a chuckle, 'that California girl we met at Stiver's studio last week? Well, I'm on my way to see her. She repeated that poem of mine, "The Tribute of Spring," word for word. She's the smartest proposition in this town just at present. Say, how does this confounded tie look? I spoiled four before I got one to set right.'

'And the Voice that I asked you about?' I inquired.

'Oh, she doesn't sing,' said Cleon. 'But you ought to hear her recite my "Angel of the Inshore Wind."' I passed on. I cornered a newsboy and he flashed at me prophetic pink papers that outstripped the news by two revolutions of the clock's longest hand.

'Son,' I said, while I pretended to chase coins in my penny pocket, 'doesn't it sometimes seem to you as if the city ought to be able to talk? All these ups and downs and funny business and queer things happening every day—what would it say, do you think, if it could speak?'

'Quit yer kiddin',' said the boy. 'Wot paper yer want? I got no time to waste. It's Mag's birthday, and I want thirty cents to git her a present.'

Here was no interpreter of the city's mouthpiece. I bought a paper, and consigned its undeclared treaties, its premeditated murders and unfought battles to an ash can.

Again I repaired to the park and sat in the moon shade. I thought and thought, and wondered why none could tell me what I asked for.

And then, as swift as light from a fixed star, the answer came to me. I arose and hurried—hurried as so many reasoners must, back around my circle. I knew the answer and I bugged it in my breast as I flew, fearing lest some one would stop me and demand my secret.

Aurelia was still on the stoop. The moon was higher and the ivy shadows were deeper. I sat at her side and we watched a little cloud tilt at the drifting moon and go asunder, quite pale and discomfited.

And then, wonder of wonders and delight of delights! our hands somehow touched, and our fingers closed together and did not part.

After half an hour Aurelia said, with that smile of hers:

'Do you know, you haven't spoken a word since you came back!'

'That,' said I, nodding wisely, 'is the Voice of the City.'

21

VANKA

Anton Chekhov

Vanka Zhukov, a boy of nine, who had been for three months apprenticed to Alyahin the shoemaker, was sitting up on Christmas Eve. Waiting till his master and mistress and their workmen had gone to the midnight service, he took out of his master's cupboard a bottle of ink and a pen with a rusty nib, and, spreading out a crumpled sheet of paper in front of him, began writing. Before forming the first letter he several times looked round fearfully at the door and the windows, stole a glance at the dark ikon, on both sides of which stretched shelves full of lasts, and heaved a broken sigh. The paper lay on the bench while he knelt before it.

'Dear grandfather, Konstantin Makaritch,' he wrote, 'I am writing you a letter. I wish you a happy Christmas, and all blessings from God Almighty. I have neither father nor mother, you are the only one left me.'

Vanka raised his eyes to the dark ikon on which the light of his candle was reflected, and vividly recalled his grandfather, Konstantin Makaritch, who was night watchman to a family called Zhivarev. He was a thin but extraordinarily nimble and lively little old man of sixty-five, with an everlastingly laughing face and drunken eyes. By day he slept in the servants' kitchen, or made jokes with the cooks; at night, wrapped in an ample sheepskin, he walked round the grounds and tapped with his little mallet. Old Kashtanka and Eel, so-called on account of his dark colour and his long body like a weasel's, followed him with hanging heads. This Eel was exceptionally polite and affectionate, and looked with equal kindness on strangers and his own masters, but had not a very good reputation. Under his politeness and meekness was hidden the most Jesuitical cunning. No one knew better how to creep up on occasion and snap at one's legs, to slip into the store-room, or steal a hen from a peasant. His hind legs had been nearly pulled off more than once, twice he had been hanged, every week he was thrashed till he was half dead, but he always revived.

At this moment grandfather was, no doubt, standing at the gate, screwing up his eyes at the red windows of the church, stamping with his high felt boots, and joking with the servants. His little mallet was hanging on his belt. He was clasping his hands, shrugging with the cold, and, with an aged chuckle, pinching first the housemaid, then the cook.

'How about a pinch of snuff?' he was saying, offering the women his snuff-box.

The women would take a sniff and sneeze. Grandfather would be indescribably delighted, go off into a merry chuckle, and cry:

'Tear it off, it has frozen on!'

They give the dogs a sniff of snuff too. Kashtanka sneezes, wriggles her head, and walks away offended. Eel does not sneeze, from politeness, but wags his tail. And the weather is glorious. The air is still, fresh, and transparent. The night is dark, but one can see the whole village with its white roofs and coils of smoke coming from the chimneys, the trees silvered with hoar frost, the snowdrifts. The whole sky spangled with gay twinkling stars, and the Milky Way is as distinct as though it had been washed and rubbed with snow for a holiday...Vanka sighed, dipped his pen, and went on writing:

'And yesterday I had a wigging. The master pulled me out into the yard by my hair, and whacked me with a boot-stretcher because I accidentally fell asleep while I was rocking their brat in the cradle. And a week ago the mistress told me to clean a herring, and I began from the tail end, and she took the herring and thrust its head in my face. The workmen laugh at me and send me to the tavern for vodka, and tell me to steal the master's cucumbers for them, and the master beats me with anything that comes to hand. And there is nothing to eat. In the morning they give me bread, for dinner, porridge, and in the evening, bread again; but as for tea, or soup, the master and mistress gobble it all up themselves. And I am put to sleep in the passage, and when their wretched brat cries I get no sleep at all, but have to rock the cradle. Dear grandfather, show the divine mercy, take me away from here, home to the village. It's more than I can bear. I bow down to your feet, and will pray to God for you for ever, take me away from here or I shall die.'

Vanka's mouth worked, he rubbed his eyes with his black fist, and gave a sob.

'I will powder your snuff for you,' he went on. 'I will pray for you, and if I do anything you can thrash me like Sidor's goat. And if you think I've no job, then I will beg the steward for Christ's sake to let me clean his boots, or I'll go for a shepherd-boy instead of Fedka. Dear grandfather, it is more than I can bear, it's simply no life at all. I wanted to run away to the village, but I have no boots, and I am afraid of the frost. When I grow up big I will take care of you for this, and not let anyone annoy you, and when you die I will pray for the rest of your soul, just as for my mammy's.'

'Moscow is a big town. It's all gentlemen's houses, and there are lots of horses, but there are no sheep, and the dogs are not spiteful. The lads here don't go out with the star, and they don't let anyone go into the choir, and once I saw in a shop window fishing-hooks for sale, fitted ready with the line and for all sorts of fish, awfully good ones, there was even one hook that would hold a forty-pound sheat-fish. And I have seen shops where there are guns of all sorts, after the pattern of the master's guns at home, so that I shouldn't wonder if they are a hundred roubles each... And in the butchers' shops there are grouse and woodcocks and fish and hares, but the shopmen don't say where they shoot them.'

'Dear grandfather, when they have the Christmas tree at the big house, get me a gilt walnut, and put it away in the green trunk. Ask the young lady Olga Ignatyevna, say it's for Vanka.'

Vanka gave a tremulous sigh, and again stared at the window. He remembered how his grandfather always went into the forest to get the Christmas tree for his master's family, and took his grandson with him. It was a merry time! Grandfather made a noise in his throat, the forest crackled with the frost, and looking at them Vanka chortled too. Before chopping down the Christmas tree, grandfather would smoke a pipe, slowly take a pinch of snuff, and laugh at frozen Vanka... The young fir trees, covered with hoar frost, stood motionless, waiting to see which of them was to die. Wherever one looked, a hare flew like an arrow over the snowdrifts... Grandfather could not refrain from shouting: 'Hold him, hold him...hold him! Ah, the bob-tailed devil!'

When he had cut down the Christmas tree, grandfather used to drag it to the big house, and there set to work to decorate it... The young lady, who was Vanka's favourite, Olga

Ignatyevna, was the busiest of all. When Vanka's mother Pelageya was alive, and a servant in the big house, Olga Ignatyevna used to give him goodies, and having nothing better to do, taught him to read and write, to count up to a hundred, and even to dance a quadrille. When Pelageya died, Vanka had been transferred to the servants' kitchen to be with his grandfather, and from the kitchen to the shoemaker's in Moscow.

'Do come, dear grandfather,' Vanka went on with his letter. 'For Christ's sake, I beg you, take me away. Have pity on an unhappy orphan like me; here everyone knocks me about, and I am fearfully hungry; I can't tell you what misery it is, I am always crying. And the other day the master hit me on the head with a last, so that I fell down. My life is wretched, worse than any dog's... I send greetings to Alyona, one-eyed Yegorka, and the coachman, and don't give my concertina to anyone. I remain, your grandson, Ivan Zhukov. Dear grandfather, do come.'

Vanka folded the sheet of writing-paper twice, and put it into an envelope he had bought the day before for a kopeck... After thinking a little, he dipped the pen and wrote the address:

To grandfather in the village.

Then he scratched his head, thought a little, and added: Konstantin Makaritch. Glad that he had not been prevented from writing, he put on his cap and, without putting on his little greatcoat, ran out into the street as he was in his shirt... The shopmen at the butcher's, whom he had questioned the day before, told him that letters were put in post-boxes, and from the boxes were carried about all over the earth in mailcarts with drunken drivers and ringing bells. Vanka ran to the nearest post-box, and thrust the precious letter in the slit...An hour later, lulled by sweet hopes, he was sound asleep... He dreamed of the stove. On the stove was sitting his grandfather, swinging his bare legs, and reading the letter to the cooks…By the stove was Eel, wagging his tail.

22

A DEFENSELESS CREATURE

Anton Chekhov

In spite of a violent attack of gout in the night and the nervous exhaustion left by it, Kistunov went in the morning to his office and began punctually seeing the clients of the bank and persons who had come with petitions. He looked languid and exhausted, and spoke in a faint voice hardly above a whisper, as though he were dying.

'What can I do for you?' he asked a lady in an antediluvian mantle, whose back view was extremely suggestive of a huge dung-beetle.

'You see, your Excellency,' the petitioner in question began, speaking rapidly, 'my husband Shtchukin, a collegiate assessor, was ill for five months, and while he, if you will excuse my saying so, was laid up at home, he was for no sort of reason dismissed, your Excellency; and when I went for his salary they deducted, if you please, your Excellency, twenty-four roubles thirty-six kopecks from his salary. "What for?" I asked. "He borrowed from the club fund," they told me, "and the other clerks had stood security for him." How was that? How could he have borrowed it without my consent? It's impossible, your Excellency. What's the reason of it? I am a poor woman, I earn my bread by taking in lodgers. I am a weak, defenceless woman… I have to put up with ill-usage from everyone and never hear a kind word…'

The petitioner was blinking, and dived into her mantle for her handkerchief. Kistunov took her petition from her and began reading it.

'Excuse me, what's this?' he asked, shrugging his shoulders. 'I can make nothing of it. Evidently you have come to the wrong place, madam. Your petition has nothing to do with us at all. You will have to apply to the department in which your husband was employed.'

'Why, my dear sir, I have been to five places already, and they would not even take the petition anywhere,' said Madame Shtchukin. 'I'd quite lost my head, but, thank goodness—God bless him for it—my son-in-law, Boris Matveyitch, advised me to come to you. "You go to Mr Kistunov, mamma: he is an influential man, he can do anything for you…" Help me, your Excellency!'

'We can do nothing for you, Madame Shtchukin. You must understand: your husband served in the Army Medical Department, and our establishment is a purely private commercial undertaking, a bank. Surely you must understand that!'

Kistunov shrugged his shoulders again and turned to a gentleman in a military uniform, with a swollen face.

'Your Excellency,' piped Madame Shtchukin in a pitiful voice, 'I have the doctor's certificate that my husband was ill! Here it is, if you will kindly look at it.'

'Very good, I believe you,' Kistunov said irritably, 'but I repeat it has nothing to do with us. It's queer and positively absurd! Surely your husband must know where you are to apply?'

'He knows nothing, your Excellency. He keeps on: "It's not

your business! Get away!"—that's all I can get out of him... Whose business is it, then? It's I have to keep them all!'

Kistunov again turned to Madame Shtchukin and began explaining to her the difference between the Army Medical Department and a private bank. She listened attentively, nodded in token of assent, and said:

'Yes...yes...yes... I understand, sir. In that case, your Excellency, tell them to pay me fifteen roubles at least! I agree to take part on account!

'Ough!' sighed Kistunov, letting his head drop back. 'There's no making you see reason. Do understand that to apply to us with such a petition is as strange as to send in a petition concerning divorce, for instance, to a chemist's or to the Assaying Board. You have not been paid your due, but what have we to do with it?'

'Your Excellency, make me remember you in my prayers for the rest of my days, have pity on a lone, lorn woman,' wailed Madame Shtchukin; 'I am a weak, defenceless woman... I am worried to death, I've to settle with the lodgers and see to my husband's affairs and fly round looking after the house, and I am going to church every day this week, and my son-in-law is out of a job... I might as well not eat or drink... I can scarcely keep on my feet... I haven't slept all night...'

Kistunov was conscious of the palpitation of his heart. With a face of anguish, pressing his hand on his heart, he began explaining to Madame Shtchukin again, but his voice failed him.

'No, excuse me, I cannot talk to you,' he said with a wave of his hand. 'My head's going round. You are hindering us and wasting your time. Ough! Alexey Nikolaitch,' he said, addressing one of his clerks, 'please will you explain to Madame Shtchukin?'

Kistunov, passing by all the petitioners, went to his private room and signed about a dozen papers while Alexey Nikolaitch was still engaged with Madame Shtchukin. As he sat in his room Kistunov heard two voices: the monotonous, restrained bass of Alexey Nikolaitch and the shrill, wailing voice of Madame Shtchukin.

'I am a weak, defenceless woman, I am a woman in delicate health,' said Madame Shtchukin. 'I look strong, but if you were to overhaul me there is not one healthy fibre in me. I can scarcely keep on my feet, and my appetite is gone... I drank my cup of coffee this morning without the slightest relish...'

Alexey Nikolaitch explained to her the difference between the departments and the complicated system of sending in papers. He was soon exhausted, and his place was taken by the accountant.

'A wonderfully disagreeable woman!' said Kistunov, revolted, nervously cracking his fingers and continually going to the decanter of water. 'She's a perfect idiot! She's worn me out and she'll exhaust them, the nasty creature! Ough!...my heart is throbbing.'

Half an hour later he rang his bell. Alexey Nikolaitch made his appearance.

'How are things going?' Kistunov asked languidly.

'We can't make her see anything, Pyotr Alexandritch! We are simply done. We talk of one thing and she talks of something else.'

'I...I can't stand the sound of her voice... I am ill... I can't bear it.'

'Send for the porter, Pyotr Alexandritch, let him put her out.'

'No, no,' cried Kistunov in alarm. 'She will set up a squeal, and there are lots of flats in this building, and goodness knows what they would think of us... Do try and explain to her, my dear fellow...'

A minute later the deep drone of Alexey Nikolaitch's voice was audible again. A quarter of an hour passed, and instead of his bass there was the murmur of the accountant's powerful tenor.'

'Re-mark-ably nasty woman,' Kistunov thought indignantly, nervously shrugging his shoulders. 'No more brains than a sheep. I believe that's a twinge of the gout again... My migraine is coming back...'

In the next room Alexey Nikolaitch, at the end of his resources, at last tapped his finger on the table and then on his own forehead.

'The fact of the matter is you haven't a head on your shoulders,' he said, 'but this.'

'Come, come,' said the old lady, offended. 'Talk to your own wife like that... You screw!... Don't be too free with your hands.'

And looking at her with fury, with exasperation, as though he would devour her, Alexey Nikolaitch said in a quiet, stifled voice:

'Clear out.'

'Wha-at?' squealed Madame Shtchukin. 'How dare you? I am a weak, defenceless woman; I won't endure it. My husband is a collegiate assessor. You screw!... I will go to Dmitri Karlitch, the lawyer, and there will be nothing left of you! I've had the law of three lodgers, and I will make you flop down at my feet for your saucy words! I'll go to your general. Your Excellency, your Excellency!'

'Be off, you pest,' hissed Alexey Nikolaitch.

Kistunov opened his door and looked into the office.

'What is it?' he asked in a tearful voice.

Madame Shtchukin, as red as a crab, was standing in the middle of the room, rolling her eyes and prodding the air with her fingers. The bank clerks were standing round red in the face too, and, evidently harassed, were looking at each other distractedly.

'Your Excellency,' cried Madame Shtchukin, pouncing upon Kistunov. 'Here, this man, he here…this man…' (she pointed to Alexey Nikolaitch) 'tapped himself on the forehead and then tapped the table… You told him to go into my case, and he's jeering at me! I am a weak, defenceless woman… My husband is a collegiate assessor, and I am a major's daughter myself! '

'Very good, madam,' moaned Kistunov. 'I will go into it…I will take steps… Go away…later!'

'And when shall I get the money, your Excellency? I need it to-day!'

Kistunov passed his trembling hand over his forehead, heaved a sigh, and began explaining again.

'Madam, I have told you already this is a bank, a private commercial establishment… What do you want of us? And do understand that you are hindering us.'

Madame Shtchukin listened to him and sighed.

'To be sure, to be sure,' she assented. 'Only, your Excellency, do me the kindness, make me pray for you for the rest of my life, be a father, protect me! If a medical certificate is not enough I can produce an affidavit from the police… Tell them to give me the money.'

Everything began swimming before Kistunov's eyes. He breathed out all the air in his lungs in a prolonged sigh and sank helpless on a chair.

'How much do you want?' he asked in a weak voice.

'Twenty-four roubles and thirty-six kopecks.'

Kistunov took his pocket-book out of his pocket, extracted

a twenty-five rouble note and gave it to Madame Shtchukin.

'Take it and...and go away!'

Madame Shtchukin wrapped the money up in her handkerchief, put it away, and pursing up her face into a sweet, mincing, even coquettish smile, asked:

'Your Excellency, and would it be possible for my husband to get a post again?'

'I am going...I am ill...' said Kistunov in a weary voice. 'I have dreadful palpitations.'

When he had driven home Alexey Nikolaitch sent Nikita for some laurel drops, and, after taking twenty drops each, all the clerks set to work, while Madame Shtchukin stayed another two hours in the vestibule, talking to the porter and waiting for Kistunov to return... She came again next day.

23

THE DEATH OF
A GOVERNMENT CLERK

Anton Chekhov

One fine evening, a no less fine government clerk called Ivan Dmitritch Tchervyakov was sitting in the second row of the stalls, gazing through an opera glass at the Cloches de Corneville. He gazed and felt at the acme of bliss. But suddenly.... In stories one so often meets with this 'But suddenly.' The authors are right: life is so full of surprises! But suddenly his face puckered up, his eyes disappeared, his breathing was arrested...he took the opera glass from his eyes, bent over and... 'Aptchee!!' he sneezed as you perceive. It is not reprehensible for anyone to sneeze anywhere. Peasants sneeze and so do police superintendents, and sometimes even privy councillors. All men sneeze. Tchervyakov was not in the least confused, he wiped his face with his handkerchief, and like a polite man, looked round to see whether he had disturbed any one by his sneezing. But then he was overcome with confusion. He saw that an old gentleman sitting in front of him in the first row of the stalls was carefully wiping his bald head and his neck with his glove and muttering something to himself. In the old gentleman, Tchervyakov recognized Brizzhalov, a civilian general serving in the Department of Transport.

'I have spattered him,' thought Tchervyakov, 'he is not the head of my department, but still it is awkward. I must apologise.'

Tchervyakov gave a cough, bent his whole person forward, and whispered in the general's ear.

'Pardon, your Excellency, I spattered you accidentally...'

'Never mind, never mind.'

'For goodness sake excuse me, I...I did not mean to.'

'Oh, please, sit down! let me listen!'

Tchervyakov was embarrassed, he smiled stupidly and fell to gazing at the stage. He gazed at it but was no longer feeling bliss. He began to be troubled by uneasiness. In the interval, he went up to Brizzhalov, walked beside him, and overcoming his shyness, muttered:

'I spattered you, your Excellency, forgive me...you see...I didn't do it to...'

'Oh, that's enough...I'd forgotten it, and you keep on about it!' said the general, moving his lower lip impatiently.

'He has forgotten, but there is a fiendish light in his eye,' thought Tchervyakov, looking suspiciously at the general. 'And he doesn't want to talk. I ought to explain to him...that I really didn't intend...that it is the law of nature or else he will think I meant to spit on him. He doesn't think so now, but he will think so later!'

On getting home, Tchervyakov told his wife of his breach of good manners. It struck him that his wife took too frivolous a view of the incident; she was a little frightened, but when she learned that Brizzhalov was in a different department, she was reassured.

'Still, you had better go and apologize,' she said, 'or he will think you don't know how to behave in public.'

'That's just it! I did apologize, but he took it somehow queerly...he didn't say a word of sense. There wasn't time to talk properly.'

Next day Tchervyakov put on a new uniform, had his hair cut and went to Brizzhalov's to explain; going into the general's reception room he saw there a number of petitioners and among them the general himself, who was beginning to interview them. After questioning several petitioners the general raised his eyes and looked at Tchervyakov.

'Yesterday at the Arcadia, if you recollect, your Excellency,' the latter began, 'I sneezed and...accidentally spattered...Exc...'

'What nonsense... It's beyond anything! What can I do for you,' said the general addressing the next petitioner.

'He won't speak,' thought Tchervyakov, turning pale; 'that means that he is angry... No, it can't be left like this... I will explain to him.'

When the general had finished his conversation with the last of the petitioners and was turning towards his inner apartments, Tchervyakov took a step towards him and muttered:

'Your Excellency! If I venture to trouble your Excellency, it is simply from a feeling I may say of regret!... It was not intentional if you will graciously believe me.'

The general made a lachrymose face, and waved his hand.

'Why, you are simply making fun of me, sir,' he said as he closed the door behind him.

'Where's the making fun in it?' thought Tchervyakov, 'there is nothing of the sort! He is a general, but he can't understand. If that is how it is I am not going to apologize to that *fanfaron* any more! The devil take him. I'll write a letter to him, but I won't go. By Jove, I won't.'

So thought Tchervyakov as he walked home; he did not write a letter to the general, he pondered and pondered and could not make up that letter. He had to go next day to explain in person.

'I ventured to disturb your Excellency yesterday,' he muttered, when the general lifted enquiring eyes upon him, 'not to make fun as you were pleased to say. I was apologizing for having spattered you in sneezing... And I did not dream of making fun of you. Should I dare to make fun of you, if we should take to making fun, then there would be no respect for persons, there would be...'

'Be off!' yelled the general, turning suddenly purple, and shaking all over.

'What?' asked Tchervyakov, in a whisper turning numb with horror.

'Be off!' repeated the general, stamping.

Something seemed to give way in Tchervyakov's stomach. Seeing nothing and hearing nothing he reeled to the door, went out into the street, and went staggering along... Reaching home mechanically, without taking off his uniform, he lay down on the sofa and died.

24

A PAIR OF SILK STOCKINGS

Kate Chopin

Little Mrs Sommers one day found herself the unexpected possessor of fifteen dollars. It seemed to her a very large amount of money, and the way in which it stuffed and bulged her worn old *porte-monnaie* gave her a feeling of importance such as she had not enjoyed for years.

The question of investment was one that occupied her greatly. For a day or two she walked about apparently in a dreamy state, but really absorbed in speculation and calculation. She did not wish to act hastily, to do anything she might afterward regret. But it was during the still hours of the night when she lay awake revolving plans in her mind that she seemed to see her way clearly toward a proper and judicious use of the money.

A dollar or two should be added to the price usually paid for Janie's shoes, which would insure their lasting an appreciable time longer than they usually did. She would buy so and so many yards of percale for new shirt waists for the boys and Janie and Mag. She had intended to make the old ones do by skilful patching. Mag should have another gown. She had seen some beautiful patterns, veritable bargains in the shop windows. And still there would be left enough for new stockings—two pairs apiece—and what darning that would save for a while! She would get caps for the boys and sailor-hats for the girls. The vision of her little brood looking fresh and dainty and new for once in their lives excited her and made her restless and wakeful with anticipation.

The neighbors sometimes talked of certain 'better days' that little Mrs Sommers had known before she had ever thought of being Mrs Sommers. She herself indulged in no such morbid retrospection. She had no time—no second of time to devote to the past. The needs of the present absorbed her every faculty. A vision of the future like some dim, gaunt monster sometimes appalled her, but luckily tomorrow never comes.

Mrs Sommers was one who knew the value of bargains; who could stand for hours making her way inch by inch toward the desired object that was selling below cost. She could elbow her way if need be; she had learned to clutch a piece of goods and hold it and stick to it with persistence and determination till her turn came to be served, no matter when it came.

But that day she was a little faint and tired. She had swallowed a light luncheon—no! when she came to think of it, between getting the children fed and the place righted, and preparing herself for the shopping bout, she had actually forgotten to eat any luncheon at all!

She sat herself upon a revolving stool before a counter that was comparatively deserted, trying to gather strength and courage to charge through an eager multitude that was besieging breastworks of shirting and figured lawn. An all-gone limp feeling had come over her and she rested her hand aimlessly upon the counter. She wore no gloves. By degrees she grew aware that her hand had encountered something very soothing, very pleasant to touch. She looked down to see that her hand lay upon a pile of silk stockings. A placard nearby announced that they had been reduced in price from two dollars and fifty cents to one dollar and ninety-eight cents; and a young girl who stood behind the counter asked her if she wished to examine their line of silk hosiery. She smiled, just as if she had been asked to inspect a tiara of diamonds with the ultimate view of purchasing it. But she went on feeling the soft, sheeny luxurious things—with both hands now, holding them up to see them glisten, and to feel them glide serpent-like through her fingers.

Two hectic blotches came suddenly into her pale cheeks. She looked up at the girl.

'Do you think there are any eights-and-a-half among these?'

There were any number of eights-and-a-half. In fact, there were more of that size than any other. Here was a light-blue pair; there were some lavender, some all black and various shades of tan and grey. Mrs Sommers selected a black pair and looked at them very long and closely. She pretended to be examining their texture, which the clerk assured her was excellent.

'A dollar and ninety-eight cents,' she mused aloud. 'Well, I'll take this pair.' She handed the girl a five-dollar bill and waited for her change and for her parcel. What a very small parcel it was! It seemed lost in the depths of her shabby old shopping-bag.

Mrs Sommers after that did not move in the direction of the bargain counter. She took the elevator, which carried her to an upper floor into the region of the ladies' waiting-rooms. Here, in a retired corner, she exchanged her cotton stockings for the new silk ones which she had just bought. She was not going through any acute mental process or reasoning with herself, nor was she striving to explain to her satisfaction the motive of her action. She was not thinking at all. She seemed for the time to be taking a rest from that laborious and fatiguing function and to have abandoned herself to some mechanical impulse that directed her actions and freed her of responsibility.

How good was the touch of the raw silk to her flesh! She felt like lying back in the cushioned chair and revelling for a while in the luxury of it. She did for a little while. Then she replaced her shoes, rolled the cotton stockings together and thrust them into her bag. After doing this she crossed straight over to the shoe department and took her seat to be fitted.

She was fastidious. The clerk could not make her out; he could not reconcile her shoes with her stockings, and she was not too easily pleased. She held back her skirts and turned her feet one way and her head another way as she glanced down at the polished, pointed-tipped boots. Her foot and ankle looked very pretty. She could not realize that they belonged to her and were a part of herself. She wanted an excellent and stylish fit, she told the young fellow who served her, and she did not mind the difference of a dollar or two more in the price so long as she got what she desired.

It was a long time since Mrs Sommers had been fitted with gloves. On rare occasions when she had bought a pair they were always 'bargains,' so cheap that it would have been preposterous and unreasonable to have expected them to be fitted to the hand.

Now she rested her elbow on the cushion of the glove counter, and a pretty, pleasant young creature, delicate and deft of touch, drew a long-wristed 'kid' over Mrs Sommers's hand. She smoothed it down over the wrist and buttoned it neatly, and both lost themselves for a second or two in admiring contemplation of the little symmetrical gloved hand. But there were other places where money might be spent.

There were books and magazines piled up in the window of a stall a few paces down the street. Mrs Sommers bought two high-priced magazines such as she had been accustomed to read in the days when she had been accustomed to other pleasant things. She carried them without wrapping. As well as she could she lifted her skirts at the crossings. Her stockings and boots and well-fitting gloves had worked marvels in her bearing—had given her a feeling of assurance, a sense of belonging to the well-dressed multitude.

She was very hungry. Another time she would have stilled the cravings for food until reaching her own home, where she would have brewed herself a cup of tea and taken a snack of anything that was available. But the impulse that was guiding her would not suffer her to entertain any such thought.

There was a restaurant at the corner. She had never entered its doors; from the outside she had sometimes caught glimpses of spotless damask and shining crystal, and soft-stepping waiters serving people of fashion.

When she entered her appearance created no surprise, no consternation, as she had half feared it might. She seated herself at a small table alone, and an attentive waiter at once approached to take her order. She did not want a profusion; she craved a nice and tasty bite—a half dozen blue-points, a plump chop with cress, a something sweet—a crème-frappée, for instance; a glass of Rhine wine, and after all a small cup of black coffee.

While waiting to be served she removed her gloves very leisurely and laid them beside her. Then she picked up a magazine and glanced through it, cutting the pages with a blunt edge of her knife. It was all very agreeable. The damask was even more spotless than it had seemed through the window, and the crystal more sparkling. There were quiet ladies and gentlemen, who did not notice her, lunching at the small tables like her own. A soft, pleasing strain of music could be heard, and a gentle breeze was blowing through the window. She tasted a bite, and she read a word or two, and she sipped the amber wine and wiggled her toes in the silk stockings. The price of it made no difference. She counted the money out to the waiter and left an extra coin on his tray, whereupon he bowed before her as before a princess of royal blood.

There was still money in her purse, and her next temptation presented itself in the shape of a matinee poster.

It was a little later when she entered the theatre, the play had begun and the house seemed to her to be packed. But there were vacant seats here and there, and into one of them she was ushered, between brilliantly dressed women who had gone there to kill time and eat candy and display their gaudy attire. There were many others who were there solely for the play and acting. It is safe to say there was no one present who bore quite the attitude which Mrs Sommers did to her surroundings. She gathered in the whole—stage and players and people in one wide impression, and absorbed it and enjoyed it. She laughed at the comedy and wept—she and the gaudy woman next to her wept over the tragedy. And they talked a little together over it. And the gaudy woman wiped her eyes and sniffled on a tiny square of filmy, perfumed lace and passed little Mrs Sommers her box of candy.

The play was over, the music ceased, the crowd filed out. It was like a dream ended. People scattered in all directions. Mrs Sommers went to the corner and waited for the cable car.

A man with keen eyes, who sat opposite to her, seemed to like the study of her small, pale face. It puzzled him to decipher what he saw there. In truth, he saw nothing—unless he were wizard enough to detect a poignant wish, a powerful longing that the cable car would never stop anywhere, but go on and on with her forever.

THE CALINE

Kate Chopin

The sun was just far enough in the west to send inviting shadows. In the centre of a small field, and in the shade of a haystack which was there, a girl lay sleeping. She had slept long and soundly, when something awoke her as suddenly as if it had been a blow. She opened her eyes and stared a moment up in the cloudless sky. She yawned and stretched her long brown legs and arms, lazily. Then she arose, never minding the bits of straw that clung to her black hair, to her red bodice, and the blue cotonade skirt that did not reach her naked ankles.

The log cabin in which she dwelt with her parents was just outside the enclosure in which she had been sleeping. Beyond was a small clearing that did duty as a cotton field. All else was dense wood, except the long stretch that curved round the brow of the hill, and in which glittered the steel rails of the Texas and Pacific road.

When Caline emerged from the shadow she saw a long train of passenger coaches standing in view, where they must have stopped abruptly. It was that sudden stopping which had awakened her; for such a thing had not happened before within her recollection, and she looked stupid, at first, with astonishment. There seemed to be something wrong with the engine; and some of the passengers who dismounted went forward to investigate the trouble. Others came strolling along in the direction of the cabin, where Caline stood under an old gnarled mulberry tree, staring. Her father had halted his mule at the end of the cotton row, and stood staring also, leaning upon his plow.

There were ladies in the party. They walked awkwardly in their high-heeled boots over the rough, uneven ground, and held up their skirts mincingly. They twirled parasols over their shoulders, and laughed immoderately at the funny things which their masculine companions were saying.

They tried to talk to Caline, but could not understand the French patois with which she answered them.

One of the men—a pleasant-faced youngster—drew a sketch book from his pocket and began to make a picture of the girl. She stayed motionless, her hands behind her, and her wide eyes fixed earnestly upon him.

Before he had finished there was a summons from the train; and all went scampering hurriedly away. The engine screeched, it sent a few lazy puffs into the still air, and in another moment or two had vanished, bearing its human cargo with it.

Caline could not feel the same after that. She looked with new and strange interest upon the trains of cars that passed so swiftly back and forth across her vision, each day; and wondered whence these people came, and whither they were going.

Her mother and father could not tell her, except to say that they came from 'loin là bas,' and were going 'Djieu sait é où.'

One day she walked miles down the track to talk with the old flagman, who stayed down there by the big water tank. Yes, he knew. Those people came from the great cities in the north, and were going to the city in the south. He knew all about the city; it was a grand place. He had lived there once.

His sister lived there now; and she would be glad enough to have so fine a girl as Caline to help her cook and scrub, and tend the babies. And he thought Caline might earn as much as five dollars a month, in the city.

So she went; in a new cotonade, and her Sunday shoes; with a sacredly guarded scrawl that the flagman sent to his sister.

The woman lived in a tiny, stuccoed house, with green blinds, and three wooden steps leading down to the banquette. There seemed to be hundreds like it along the street. Over the house tops loomed the tall masts of ships, and the hum of the French market could be heard on a still morning.

Caline was at first bewildered. She had to readjust all her preconceptions to fit the reality of it. The flagman's sister was a kind and gentle task-mistress. At the end of a week or two she wanted to know how the girl liked it all. Caline liked it very well, for it was pleasant, on Sunday afternoons, to stroll with the children under the great, solemn sugar sheds; or to sit upon the compressed cotton bales, watching the stately steamers, the graceful boats, and noisy little tugs that plied the waters of the Mississippi. And it filled her with agreeable excitement to go to the French market, where the handsome Gascon butchers were eager to present their compliments and little Sunday bouquets to the pretty Acadian girl; and to throw fistfuls of *lagniappe* into her basket.

When the woman asked her again after another week if she were still pleased, she was not so sure. And again when she questioned Caline the girl turned away, and went to sit behind the big, yellow cistern, to cry unobserved. For she knew now that it was not the great city and its crowds of people she had so eagerly sought; but the pleasant-faced boy, who had made her picture that day under the mulberry tree.

26

A DEAD WOMAN'S SECRETS

Guy de Maupassant

The woman had died without pain, quietly, as a woman should whose life had been blameless. Now she was resting in her bed, lying on her back, her eyes closed, her features calm, her long white hair carefully arranged as though she had done it up ten minutes before dying. The whole pale countenance of the dead woman was so collected, so calm, so resigned that one could feel what a sweet soul had lived in that body, what a quiet existence this old soul had led, how easy and pure the death of this parent had been.

Kneeling beside the bed, her son, a magistrate with inflexible principles, and her daughter, Marguerite, known as Sister Eulalie, were weeping as though their hearts would break. She had, from childhood up, armed them with a strict moral code, teaching them religion, without weakness, and duty, without compromise. He, the man, had become a judge and handled the law as a weapon with which he smote the weak ones without pity. She, the girl, influenced by the virtue which had bathed her in this austere family, had become the bride of the Church through her loathing for man.

They had hardly known their father, knowing only that he

had made their mother most unhappy, without being told any other details.

The nun was wildly-kissing the dead woman's hand, an ivory hand as white as the large crucifix lying across the bed. On the other side of the long body the other hand seemed still to be holding the sheet in the death grasp; and the sheet had preserved the little creases as a memory of those last movements which precede eternal immobility.

A few light taps on the door caused the two sobbing heads to look up, and the priest, who had just come from dinner, returned. He was red and out of breath from his interrupted digestion, for he had made himself a strong mixture of coffee and brandy in order to combat the fatigue of the last few nights and of the wake which was beginning.

He looked sad, with that assumed sadness of the priest for whom death is a bread winner. He crossed himself and approaching with his professional gesture: 'Well, my poor children! I have come to help you pass these last sad hours.' But Sister Eulalie suddenly arose. 'Thank you, father, but my brother and I prefer to remain alone with her. This is our last chance to see her, and we wish to be together, all three of us, as we—we—used to be when we were small and our poor mo—mother—'

Grief and tears stopped her; she could not continue.

Once more serene, the priest bowed, thinking of his bed. 'As you wish, my children.' He knelt, crossed himself, prayed, arose and went out quietly, murmuring: 'She was a saint!'

They remained alone, the dead woman and her children. The ticking of the clock, hidden in the shadow, could be heard distinctly, and through the open window drifted in the sweet smell of hay and of woods, together with the soft moonlight. No other noise could be heard over the land except the occasional croaking of the frog or the chirping of some belated insect. An infinite peace, a divine melancholy, a silent serenity surrounded this dead woman, seemed to be breathed out from her and to appease nature itself.

Then the judge, still kneeling, his head buried in the bed clothes, cried in a voice altered by grief and deadened by the sheets and blankets: 'Mamma, mamma, mamma!' And his sister, frantically striking her forehead against the woodwork, convulsed, twitching and trembling as in an epileptic fit, moaned: 'Jesus, Jesus, mamma, Jesus!' And both of them, shaken by a storm of grief, gasped and choked.

The crisis slowly calmed down and they began to weep quietly, just as on the sea when a calm follows a squall.

A rather long time passed and they arose and looked at their dead. And the memories, those distant memories, yesterday so dear, to-day so torturing, came to their minds with all the little forgotten details, those little intimate familiar details which bring back to life the one who has left. They recalled to each other circumstances, words, smiles, intonations of the mother who was no longer to speak to them. They saw her again happy and calm. They remembered things which she had said, and a little motion of the hand, like beating time, which she often used when emphasizing something important.

And they loved her as they never had loved her before. They measured the depth of their grief, and thus they discovered how lonely they would find themselves.

It was their prop, their guide, their whole youth, all the best part of their lives which was disappearing. It was their bond with life, their mother, their mamma, the connecting link with their forefathers which they would thenceforth miss. They now became solitary, lonely beings; they could no longer look back.

The nun said to her brother: 'You remember how mamma

used always to read her old letters; they are all there in that drawer. Let us, in turn, read them; let us live her whole life through tonight beside her! It would be like a road to the cross, like making the acquaintance of her mother, of our grandparents, whom we never knew, but whose letters are there and of whom she so often spoke, do you remember?'

Out of the drawer they took about ten little packages of yellow paper, tied with care and arranged one beside the other. They threw these relics on the bed and chose one of them on which the word 'Father' was written. They opened and read it.

It was one of those old-fashioned letters which one finds in old family desk drawers, those epistles which smell of another century. The first one started: 'My dear,' another one: 'My beautiful little girl,' others: 'My dear child,' or: 'My dear (laughter).' And suddenly the nun began to read aloud, to read over to the dead woman her whole history, all her tender memories. The judge, resting his elbow on the bed, was listening with his eyes fastened on his mother. The motionless body seemed happy.

Sister Eulalie, interrupting herself, said suddenly:

'These ought to be put in the grave with her; they ought to be used as a shroud and she ought to be buried in it.' She took another package, on which no name was written. She began to read in a firm voice: 'My adored one, I love you wildly. Since yesterday I have been suffering the tortures of the damned, haunted by our memory. I feel your lips against mine, your eyes in mine, your breast against mine. I love you, I love you! You have driven me mad. My arms open, I gasp, moved by a wild desire to hold you again. My whole soul and body cries out for you, wants you. I have kept in my mouth the taste of your kisses—'

The judge had straightened himself up. The nun stopped

reading. He snatched the letter from her and looked for the signature. There was none, but only under the words, 'The man who adores you,' the name 'Henry.' Their father's name was Rene. Therefore this was not from him. The son then quickly rummaged through the package of letters, took one out and read: 'I can no longer live without your caresses.' Standing erect, severe as when sitting on the bench, he looked unmoved at the dead woman. The nun, straight as a statue, tears trembling in the corners of her eyes, was watching her brother, waiting. Then he crossed the room slowly, went to the window and stood there, gazing out into the dark night.

When he turned around again Sister Eulalie, her eyes dry now, was still standing near the bed, her head bent down.

He stepped forward, quickly picked up the letters and threw them pell-mell back into the drawer. Then he closed the curtains of the bed.

When daylight made the candles on the table turn pale the son slowly left his armchair, and without looking again at the mother upon whom he had passed sentence, severing the tie that united her to son and daughter, he said slowly: 'Let us now retire, sister.'

27

A FAMILY

Guy de Maupassant

I was to see my old friend, Simon Radevin, of whom I had lost sight for fifteen years. At one time he was my most intimate friend, the friend who knows one's thoughts, with whom one passes long, quiet, happy evenings, to whom one tells one's secret love affairs, and who seems to draw out those rare, ingenious, delicate thoughts born of that sympathy that gives a sense of repose.

For years we had scarcely been separated; we had lived, travelled, thought and dreamed together; had liked the same things, had admired the same books, understood the same authors, trembled with the same sensations, and very often laughed at the same individuals, whom we understood completely by merely exchanging a glance.

Then he married. He married, quite suddenly, a little girl from the provinces, who had come to Paris in search of a husband. How in the world could that little thin, insipidly fair girl, with her weak hands, her light, vacant eyes, and her clear, silly voice, who was exactly like a hundred thousand marriageable dolls, have picked up that intelligent, clever young fellow? Can any one understand these things? No doubt he had hoped for happiness, simple, quiet and long-enduring happiness, in the arms of a good, tender and faithful woman; he had seen all that in the transparent looks of that schoolgirl with light hair.

He had not dreamed of the fact that an active, living and vibrating man grows weary of everything as soon as he understands the stupid reality, unless, indeed, he becomes so brutalized that he understands nothing whatever.

What would he be like when I met him again? Still lively, witty, light-hearted and enthusiastic, or in a state of mental torpor induced by provincial life? A man may change greatly in the course of fifteen years!

The train stopped at a small station, and as I got out of the carriage, a stout, a very stout man with red cheeks and a big stomach rushed up to me with open arms, exclaiming: 'George!' I embraced him, but I had not recognized him, and then I said, in astonishment: 'By Jove! You have not grown thin!' And he replied with a laugh:

'What did you expect? Good living, a good table and good nights! Eating and sleeping, that is my existence!'

I looked at him closely, trying to discover in that broad face the features I held so dear. His eyes alone had not changed, but I no longer saw the same expression in them, and I said to myself: 'If the expression be the reflection of the mind, the thoughts in that head are not what they used to be formerly; those thoughts which I knew so well.'

Yet his eyes were bright, full of happiness and friendship, but they had not that clear, intelligent expression which shows as much as words the brightness of the intellect. Suddenly he said:

'Here are my two eldest children.' A girl of fourteen, who was almost a woman, and a boy of thirteen, in the dress of a boy from a Lycee, came forward in a hesitating and awkward manner, and I said in a low voice: 'Are they yours?' 'Of course they are,' he replied, laughing. 'How many have you?' 'Five! There are three more at home.'

He said this in a proud, self-satisfied, almost triumphant manner, and I felt profound pity, mingled with a feeling of vague contempt, for this vainglorious and simple reproducer of his species.

I got into a carriage which he drove himself, and we set off through the town, a dull, sleepy, gloomy town where nothing was moving in the streets except a few dogs and two or three maidservants. Here and there a shopkeeper, standing at his door, took off his hat, and Simon returned his salute and told me the man's name; no doubt to show me that he knew all the inhabitants personally, and the thought struck me that he was thinking of becoming a candidate for the Chamber of Deputies, that dream of all those who bury themselves in the provinces.

We were soon out of the town, and the carriage turned into a garden that was an imitation of a park, and stopped in front of a turreted house, which tried to look like a chateau.

'That is my den,' said Simon, so that I might compliment him on it. 'It is charming,' I replied.

A lady appeared on the steps, dressed for company, and with company phrases all ready prepared. She was no longer the light-haired, insipid girl I had seen in church fifteen years previously, but a stout lady in curls and flounces, one of those ladies of uncertain age, without intellect, without any of those things that go to make a woman. In short, she was a mother, a stout, commonplace mother, a human breeding machine which procreates without any other preoccupation but her children and her cook-book.

She welcomed me, and I went into the hall, where three children, ranged according to their height, seemed set out for review, like firemen before a mayor, and I said: 'Ah! ah! so there are the others?' Simon, radiant with pleasure, introduced them: 'Jean, Sophie and Gontran.'

The door of the drawing-room was open. I went in, and in the depths of an easy-chair, I saw something trembling, a man, an old, paralysed man. Madame Radevin came forward and said: 'This is my grandfather, monsieur; he is eighty-seven.' And then she shouted into the shaking old man's ears: 'This is a friend of Simon's, papa.' The old gentleman tried to say 'good-day' to me, and he muttered: 'Oua, oua, oua,' and waved his hand, and I took a seat saying: 'You are very kind, monsieur.'

Simon had just come in, and he said with a laugh: 'So! You have made grandpapa's acquaintance. He is a treasure, that old man; he is the delight of the children. But he is so greedy that he almost kills himself at every meal; you have no idea what he would eat if he were allowed to do as he pleased. But you will see, you will see. He looks at all the sweets as if they were so many girls. You never saw anything so funny; you will see presently.'

I was then shown to my room, to change my dress for dinner, and hearing a great clatter behind me on the stairs, I turned round and saw that all the children were following me behind their father; to do me honour, no doubt.

My windows looked out across a dreary, interminable plain, an ocean of grass, of wheat and of oats, without a clump of trees or any rising ground, a striking and melancholy picture of the life which they must be leading in that house.

A bell rang; it was for dinner, and I went downstairs. Madame Radevin took my arm in a ceremonious manner, and we passed into the dining-room. A footman wheeled in the old man in his armchair. He gave a greedy and curious look at the dessert, as he turned his shaking head with difficulty from one dish to the other.

Simon rubbed his hands: 'You will be amused,' he said; and all the children understanding that I was going to be indulged with the sight of their greedy grandfather, began to laugh, while their mother merely smiled and shrugged her shoulders, and Simon, making a speaking trumpet of his hands, shouted at the old man: 'This evening there is sweet creamed rice!' The wrinkled face of the grandfather brightened, and he trembled more violently, from head to foot, showing that he had understood and was very pleased. The dinner began.

'Just look!' Simon whispered. The old man did not like the soup, and refused to eat it; but he was obliged to do it for the good of his health, and the footman forced the spoon into his mouth, while the old man blew so energetically, so as not to swallow the soup, that it was scattered like a spray all over the table and over his neighbors. The children writhed with laughter at the spectacle, while their father, who was also amused, said: 'Is not the old man comical?'

During the whole meal they were taken up solely with him. He devoured the dishes on the table with his eyes, and tried to seize them and pull them over to him with his trembling hands. They put them almost within his reach, to see his useless efforts, his trembling clutches at them, the piteous appeal of his whole nature, of his eyes, of his mouth and of his nose as he smelt them, and he slobbered on his table napkin with eagerness, while uttering inarticulate grunts. And the whole family was highly amused at this horrible and grotesque scene.

Then they put a tiny morsel on his plate, and he ate with feverish gluttony, in order to get something more as soon as possible, and when the sweetened rice was brought in, he nearly had a fit, and groaned with greediness, and Gontran called out to him:

'You have eaten too much already; you can have no more.'

And they pretended not to give him any. Then he began to cry; he cried and trembled more violently than ever, while all the children laughed. At last, however, they gave him his helping, a very small piece; and as he ate the first mouthful, he made a comical noise in his throat, and a movement with his neck as ducks do when they swallow too large a morsel, and when he had swallowed it, he began to stamp his feet, so as to get more.

I was seized with pity for this saddening and ridiculous Tantalus, and interposed on his behalf:

'Come, give him a little more rice!' But Simon replied: 'Oh! no, my dear fellow, if he were to eat too much, it would harm him, at his age.'

I held my tongue, and thought over those words. Oh, ethics! Oh, logic! Oh, wisdom! At his age! So they deprived him of his only remaining pleasure out of regard for his health! His health! What would he do with it, inert and trembling wreck that he was? They were taking care of his life, so they said. His life? How many days? Ten, twenty, fifty, or a hundred? Why? For his own sake? Or to preserve for some time longer the spectacle of his impotent greediness in the family.

There was nothing left for him to do in this life, nothing whatever. He had one single wish left, one sole pleasure; why not grant him that last solace until he died?

After we had played cards for a long time, I went up to my room and to bed; I was low-spirited and sad, sad, sad! and I sat at my window. Not a sound could be heard outside but the beautiful warbling of a bird in a tree, somewhere in the distance. No doubt the bird was singing in a low voice during the night, to lull his mate, who was asleep on her eggs. And I thought of my poor friend's five children, and pictured him to myself, snoring by the side of his ugly wife.

28

THE BEGGAR

Guy de Maupassant

He had seen better days, despite his present misery and infirmities.

At the age of fifteen both his legs had been crushed by a carriage on the Varville highway. From that time forth he begged, dragging himself along the roads and through the farmyards, supported by crutches which forced his shoulders up to his ears. His head looked as if it were squeezed in between two mountains.

A foundling, picked up out of a ditch by the priest of Les Billettes on the eve of All Saints' Day and baptized, for that reason, Nicholas Toussaint, reared by charity, utterly without education, crippled in consequence of having drunk several glasses of brandy given him by the baker (such a funny story!) and a vagabond all his life afterward—the only thing he knew how to do was to hold out his hand for alms.

At one time the Baroness d'Avary allowed him to sleep in a kind of recess spread with straw, close to the poultry yard in the farm adjoining the chateau, and if he was in great need he was sure of getting a glass of cider and a crust of bread in the kitchen. Moreover, the old lady often threw him a few pennies from her window. But she was dead now.

In the villages people gave him scarcely anything—he was too well known. Everybody had grown tired of seeing him, day after day for forty years, dragging his deformed and tattered person from door to door on his wooden crutches. But he could not make up his mind to go elsewhere, because he knew no place on earth but this particular corner of the country, these three or four villages where he had spent the whole of his miserable existence. He had limited his begging operations and would not for worlds have passed his accustomed bounds.

He did not even know whether the world extended for any distance beyond the trees which had always bounded his vision. He did not ask himself the question. And when the peasants, tired of constantly meeting him in their fields or along their lanes, exclaimed: 'Why don't you go to other villages instead of always limping about here?' he did not answer, but slunk away, possessed with a vague dread of the unknown—the dread of a poor wretch who fears confusedly a thousand things—new faces, taunts, insults, the suspicious glances of people who do not know him and the policemen walking in couples on the roads. These last he always instinctively avoided, taking refuge in the bushes or behind heaps of stones when he saw them coming.

When he perceived them in the distance, with uniforms gleaming in the sun, he was suddenly possessed with unwonted agility—the agility of a wild animal seeking its lair. He threw aside his crutches, fell to the ground like a limp rag, made himself as small as possible and crouched like a hare under cover, his tattered vestments blending in hue with the earth on which he cowered.

He had never had any trouble with the police, but the instinct to avoid them was in his blood. He seemed to have inherited it from the parents he had never known.

He had no refuge, no roof for his head, no shelter of any kind. In summer he slept out of doors and in winter he showed remarkable skill in slipping unperceived into barns and stables. He always decamped before his presence could be discovered. He knew all the holes through which one could creep into farm buildings, and the handling of his crutches having made his arms surprisingly muscular he often hauled himself up through sheer strength of wrist into hay-lofts, where he sometimes remained for four or five days at a time, provided he had collected a sufficient store of food beforehand.

He lived like the beasts of the field. He was in the midst of men, yet knew no one, loved no one, exciting in the breasts of the peasants only a sort of careless contempt and smouldering hostility. They nicknamed him 'Bell,' because he hung between his two crutches like a church bell between its supports.

For two days he had eaten nothing. No one gave him anything now. Every one's patience was exhausted. Women shouted to him from their doorsteps when they saw him coming:

'Be off with you, you good-for-nothing vagabond! Why, I gave you a piece of bread only three days ago!

And he turned on his crutches to the next house, where he was received in the same fashion.

The women declared to one another as they stood at their doors:

'We can't feed that lazy brute all the year round!'

And yet the 'lazy brute' needed food every day.

He had exhausted Saint-Hilaire, Varville and Les Billettes without getting a single copper or so much as a dry crust. His only hope was in Tournolles, but to reach this place he would have to walk five miles along the high-road, and he felt so weary that he could hardly drag himself another yard. His stomach and his pocket were equally empty, but he started on his way.

It was December and a cold wind blew over the fields and whistled through the bare branches of the trees; the clouds careered madly across the black, threatening sky. The cripple dragged himself slowly along, raising one crutch after the other with a painful effort, propping himself on the one distorted leg which remained to him.

Now and then he sat down beside a ditch for a few moments' rest. Hunger was gnawing his vitals, and in his confused, slow-working mind he had only one idea—to eat—but how this was to be accomplished he did not know. For three hours he continued his painful journey. Then at last the sight of the trees of the village inspired him with new energy.

The first peasant he met, and of whom he asked alms, replied:

'So it's you again, is it, you old scamp? Shall I never be rid of you?'

And 'Bell' went on his way. At every door he got nothing but hard words. He made the round of the whole village, but received not a halfpenny for his pains.

Then he visited the neighbouring farms, toiling through the muddy land, so exhausted that he could hardly raise his crutches from the ground. He met with the same reception everywhere. It was one of those cold, bleak days, when the heart is frozen and the temper irritable, and hands do not open either to give money or food.

When he had visited all the houses he knew, 'Bell' sank down in the corner of a ditch running across Chiquet's farmyard. Letting his crutches slip to the ground, he remained motionless, tortured by hunger, but hardly intelligent enough to realize to the full his unutterable misery.

He awaited he knew not what, possessed with that vague hope which persists in the human heart in spite of everything.

He awaited in the corner of the farmyard in the biting December wind, some mysterious aid from Heaven or from men, without the least idea whence it was to arrive. A number of black hens ran hither and thither, seeking their food in the earth which supports all living things. Ever now and then they snapped up in their beaks a grain of corn or a tiny insect; then they continued their slow, sure search for nutriment.

'Bell' watched them at first without thinking of anything. Then a thought occurred rather to his stomach than to his mind—the thought that one of those fowls would be good to eat if it were cooked over a fire of dead wood.

He did not reflect that he was going to commit a theft. He took up a stone which lay within reach, and, being of skilful aim, killed at the first shot the fowl nearest to him. The bird fell on its side, flapping its wings. The others fled wildly hither and thither, and 'Bell,' picking up his crutches, limped across to where his victim lay.

Just as he reached the little black body with its crimsoned head he received a violent blow in his back which made him let go his hold of his crutches and sent him flying ten paces distant. And Farmer Chiquet, beside himself with rage, cuffed and kicked the marauder with all the fury of a plundered peasant as 'Bell' lay defenceless before him.

The farm hands came up also and joined their master in cuffing the lame beggar. Then when they were tired of beating him they carried him off and shut him up in the woodshed, while they went to fetch the police.

'Bell,' half dead, bleeding and perishing with hunger, lay on the floor. Evening came—then night—then dawn. And still he had not eaten.

About midday the police arrived. They opened the door of the woodshed with the utmost precaution, fearing resistance on the beggar's part, for Farmer Chiquet asserted that he had been attacked by him and had had great difficulty in defending himself.

The sergeant cried:

'Come, get up!'

But 'Bell' could not move. He did his best to raise himself on his crutches, but without success. The police, thinking his weakness feigned, pulled him up by main force and set him between the crutches.

Fear seized him—his native fear of a uniform, the fear of the game in presence of the sportsman, the fear of a mouse for a cat—and by the exercise of almost superhuman effort he succeeded in remaining upright.

'Forward!' said the sergeant. He walked. All the inmates of the farm watched his departure. The women shook their fists at him the men scoffed at and insulted him. He was taken at last! Good riddance! He went off between his two guards. He mustered sufficient energy—the energy of despair—to drag himself along until the evening, too dazed to know what was happening to him, too frightened to understand.

People whom he met on the road stopped to watch him go by and peasants muttered:

'It's some thief or other.'

Toward evening he reached the country town. He had never been so far before. He did not realize in the least what he was there for or what was to become of him. All the terrible and unexpected events of the last two days, all these unfamiliar faces and houses struck dismay into his heart.

He said not a word, having nothing to say because he understood nothing. Besides, he had spoken to no one for so many years past that he had almost lost the use of his tongue, and his thoughts were too indeterminate to be put into words.

He was shut up in the town jail. It did not occur to the police that he might need food, and he was left alone until the following day. But when in the early morning they came to examine him he was found dead on the floor. Such an astonishing thing!

29

THE BLIND MAN

Guy de Maupassant

How is it that the sunlight gives us such joy? Why does this radiance when it falls on the earth fill us with the joy of living? The whole sky is blue, the fields are green, the houses all white, and our enchanted eyes drink in those bright colours which bring delight to our souls. And then there springs up in our hearts a desire to dance, to run, to sing, a happy lightness of thought, a sort of enlarged tenderness; we feel a longing to embrace the sun.

The blind, as they sit in the doorways, impassive in their eternal darkness, remain as calm as ever in the midst of this fresh gaiety, and, not understanding what is taking place around them, they continually check their dogs as they attempt to play.

When, at the close of the day, they are returning home on the arm of a young brother or a little sister, if the child says: 'It was a very fine day!' the other answers: 'I could notice that it was fine. Loulou wouldn't keep quiet.'

I knew one of these men whose life was one of the most cruel martyrdoms that could possibly be conceived.

He was a peasant, the son of a Norman farmer. As long as his father and mother lived, he was more or less taken care of; he suffered little save from his horrible infirmity; but as soon as the old people were gone, an atrocious life of misery commenced for him. Dependent on a sister of his, everybody in the farmhouse treated him as a beggar who is eating the bread of strangers. At every meal the very food he swallowed was made a subject of reproach against him; he was called a drone, a clown, and although his brother-in-law had taken possession of his portion of the inheritance, he was helped grudgingly to soup, getting just enough to save him from starving.

His face was very pale and his two big white eyes looked like wafers. He remained unmoved at all the insults hurled at him, so reserved that one could not tell whether he felt them.

Moreover, he had never known any tenderness, his mother having always treated him unkindly and caring very little for him; for in country places useless persons are considered a nuisance, and the peasants would be glad to kill the infirm of their species, as poultry do.

As soon as he finished his soup he went and sat outside the door in summer and in winter beside the fireside, and did not stir again all the evening. He made no gesture, no movement; only his eyelids, quivering from some nervous affection, fell down sometimes over his white, sightless orbs. Had he any intellect, any thinking faculty, any consciousness of his own existence? Nobody cared to inquire.

For some years things went on in this fashion. But his incapacity for work as well as his impassiveness eventually exasperated his relatives, and he became a laughingstock, a sort of butt for merriment, a prey to the inborn ferocity, to the savage gaiety of the brutes who surrounded him.

It is easy to imagine all the cruel practical jokes inspired by his blindness. And, in order to have some fun in return for feeding him, they now converted his meals into hours of pleasure for the neighbours and of punishment for the helpless creature himself.

The peasants from the nearest houses came to this entertainment; it was talked about from door to door, and every day the kitchen of the farmhouse was full of people. Sometimes they placed before his plate, when he was beginning to eat his soup, some cat or dog. The animal instinctively perceived the man's infirmity, and, softly approaching, commenced eating noiselessly, lapping up the soup daintily; and, when they lapped the food rather noisily, rousing the poor fellow's attention, they would prudently scamper away to avoid the blow of the spoon directed at random by the blind man!

Then the spectators ranged along the wall would burst out laughing, nudge each other and stamp their feet on the floor. And he, without ever uttering a word, would continue eating with his right hand, while stretching out his left to protect his plate.

Another time they made him chew corks, bits of wood, leaves or even filth, which he was unable to distinguish.

After this they got tired even of these practical jokes, and the brother-in-law, angry at having to support him always, struck him, cuffed him incessantly, laughing at his futile efforts to ward off or return the blows. Then came a new pleasure—the pleasure of smacking his face. And the plough-men, the servant girls and even every passing vagabond were every moment giving him cuffs, which caused his eyelashes to twitch spasmodically. He did not know where to hide himself and remained with his arms always held out to guard against people coming too close to him.

At last he was forced to beg.

He was placed somewhere on the high-road on market-days, and as soon as he heard the sound of footsteps or the rolling of a vehicle, he reached out his hat, stammering:

'Charity, if you please!'

But the peasant is not lavish, and for whole weeks he did not bring back a sou.

Then he became the victim of furious, pitiless hatred. And this is how he died.

One winter the ground was covered with snow, and it was freezing hard. His brother-in-law led him one morning a great distance along the high road in order that he might solicit alms. The blind man was left there all day; and when night came on, the brother-in-law told the people of his house that he could find no trace of the mendicant. Then he added:

'Pooh! best not bother about him! He was cold and got someone to take him away. Never fear! he's not lost. He'll turn up soon enough tomorrow to eat the soup.'

Next day he did not come back.

After long hours of waiting, stiffened with the cold, feeling that he was dying, the blind man began to walk. Being unable to find his way along the road, owing to its thick coating of ice, he went on at random, falling into ditches, getting up again, without uttering a sound, his sole object being to find some house where he could take shelter.

But, by degrees, the descending snow made a numbness steal over him, and his feeble limbs being incapable of carrying him farther, he sat down in the middle of an open field. He did not get up again.

The white flakes which fell continuously buried him, so that his body, quite stiff and stark, disappeared under the incessant accumulation of their rapidly thickening mass, and nothing was left to indicate the place where he lay.

His relatives made a pretence of inquiring about him and searching for him for about a week. They even made a show of weeping.

The winter was severe, and the thaw did not set in quickly. Now, one Sunday, on their way to mass, the farmers noticed a great flight of crows, who were whirling incessantly above the open field, and then descending like a shower of black rain at the same spot, ever going and coming.

The following week these gloomy birds were still there. There was a crowd of them up in the air, as if they had gathered from all corners of the horizon, and they swooped down with a great cawing into the shining snow, which they covered like black patches, and in which they kept pecking obstinately. A young fellow went to see what they were doing and discovered the body of the blind man, already half devoured, mangled. His wan eyes had disappeared, pecked out by the long, voracious beaks.

And I can never feel the glad radiance of sunlit days without sadly remembering and pondering over the fate of the beggar who was such an outcast in life that his horrible death was a relief to all who had known him.

30

THE OPEN WINDOW

Saki

'My aunt will be down presently, Mr Nuttel,' said a very self-possessed young lady of fifteen; 'in the meantime you must try and put up with me.'

Framton Nuttel endeavoured to say the correct something which should duly flatter the niece of the moment without unduly discounting the aunt that was to come. Privately he doubted more than ever whether these formal visits on a succession of total strangers would do much towards helping the nerve cure which he was supposed to be undergoing.

'I know how it will be,' his sister had said when he was preparing to migrate to this rural retreat; 'you will bury yourself down there and not speak to a living soul, and your nerves will be worse than ever from moping. I shall just give you letters of introduction to all the people I know there. Some of them, as far as I can remember, were quite nice.'

Framton wondered whether Mrs Sappleton, the lady to whom he was presenting one of the letters of introduction, came into the nice division.

'Do you know many of the people round here?' asked the niece, when she judged that they had had sufficient silent communion.

'Hardly a soul,' said Framton. 'My sister was staying here, at the rectory, you know, some four years ago, and she gave me letters of introduction to some of the people here.'

He made the last statement in a tone of distinct regret.

'Then you know practically nothing about my aunt?' pursued the self-possessed young lady.

'Only her name and address,' admitted the caller. He was wondering whether Mrs Sappleton was in the married or widowed state. An undefinable something about the room seemed to suggest masculine habitation.

'Her great tragedy happened just three years ago,' said the child; 'that would be since your sister's time.'

'Her tragedy?' asked Framton; somehow in this restful country spot tragedies seemed out of place.

'You may wonder why we keep that window wide open on an October afternoon,' said the niece, indicating a large French window that opened on to a lawn.

'It is quite warm for the time of the year,' said Framton; 'but has that window got anything to do with the tragedy?'

'Out through that window, three years ago to a day, her husband and her two young brothers went off for their day's shooting. They never came back. In crossing the moor to their favourite snipe-shooting ground they were all three engulfed in a treacherous piece of bog. It had been that dreadful wet summer, you know, and places that were safe in other years gave way suddenly without warning. Their bodies were never recovered. That was the dreadful part of it.' Here the child's voice lost its self-possessed note and became falteringly human. 'Poor aunt always thinks that they will come back someday, they and the little brown spaniel that was lost with them, and walk in at that window just as they used to do. That is why the window is kept open every evening till it is quite dusk. Poor dear aunt, she has often told me how they went out, her husband with his white waterproof coat over his arm, and Ronnie, her youngest brother, singing "Bertie, why do you bound?" as he always did to tease her, because she said it got on her nerves. Do you know, sometimes on still, quiet evenings like this, I almost get a creepy feeling that they will all walk in through that window—'

She broke off with a little shudder. It was a relief to Framton when the aunt bustled into the room with a whirl of apologies for being late in making her appearance.

'I hope Vera has been amusing you?' she said.

'She has been very interesting,' said Framton.

'I hope you don't mind the open window,' said Mrs Sappleton briskly; 'my husband and brothers will be home directly from shooting, and they always come in this way. They've been out for snipe in the marshes today, so they'll make a fine mess over my poor carpets. So like you menfolk, isn't it?'

She rattled on cheerfully about the shooting and the scarcity of birds, and the prospects for duck in the winter. To Framton it was all purely horrible. He made a desperate but only partially successful effort to turn the talk on to a less ghastly topic; he was conscious that his hostess was giving him only a fragment of her attention, and her eyes were constantly straying past him to the open window and the lawn beyond. It was certainly an unfortunate coincidence that he should have paid his visit on this tragic anniversary.

'The doctors agree in ordering me complete rest, an absence of mental excitement and avoidance of anything in the nature of violent physical exercise,' announced Framton, who laboured under the tolerably widespread delusion that total strangers and chance acquaintances are hungry for the least detail of one's ailments and infirmities, their cause and cure. 'On the matter of diet they are not so much in agreement,' he continued.

'No?' said Mrs Sappleton, in a voice which only replaced a yawn at the last moment. Then she suddenly brightened into alert attention—but not to what Framton was saying.

'Here they are at last!' she cried. 'Just in time for tea, and don't they look as if they were muddy up to the eyes!'

Framton shivered slightly and turned towards the niece with a look intended to convey sympathetic comprehension. The child was staring out through the open window with a dazed horror in her eyes. In a chill shock of nameless fear Framton swung round in his seat and looked in the same direction.

In the deepening twilight three figures were walking across the lawn towards the window, they all carried guns under their arms, and one of them was additionally burdened with a white coat hung over his shoulders. A tired brown spaniel kept close at their heels. Noiselessly they neared the house, and then a hoarse young voice chanted out of the dusk: 'I said, Bertie, why do you bound?'

Framton grabbed wildly at his stick and hat; the hall door, the gravel drive and the front gate were dimly noted stages in his headlong retreat. A cyclist coming along the road had to run into the hedge to avoid imminent collision.

'Here we are, my dear,' said the bearer of the white mackintosh, coming in through the window, 'fairly muddy, but most of it's dry. Who was that who bolted out as we came up?'

'A most extraordinary man, a Mr Nuttel,' said Mrs Sappleton; 'could only talk about his illnesses, and dashed off without a word of good-bye or apology when you arrived. One would think he had seen a ghost.'

'I expect it was the spaniel,' said the niece calmly; 'he told me he had a horror of dogs. He was once hunted into a cemetery somewhere on the banks of the Ganges by a pack of pariah dogs, and had to spend the night in a newly dug grave with the creatures snarling and grinning and foaming just above him. Enough to make anyone lose their nerve.'

Romance at short notice was her speciality.

31

THE DREAMER

Saki

It was the season of sales. The august establishment of Walpurgis and Nettlepink had lowered its prices for an entire week as a concession to trade observances, much as an Archduchess might protestingly contract an attack of influenza for the unsatisfactory reason that influenza was locally prevalent. Adela Chemping, who considered herself in some measure superior to the allurements of an ordinary bargain sale, made a point of attending the reduction week at Walpurgis and Nettlepink's.

'I'm not a bargain hunter,' she said, 'but I like to go where bargains are.'

Which showed that beneath her surface strength of character there flowed a gracious undercurrent of human weakness.

With a view to providing herself with a male escort Mrs Chemping had invited her youngest nephew to accompany her on the first day of the shopping expedition, throwing in the additional allurement of a cinematograph theatre and the prospect of light refreshment. As Cyprian was not yet eighteen she hoped he might not have reached that stage in masculine development when parcel-carrying is looked on as a thing abhorrent.

'Meet me just outside the floral department,' she wrote to him, 'and don't be a moment later than eleven.'

Cyprian was a boy who carried with him through early life the wondering look of a dreamer, the eyes of one who sees things that are not visible to ordinary mortals, and invests the commonplace things of this world with qualities unsuspected by plainer folk—the eyes of a poet or a house agent. He was quietly dressed—that sartorial quietude which frequently accompanies early adolescence, and is usually attributed by novel-writers to the influence of a widowed mother. His hair was brushed back in a smoothness as of ribbon seaweed and seamed with a narrow furrow that scarcely aimed at being a parting. His aunt particularly noted this item of his toilet when they met at the appointed rendezvous, because he was standing waiting for her bare-headed.

'Where is your hat?' she asked.

'I didn't bring one with me,' he replied.

Adela Chemping was slightly scandalized.

'You are not going to be what they call a Nut, are you?' she inquired with some anxiety, partly with the idea that a Nut would be an extravagance which her sister's small household would scarcely be justified in incurring, partly, perhaps, with the instinctive apprehension that a Nut, even in its embryo stage, would refuse to carry parcels.

Cyprian looked at her with his wondering, dreamy eyes.

'I didn't bring a hat,' he said, 'because it is such a nuisance when one is shopping; I mean it is so awkward if one meets anyone one knows and has to take one's hat off when one's hands are full of parcels. If one hasn't got a hat on one can't take it off.'

Mrs Chemping sighed with great relief; her worst fear had been laid at rest.

'It is more orthodox to wear a hat,' she observed, and then turned her attention briskly to the business in hand.

'We will go first to the table-linen counter,' she said, leading the way in that direction; 'I should like to look at some napkins.'

The wondering look deepened in Cyprian's eyes as he followed his aunt; he belonged to a generation that is supposed to be over-fond of the role of mere spectator, but looking at napkins that one did not mean to buy was a pleasure beyond his comprehension. Mrs Chemping held one or two napkins up to the light and stared fixedly at them, as though she half expected to find some revolutionary cypher written on them in scarcely visible ink; then she suddenly broke away in the direction of the glassware department.

'Millicent asked me to get her a couple of decanters if there were any going really cheap,' she explained on the way, 'and I really do want a salad bowl. I can come back to the napkins later on.'

She handled and scrutinized a large number of decanters and a long series of salad bowls, and finally bought seven chrysanthemum vases.

'No one uses that kind of vase nowadays,' she informed Cyprian, 'but they will do for presents next Christmas.'

Two sunshades that were marked down to a price that Mrs Chemping considered absurdly cheap were added to her purchases.

'One of them will do for Ruth Colson; she is going out to the Malay States, and a sunshade will always be useful there. And I must get her some thin writing paper. It takes up no room in one's baggage.'

Mrs Chemping bought stacks of writing paper; it was so cheap, and it went so flat in a trunk or portmanteau. She also bought a few envelopes—envelopes somehow seemed rather an extravagance compared with notepaper.

'Do you think Ruth will like blue or grey paper?' she asked Cyprian.

'Grey,' said Cyprian, who had never met the lady in question.

'Have you any mauve notepaper of this quality?' Adela asked the assistant.

'We haven't any mauve,' said the assistant, 'but we've two shades of green and a darker shade of grey.'

Mrs Chemping inspected the greens and the darker grey, and chose the blue.

'Now we can have some lunch,' she said.

Cyprian behaved in an exemplary fashion in the refreshment department, and cheerfully accepted a fish cake and a mince pie and a small cup of coffee as adequate restoratives after two hours of concentrated shopping. He was adamant, however, in resisting his aunt's suggestion that a hat should be bought for him at the counter where men's headwear was being disposed of at temptingly reduced prices.

'I've got as many hats as I want at home,' he said, 'and besides, it rumples one's hair so, trying them on.'

Perhaps he was going to develop into a Nut after all. It was a disquieting symptom that he left all the parcels in charge of the cloak-room attendant.

'We shall be getting more parcels presently,' he said, 'so we need not collect these till we have finished our shopping.'

His aunt was doubtfully appeased; some of the pleasure and excitement of a shopping expedition seemed to evaporate when one was deprived of immediate personal contact with one's purchases.

'I'm going to look at those napkins again,' she said, as they descended the stairs to the ground floor. 'You need not come,' she added, as the dreaming look in the boy's eyes changed for a moment into one of mute protest, 'you can meet me afterwards in the cutlery department; I've just remembered that I haven't a corkscrew in the house that can be depended on.'

Cyprian was not to be found in the cutlery department when his aunt in due course arrived there, but in the crush and bustle of anxious shoppers and busy attendants it was an easy matter to miss anyone. It was in the leather goods department some quarter of an hour later that Adela Chemping caught sight of her nephew, separated from her by a rampart of suitcases and portmanteaux and hemmed in by the jostling crush of human beings that now invaded every corner of the great shopping emporium. She was just in time to witness a pardonable but rather embarrassing mistake on the part of a lady who had wriggled her way with unstayable determination towards the bareheaded Cyprian, and was now breathlessly demanding the sale price of a handbag which had taken her fancy.

'There now,' exclaimed Adela to herself, 'she takes him for one of the shop assistants because he hasn't got a hat on. I wonder it hasn't happened before.'

Perhaps it had. Cyprian, at any rate, seemed neither startled nor embarrassed by the error into which the good lady had fallen. Examining the ticket on the bag, he announced in a clear, dispassionate voice:

'Black seal, thirty-four shillings, marked down to twenty-eight. As a matter of fact, we are clearing them out at a special reduction price of twenty-six shillings. They are going off rather fast.'

'I'll take it,' said the lady, eagerly digging some coins out of her purse.

'Will you take it as it is?' asked Cyprian; 'it will be a matter of a few minutes to get it wrapped up, there is such a crush.'

'Never mind, I'll take it as it is,' said the purchaser, clutching her treasure and counting the money into Cyprian's palm.

Several kind strangers helped Adela into the open air.

'It's the crush and the heat,' said one sympathizer to another; 'it's enough to turn anyone giddy.'

When she next came across Cyprian he was standing in the crowd that pushed and jostled around the counters of the book department. The dream look was deeper than ever in his eyes. He had just sold two books of devotion to an elderly Canon.

32

THE WOLVES OF CERNOGRATZ

Saki

'Are they any old legends attached to the castle?' asked Conrad of his sister. Conrad was a prosperous Hamburg merchant, but he was the one poetically-disposed member of an eminently practical family.

The Baroness Gruebel shrugged her plump shoulders.

'There are always legends hanging about these old places. They are not difficult to invent and they cost nothing. In this case there is a story that when any one dies in the castle all the dogs in the village and the wild beasts in forest howl the night long. It would not be pleasant to listen to, would it?'

'It would be weird and romantic,' said the Hamburg merchant.

'Anyhow, it isn't true,' said the Baroness complacently; 'since we bought the place we have had proof that nothing of the sort happens. When the old mother-in-law died last springtime we all listened, but there was no howling. It is just a story that lends dignity to the place without costing anything.'

'The story is not as you have told it,' said Amalie, the grey old governess. Every one turned and looked at her in astonishment. She was wont to sit silent and prim and faded in her place at table, never speaking unless some one spoke to her, and there were few who troubled themselves to make conversation with her. Today a sudden volubility had descended on her; she continued to talk, rapidly and nervously, looking straight in front of her and seeming to address no one in particular.

'It is not when *any one* dies in the castle that the howling is heard. It was when one of the Cernogratz family died here that the wolves came from far and near and howled at the edge of the forest just before the death hour. There were only a few couple of wolves that had their lairs in this part of the forest, but at such a time the keepers say there would be scores of them, gliding about in the shadows and howling in chorus, and the dogs of the castle and the village and all the farms round would bay and howl in fear and anger at the wolf chorus, and as the soul of the dying one left its body a tree would crash down in the park. That is what happened when a Cernogratz died in his family castle. But for a stranger dying here, of course no wolf would howl and no tree would fall. Oh, no.'

There was a note of defiance, almost of contempt, in her voice as she said the last words. The well-fed, much-too-well dressed Baroness stared angrily at the dowdy old woman who had come forth from her usual and seemly position of effacement to speak so disrespectfully.

'You seem to know quite a lot about the von Cernogratz legends, Fraulein Schmidt,' she said sharply; 'I did not know that family histories were among the subjects you are supposed to be proficient in.'

The answer to her taunt was even more unexpected and astonishing than the conversational outbreak which had provoked it.

'I am a von Cernogratz myself,' said the old woman, 'that is why I know the family history.'

'You a von Cernogratz? You!' came in an incredulous chorus.

'When we became very poor,' she explained, 'and I had to go out and give teaching lessons, I took another name; I thought it would be more in keeping. But my grandfather spent much of his time as a boy in this castle, and my father used to tell me many stories about it, and, of course, I knew all the family legends and stories. When one has nothing left to one but memories, one guards and dusts them with especial care. I little thought when I took service with you that I should one day come with you to the old home of my family. I could wish it had been anywhere else.'

There was silence when she finished speaking, and then the Baroness turned the conversation to a less embarrassing topic than family histories. But afterwards, when the old governess had slipped away quietly to her duties, there arose a clamour of derision and disbelief.

'It was an impertinence,' snapped out the Baron, his protruding eyes taking on a scandalized expression; 'fancy the woman talking like that at our table. She almost told us we were nobodies, and I don't believe a word of it. She is just Schmidt and nothing more. She has been talking to some of the peasants about the old Cernogratz family, and raked up their history and their stories.'

'She wants to make herself out of some consequence,' said the Baroness; 'she knows she will soon be past work and she wants to appeal to our sympathies. Her grandfather, indeed!'

The Baroness had the usual number of grandfathers, but she never, never boasted about them.

'I dare say her grandfather was a pantry boy or something of the sort in the castle,' sniggered the Baron; 'that part of the story may be true.'

The merchant from Hamburg said nothing; he had seen

tears in the old woman's eyes when she spoke of guarding her memories—or, being of an imaginative disposition, he thought he had.

'I shall give her notice to go as soon as the New Year festivities are over,' said the Baroness; 'till then I shall be too busy to manage without her.'

But she had to manage without her all the same, for in the cold biting weather after Christmas, the old governess fell ill and kept to her room.

'It is most provoking,' said the Baroness, as her guests sat round the fire on one of the last evenings of the dying year; 'all the time that she has been with us I cannot remember that she was ever seriously ill, too ill to go about and do her work, I mean. And now, when I have the house full, and she could be useful in so many ways, she goes and breaks down. One is sorry for her, of course, she looks so withered and shrunken, but it is intensely annoying all the same.'

'Most annoying,' agreed the banker's wife, sympathetically; 'it is the intense cold, I expect, it breaks the old people up. It has been unusually cold this year.'

'The frost is the sharpest that has been known in December for many years,' said the Baron.

'And, of course, she is quite old,' said the Baroness; 'I wish I had given her notice some weeks ago, then she would have left before this happened to her. Why, Wappi, what is the matter with you?'

The small, woolly lapdog had leapt suddenly down from its cushion and crept shivering under the sofa. At the same moment an outburst of angry barking came from the dogs in the castle-yard, and other dogs could be heard yapping and barking in the distance.

'What is disturbing the animals?' asked the Baron.

And then the humans, listening intently, heard the sound that had roused the dogs to their demonstrations of fear and rage; heard a long-drawn whining howl, rising and falling, seeming at one moment leagues away, at others sweeping across the snow until it appeared to come from the foot of the castle walls. All the starved, cold misery of a frozen world, all the relentless hunger-fury of the wild, blended with other forlorn and haunting melodies to which one could give no name, seemed concentrated in that wailing cry.

'Wolves!' cried the Baron.

Their music broke forth in one raging burst, seeming to come from everywhere.

'Hundreds of wolves,' said the Hamburg merchant, who was a man of strong imagination.

Moved by some impulse which she could not have explained, the Baroness left her guests and made her way to the narrow, cheerless room where the old governess lay watching the hours of the drying year slip by. In spite of the biting cold of the winter night, the window stood open. With a scandalized exclamation on her lips, the Baroness rushed forward to close it.

'Leave it open,' said the old woman in a voice that for all its weakness carried an air of command such as the Baroness had never heard before from her lips.

'But you will die of cold!' she expostulated.

'I am dying in any case,' said the voice, 'and I want to hear their music. They have come from far and wide to sing the death-music of my family. It is beautiful that they have come; I am the last von Cernogratz that will die in our old castle, and they have come to sing to me. Hark, how loud they are calling!'

The cry of the wolves rose on the still winter air and floated round the castle walls in long-drawn piercing wails; the old woman lay back on her couch with a look of long-delayed happiness on her face.

'Go away,' she said to the Baroness; 'I am not lonely any more. I am one of a great old family...'

'I think she is dying,' said the Baroness when she had rejoined her guests; 'I suppose we must send for a doctor. And that terrible howling! Not for much money would I have such death-music.'

'That music is not to be bought for any amount of money,' said Conrad.

'Hark! What is that other sound?' asked the Baron, as a noise of splitting and crashing was heard.

It was a tree falling in the park.

There was a moment of constrained silence, and then the banker's wife spoke.

'It is the intense cold that is splitting the trees. It is also the cold that has brought the wolves out in such numbers. It is many years since we have had such a cold winter.'

The Baroness eagerly agreed that the cold was responsible for these things. It was the cold of the open window, too, which caused the heart failure that made the doctor's ministrations unnecessary for the old Fraulein. But the notice in the newspapers looked very well—

> 'On December 29th, at Schloss Cernogratz, Amalie von Cernogratz, for many years the valued friend of Baron and Baroness Gruebel.'

33

THE IMP OF THE PERVERSE

Edgar Allan Poe

In the consideration of the faculties and impulses—of the *prima mobilia* of the human soul, the phrenologists have failed to make room for a propensity which, although obviously existing as a radical, primitive, irreducible sentiment, has been equally overlooked by all the moralists who have preceded them. In the pure arrogance of the reason, we have all overlooked it. We have suffered its existence to escape our senses solely through want of belief—of faith;—whether it be faith in Revelation, or faith in the Kabbala. The idea of it has never occurred to us, simply because of its supererogation. We saw no *need* of impulse—for the propensity. We could not perceive its necessity. We could not understand, that is to say, we could not have understood, had the notion of this *primum mobile* ever obtruded itself;—we could not have understood in what manner it might be made to further the objects of humanity, either temporal or eternal. It cannot be denied that phrenology and, in great measure, all metaphysicianism have been concocted *a priori*. The intellectual or logical man, rather than the understanding or observant man, set himself to imagine designs—to dictate purposes to God. Having thus fathomed, to his satisfaction, the intentions of Jehovah, out of these intentions he built his innumerable systems of mind. In the matter of phrenology, for example, we first determined, naturally enough, that it was the design of the Deity that man should eat. We then assigned to man an organ of alimentiveness, and this organ is the scourge with which the Deity compels man, will-I nill-I, into eating. Secondly, having settled it to be God's will that man should continue his species, we discovered an organ of amativeness, forthwith. And so with combativeness, with ideality, with causality, with constructiveness,—so, in short, with every organ, whether representing a propensity, a moral sentiment, or a faculty of the pure intellect. And in these arrangements of the *principia* of human action, the Spurzheimites, whether right or wrong, in part, or upon the whole, have but followed, in principle, the footsteps of their predecessors; deducing and establishing everything from the preconceived destiny of man, and upon the ground of the objects of this Creator.

It would have been wiser, it would have been safer, to classify (if classify we must) upon the basis of what man usually or occasionally did, and was always occasionally doing, rather than upon the basis of what he took it for granted the Deity intended him to do. If we cannot comprehend God in his visible works, how then in his inconceivable thoughts, that call the works into being? If we cannot understand him in his objective creatures, how then in his substantive moods and phases of creation?

Induction, *a posteriori*, would have brought phrenology to admit, as an innate and primitive principle of human action, a paradoxical something, which we may call *perverseness*, for want of a more characteristic term. In the sense I intend, it is, in fact, a *mobile* without motive, a motive not *motivirt*. Through its promptings we act without comprehensible object;

or, if this shall be understood as a contradiction in terms, we may so far modify the proposition as to say, that through its promptings we act, for the reason that we should *not*. In theory, no reason can be more unreasonable; but, in fact, there is none more strong. With certain minds, under certain conditions it becomes absolutely irresistible. I am not more certain that I breathe, than that the assurance of the wrong or error of any action is often the one unconquerable *force* which impels us, and alone impels us to its prosecution. Nor will this overwhelming tendency to do wrong for the wrong's sake, admit of analysis, or resolution into ulterior elements. It is radical, a primitive impulse—elementary. It will be said, I am aware, that when we persist in acts because we feel we should *not* persist in them, our conduct is but a modification of that which ordinarily springs from the *combativeness* of phrenology. But a glance will show the fallacy of this idea. The phrenological combativeness has, for its essence, the necessity of self-defence. It is our safeguard against injury. Its principle regards our well-being; and thus the desire to be well is excited simultaneously with its development. It follows, that the desire to be well must be excited simultaneously with any principle which shall be merely a modification of combativeness, but in the case of that something which I term *perverseness*, the desire to be well is not only aroused, but a strongly antagonistical sentiment exists.

An appeal to one's own heart is, after all, the best reply to the sophistry just noticed. No one who trustingly consults and thoroughly questions his own soul, will be disposed to deny the entire radicalness of the propensity in question. It is not more incomprehensible than distinctive. There lives no man who at some period has not been tormented, for example, by an earnest desire to tantalize a listener by circumlocution. The speaker is aware that he displeases, he has every intention to please; he is usually curt, precise, and clear; the most laconic and luminous language is struggling for utterance upon his tongue; it is only with difficulty that he restrains himself from giving it flow; he dreads and deprecates the anger of him whom he addresses; yet, the thought strikes him, that by certain involutions and parentheses this anger may be engendered. That single thought is enough. The impulse increases to a wish, the wish to a desire, the desire to an uncontrollable longing, and the longing (to the deep regret and mortification of the speaker, and in defiance of all consequences) is indulged.

We have a task before us which must be speedily performed. We know that it will be ruinous to make delay. The most important crisis of our life calls, trumpet-tongued, for immediate energy and action. We glow, we are consumed with eagerness to commence the work, with the anticipation of whose glorious result our whole souls are on fire. It must, it shall be undertaken today, and yet we put it off until tomorrow; and why? There is no answer, except that we feel perverse, using the word with no comprehension of the principle. Tomorrow arrives, and with it a more impatient anxiety to do our duty, but with this very increase of anxiety arrives, also, a nameless, a positively fearful, because unfathomable, craving for delay. This craving gathers strength as the moments fly. The last hour for action is at hand. We tremble with the violence of the conflict within us,—of the definite with the indefinite—of the substance with the shadow. But, if the contest has proceeded thus far, it is the shadow which prevails—we struggle in vain. The clock strikes, and is the knell of our welfare. At the same time, it is the chanticleer-note to the ghost that has so long overawed us. It flies—it disappears—we are free. The old energy returns. We will labour now. Alas, it is too late!

We stand upon the brink of a precipice. We peer into

the abyss—we grow sick and dizzy. Our first impulse is to shrink from the danger. Unaccountably we remain. By slow degrees our sickness and dizziness and horror become merged in a cloud of unnamable feeling. By gradations, still more imperceptible, this cloud assumes shape, as did the vapour from the bottle out of which arose the genius in the Arabian Nights. But out of this our cloud upon the precipice's edge, there grows into palpability, a shape, far more terrible than any genius or any demon of a tale, and yet it is but a thought, although a fearful one, and one which chills the very marrow of our bones with the fierceness of the delight of its horror. It is merely the idea of what would be our sensations during the sweeping precipitancy of a fall from such a height. And this fall—this rushing annihilation—for the very reason that it involves that one most ghastly and loathsome of all the most ghastly and loathsome images of death and suffering which have ever presented themselves to our imagination—for this very cause do we now the most vividly desire it. And because our reason violently deters us from the brink, therefore do we the most impetuously approach it. There is no passion in nature so demoniacally impatient as that of him who, shuddering upon the edge of a precipice, thus meditates a plunge. To indulge, for a moment, in any attempt at thought, is to be inevitably lost; for reflection but urges us to forbear, and therefore it is, I say, that we cannot. If there be no friendly arm to check us, or if we fail in a sudden effort to prostrate ourselves backward from the abyss, we plunge, and are destroyed.

Examine these and similar actions as we will, we shall find them resulting solely from the spirit of the Perverse. We perpetrate them merely because we feel that we should not. Beyond or behind this there is no intelligible principle; and we might, indeed, deem this perverseness a direct instigation of the Arch-Fiend, were it not occasionally known to operate in furtherance of good.

I have said thus much, that in some measure I may answer your question—that I may explain to you why I am here—that I may assign to you something that shall have at least the faint aspect of a cause for my wearing these fetters, and for my tenanting this cell of the condemned. Had I not been thus prolix, you might either have misunderstood me altogether, or, with the rabble, have fancied me mad. As it is, you will easily perceive that I am one of the many uncounted victims of the Imp of the Perverse.

It is impossible that any deed could have been wrought with a more thorough deliberation. For weeks, for months, I pondered upon the means of the murder. I rejected a thousand schemes, because their accomplishment involved a *chance* of detection. At length, in reading some French memoirs, I found an account of a nearly fatal illness that occurred to Madame Pilau, through the agency of a candle accidentally poisoned. The idea struck my fancy at once. I knew my victim's habit of reading in bed. I knew, too, that his apartment was narrow and ill-ventilated. But I need not vex you with impertinent details. I need not describe the easy artifices by which I substituted, in his bed-room candle stand, a wax-light of my own making for the one which I there found. The next morning he was discovered dead in his bed, and the coroner's verdict was—'Death by the visitation of God.' Having inherited his estate, all went well with me for years. The idea of detection never once entered my brain. Of the remains of the fatal taper I had myself carefully disposed. I had left no shadow of a clue by which it would be possible to convict, or even suspect, me of the crime. It is inconceivable how rich a sentiment of satisfaction arose in my bosom as I reflected upon my absolute security. For a very long period of time I was accustomed to revel in this sentiment. It afforded me more real delight than all the mere worldly advantages accruing from my sin. But there arrived at length an epoch, from which the pleasurable feeling grew, by scarcely perceptible gradations, into a haunting and harassing thought. It harassed me because it haunted. I could scarcely get rid of it for an instant. It is quite a common thing to be thus annoyed with the ringing in our ears, or rather in our memories, of the burthen of some ordinary song, or some unimpressive snatches from an opera. Nor will we be the less tormented if the song in itself be good, or the opera air meritorious. In this manner, at last, I would perpetually catch myself pondering upon my security, and repeating, in a low undertone, the phrase, 'I am safe.'

One day, whilst sauntering along the streets, I arrested myself in the act of murmuring, half aloud, these customary syllables. In a fit of petulance I remodelled them thus: 'I am safe—I am safe—yes—if I be not fool enough to make open confession.'

No sooner had I spoken these words, than I felt an icy chill creep to my heart. I had had some experience in these fits of perversity (whose nature I have been at some trouble to explain), and I remembered well that in no instance I had successfully resisted their attacks. And now my own casual self-suggestion, that I might possibly be fool enough to confess the murder of which I had been guilty, confronted me, as if the very ghost of him whom I had murdered—and beckoned me on to death.

At first, I made an effort to shake off this nightmare of the soul. I walked vigorously—faster—still faster—at length I ran. I felt a maddening desire to shriek aloud. Every succeeding wave of thought overwhelmed me with new terror, for, alas! I well, too well, understood that to think, in my situation, was to be lost. I still quickened my pace. I bounded like a madman through the crowded thoroughfares. At length, the populace took the alarm and pursued me. I felt then the consummation of my fate. Could I have torn out my tongue, I would have done it, but a rough voice resounded in my ears—a rougher grasp seized me by the shoulder. I turned—I gasped for breath. For a moment I experienced all the pangs of suffocation; I became blind, and deaf, and giddy; and then some invisible fiend, I thought, struck me with his broad palm upon the back. The long-imprisoned secret burst forth from my soul.

They say that I spoke with a distinct enunciation, but with marked emphasis and passionate hurry, as if in dread of interruption before concluding the brief but pregnant sentences that consigned me to the hangman and to hell.

Having related all that was necessary for the fullest judicial conviction, I fell prostrate in a swoon.

But why shall I say more? Today I wear these chains, and am *here*! To-morrow I shall be fetterless!—*but where*?

34

THE MASQUE OF THE RED DEATH

Edgar Allan Poe

The 'Red Death' had long devastated the country. No pestilence had ever been so fatal, or so hideous. Blood was its Avatar and its seal—the madness and the horror of blood. There were sharp pains, and sudden dizziness, and then profuse bleeding at the pores, with dissolution. The scarlet stains upon the body and especially upon the face of the victim, were the pest ban which shut him out from the aid and from the sympathy of his fellow-men. And the whole seizure, progress, and termination of the disease, were incidents of half an hour.

But Prince Prospero was happy and dauntless and sagacious. When his dominions were half depopulated, he summoned to his presence a thousand hale and light-hearted friends from among the knights and dames of his court, and with these retired to the deep seclusion of one of his crenellated abbeys. This was an extensive and magnificent structure, the creation of the prince's own eccentric yet august taste. A strong and lofty wall girdled it in. This wall had gates of iron. The courtiers, having entered, brought furnaces and massy hammers and welded the bolts.

They resolved to leave means neither of ingress nor egress to the sudden impulses of despair or of frenzy from within.

The abbey was amply provisioned. With such precautions the courtiers might bid defiance to contagion. The external world could take care of itself. In the meantime it was folly to grieve or to think. The prince had provided all the appliances of pleasure. There were buffoons, there were improvisatori, there were ballet-dancers, there were musicians, there was Beauty, there was wine. All these and security were within. Without was the 'Red Death.'

It was toward the close of the fifth or sixth month of his seclusion that the Prince Prospero entertained his thousand friends at a masked ball of the most unusual magnificence.

It was a voluptuous scene, that masquerade. But first let me tell of the rooms in which it was held. There were seven—an imperial suite, In many palaces, however, such suites form a long and straight vista, while the folding doors slide back nearly to the walls on either hand, so that the view of the whole extant is scarcely impeded. Here the case was very different; as might have been expected from the duke's love of the *bizarre*. The apartments were so irregularly disposed that the vision embraced but little more than one at a time. There was a sharp turn at the right and left, in the middle of each wall, a tall and narrow Gothic window looked out upon a closed corridor of which pursued the windings of the suite. These windows were of stained glass whose colour varied in accordance with the prevailing hue of the decorations of the chamber into which it opened. That at the eastern extremity was hung, for example, in blue—and vividly blue were its windows. The second chamber was purple in its ornaments and tapestries, and here the panes were purple. The third was green throughout, and so were the casements. The fourth was furnished and lighted with orange—the fifth with white—the sixth with violet. The seventh apartment was closely shrouded in black velvet tapestries that hung all over the ceiling and down the walls, falling in heavy folds upon a carpet of the same material and hue. But in this chamber only, the colour of the windows failed to correspond with the decorations. The panes were scarlet—a deep blood colour. Now in no one of any of the seven apartments was there any lamp or candelabrum, amid the profusion of golden ornaments that lay scattered to and fro and depended from the roof. There was no light of any kind emanating from lamp or candle within the suite of chambers. But in the corridors that followed the suite, there stood, opposite each window, a heavy tripod, bearing a brazier of fire, that projected its rays through the tinted glass and so glaringly lit the room. And thus were produced a multitude of gaudy and fantastic appearances. But in the western or back chamber the effect of the firelight that streamed upon the dark hangings through the blood-tinted panes was ghastly in the extreme, and produced so wild a look upon the countenances of those who entered, that there were few of the company bold enough to set foot within its precincts at all.

It was in this apartment, also, that there stood against the western wall, a gigantic clock of ebony. Its pendulum swung to and fro with a dull, heavy, monotonous clang; and when the minute-hand made the circuit of the face, and the hour was to be stricken, there came from the brazen lungs of the clock a sound which was clear and loud and deep and exceedingly musical, but of so peculiar a note and emphasis that, at each lapse of an hour, the musicians of the orchestra were constrained to pause, momentarily, in their performance, to hearken to the sound; and thus the waltzers perforce ceased their evolutions; and there was a brief disconcert of the whole gay company; and while the chimes of the clock yet rang, it was observed that the giddiest grew pale, and the more aged and sedate passed their hands over their brows as if in confused revery or meditation. But when the echoes had fully ceased, a light laughter at once pervaded the assembly; the musicians looked at each other and smiled as if at their own nervousness and folly, and made whispering vows, each to the other, that the next chiming of the clock should produce in them no similar emotion; and then, after the lapse of sixty minutes (which embrace three thousand and six hundred seconds of Time that flies), there came yet another chiming of the clock, and then were the same disconcert and tremulousness and meditation as before.

But, in spite of these things, it was a gay and magnificent revel. The tastes of the duke were peculiar. He had a fine eye for colour and effects. He disregarded the *decora* of mere fashion. His plans were bold and fiery, and his conceptions glowed with barbaric lustre. There are some who would have thought him mad. His followers felt that he was not. It was necessary to hear and see and touch him to be *sure* he was not.

He had directed, in great part, the movable embellishments of the seven chambers, upon occasion of this great *fête*; and it was his own guiding taste which had given character to the masqueraders. Be sure they were grotesque. There were much glare and glitter and piquancy and phantasm—much of what has been seen in 'Hernani.' There were arabesque figures with unsuited limbs and appointments. There were delirious fancies such as the madman fashions. There were much of the beautiful, much of the wanton, much of the *bizarre*, something of the terrible, and not a little of that which might have excited disgust. To and fro in the seven chambers stalked, in fact, a multitude of dreams. And these—the dreams—writhed in and about, taking hue from the rooms, and causing the wild music of the orchestra to seem as the echo of their steps. And, anon, there strikes the ebony clock which stands in the hall of the velvet. And then, for a moment, all is still, and all is silent save the voice of the clock. The dreams are stiff-frozen as they stand. But the echoes of the chime die away—they have endured but an instant—and a light, half-subdued laughter floats after them as they depart. And now again the music swells, and the dreams live, and writhe to and fro more merrily than ever, taking hue from the many tinted windows through which stream the rays of the tripods. But to the chamber which lies most westwardly of the seven, there are now none of the maskers who venture, for the night is waning away; and there flows a ruddier light through the blood-coloured panes; and the blackness of the sable drapery appals; and to him whose foot falls on the sable carpet, there comes from the near clock of ebony a muffled peal more solemnly emphatic than any which reaches *their* ears who indulge in the more remote gaieties of the other apartments.

But these other apartments were densely crowded, and in them beat feverishly the heart of life. And the revel went whirlingly on, until at length there commenced the sounding of midnight upon the clock. And then the music ceased, as I have told; and the evolutions of the waltzers were quieted; and there was an uneasy cessation of all things as before. But now there were twelve strokes to be sounded by the bell of the clock; and thus it happened, perhaps that more of thought crept, with more of time into the meditations of the thoughtful among those who revelled. And thus too, it happened, that before the last echoes of the last chime had utterly sunk into silence, there were many individuals in the crowd who had found leisure to become aware of the presence of a masked figure which had arrested the attention of no single individual before. And the rumour of this new presence having spread itself whisperingly around, there arose at length from the whole company a buzz, or murmur, of horror, and of disgust.

In an assembly of phantasms such as I have painted, it may well be supposed that no ordinary appearance could have excited such sensation. In truth the masquerade license of the night was nearly unlimited; but the figure in question had out-Heroded Herod, and gone beyond the bounds of even the prince's indefinite decorum. There are chords in the hearts of the most reckless which cannot be touched without emotion. Even with the utterly lost, to whom life and death are equally jests, there are matters of which no jest can be made. The whole company, indeed, seemed now deeply to feel that in the costume and bearing of the stranger neither wit nor propriety existed. The figure was tall and gaunt, and shrouded from head to foot in the habiliments of the grave. The mask which concealed the visage was made so nearly to resemble the countenance of a stiffened corpse that the closest scrutiny must have difficulty in detecting the cheat. And yet all this might have been endured, if not approved, by the mad revellers around. But the mummer had gone so far as to assume the type of the Red Death. His vesture was dabbled in *blood*—and his broad brow, with all the features of his face, was besprinkled with the scarlet horror.

When the eyes of Prince Prospero fell on this spectral image (which, with a slow and solemn movement, as if more fully to sustain its role, stalked to and fro among the waltzers) he was seen to be convulsed, in the first moment with a strong shudder either of terror or distaste; but in the next, his brow reddened with rage.

'Who dares'—he demanded hoarsely of the courtiers who stood near him—'who dares insult us with this blasphemous mockery? Seize him and unmask him—that we may know whom we have to hang, at sunrise, from the battlements!'

It was in the eastern or blue chamber in which stood Prince Prospero as he uttered these words. They rang throughout the seven rooms loudly and clearly, for the prince was a bold and robust man, and the music had become hushed at the waving of his hand.

It was in the blue room where stood the prince, with a group of pale courtiers by his side. At first, as he spoke, there was a slight rushing movement of this group in the direction of the intruder, who, at the moment was also near at hand, and now, with deliberate and stately step, made closer approach to the speaker. But from a certain nameless awe with which the mad assumptions of the mummer had inspired the whole party, there were found none who put forth a hand to seize him; so that, unimpeded, he passed within a yard of the prince's person; and while the vast assembly, as with one impulse, shrank from the centers of the rooms to the walls, he made his way uninterruptedly, but with the same solemn and measured step which had distinguished him from the first, through the blue chamber to the purple—to the purple to the green—through the green to the orange—through this again to the white—and even thence to the violet, ere a decided movement had been made to arrest him. It was then, however, that the Prince Prospero, maddened with rage and the shame of his own momentary cowardice, rushed hurriedly through the six chambers, while none followed him on account of a deadly terror that had seized upon all. He bore aloft a drawn dagger, and had approached, in rapid impetuosity, to within three or four feet of the retreating figure, when the latter, having attained the extremity of the velvet apartment, turned suddenly and confronted his pursuer. There was a sharp cry—and the dagger dropped gleaming upon the sable carpet, upon which most instantly afterward, fell prostrate in death the Prince Prospero. Then summoning the wild courage of despair, a throng of the revellers at once threw themselves into the black apartment, and seizing the mummer, whose tall figure stood erect and motionless within the shadow of the ebony clock, gasped in unutterable horror at finding the grave cerements and corpse-like mask, which they handled with so violent a rudeness, untenanted by any tangible form.

And now was acknowledged the presence of the Red Death. He had come like a thief in the night. And one by one dropped the revellers in the blood-bedewed halls of their revel, and died each in the despairing posture of his fall. And the life of the ebony clock went out with that of the last of the gay. And the flames of the tripods expired. And Darkness and Decay and the Red Death held illimitable dominion over all.

35

JIM BAKER'S BLUE-JAY YARN

Mark Twain

Animals talk to each other, of course. There can be no question about that; but I suppose there are very few people who can understand them. I never knew but one man who could. I knew he could, however, because he told me so himself. He was a middle-aged, simple-hearted miner who had lived in a lonely corner of California, among the woods and mountains, a good many years, and had studied the ways of his only neighbours, the beasts and the birds, until he believed he could accurately translate any remark which they made. This was Jim Baker. According to Jim Baker, some animals have only a limited education, and use only very simple words, and scarcely ever a comparison or a flowery figure; whereas, certain other animals have a large vocabulary, a fine command of language and a ready and fluent delivery; consequently these latter talk a great deal; they like it; they are conscious of their talent, and they enjoy 'showing off.' Baker said, that after long and careful observation, he had come to the conclusion that the blue-jays were the best talkers he had found among birds and beasts. Said he:—

'There's more *to* a blue-jay than any other creature. He has got more moods, and more different kinds of feelings than other creature; and mind you, whatever a blue-jay feels, he can put into language. And no mere commonplace language, either, but rattling, out-and-out book-talk—and bristling with metaphor, too—just bristling! And as for command of language—why *you* never see a blue-jay get stuck for a word. No man ever did. They just boil out of him! And another thing: I've noticed a good deal, and there's no bird, or cow, or anything that uses as good grammar as a blue-jay. You may say a cat uses good grammar. Well, a cat does—but you let a cat get excited, once; you let a cat get to pulling fur with another cat on a shed, nights, and you'll hear grammar that will give you the lockjaw. Ignorant people think it's the *noise* which fighting cats make that is so aggravating, but it ain't so; it's the sickening grammar they use. Now I've never heard a jay use bad grammar but very seldom; and when they do, they are as ashamed as a human; they shut right down and leave.

'You may call a jay a bird. Well, so he is, in a measure—because he's got feathers on him, and don't belong to no church, perhaps; but otherwise he is just as much a human as you be. And I'll tell you for why. A jay's gifts, and instincts, and feelings, and interests, cover the whole ground. A jay hasn't got any more principle than a Congressman. A jay will lie, a jay will steal, a jay will deceive, a jay will betray; and four times out of five, a jay will go back on his solemnest promise. The sacredness of an obligation is a thing which you can't cram into no blue-jay's head. Now on top of all this, there's another thing: a jay can out-swear any gentleman in the mines. You think a cat can swear. Well, a cat can; but you give a blue-jay a subject that calls for his reserve-powers, and where is your cat? Don't talk to *me*—I know too much about this thing. And there's yet another thing: in the one little particular of scolding—just good, clean, out-and-out scolding—a blue-jay can lay over anything, human or divine. Yes, sir, a jay is everything that a man is. A jay can cry, a jay can laugh, a jay can feel shame, a jay can reason and plan and discuss, a jay likes gossip and scandal, a jay has got a sense of humor, a jay knows when he is an ass just as well as you do—maybe better. If a jay ain't human, he better take in his sign, that's all. Now I'm going to tell you a perfectly true fact about some blue-jays.

'When I first begun to understand jay language correctly, there was a little incident happened here. Seven years ago, the last man in this region but me, moved away. There stands his house,—been empty ever since; a log house, with a plank roof—just one big room, and no more; no ceiling—nothing between the rafters and the floor. Well, one Sunday morning I was sitting out here in front of my cabin, with my cat, taking the sun, and looking at the blue hills, and listening to the leaves rustling so lonely in the trees, and thinking of the home away yonder in the States, that I hadn't heard from in thirteen years, when a blue jay lit on that house, with an acorn in his mouth, and says, "Hello, I reckon I've struck something." When he spoke, the acorn dropped out of his mouth and rolled down the roof, of course, but he didn't care; his mind was all on the thing he had struck. It was a knot-hole in the roof. He cocked his head to one side, shut one eye and put the other one to the hole, like a 'possum looking down a jug; then he glanced up with his bright eyes, gave a wink or two with his wings—which signifies gratification, you understand,—and says, "It looks like a hole, it's located like a hole,—blamed if I don't believe it *is* a hole!"

'Then he cocked his head down and took another look; he glances up perfectly joyful, this time; winks his wings and his tail both, and says, "O, no, this ain't no fat thing, I reckon! If I ain't in luck!—why it's a perfectly elegant hole!" So he flew down and got that acorn, and fetched it up and dropped it in, and was just tilting his head back, with the heavenliest smile on his face, when all of a sudden he was paralysed into a listening attitude and that smile faded gradually out of his countenance like breath off'n a razor, and the queerest look of surprise took its place. Then he says, "Why I didn't hear it fall!" He cocked his eye at the hole again, and took a long look; raised up and shook his head; stepped around to the other side of the hole and took another look from that side; shook his head again. He studied a while, then he just went into the details—walked round and round the hole and spied into it from every point of the compass. No use. Now he took a thinking attitude on the comb of the roof and scratched the back of his head with his right foot a minute, and finally says, "Well, it's too many for me, that's certain; must be a mighty long hole; however, I ain't got no time to fool around here, I got to 'tend to business; I reckon it's all right—chance it, anyway."

'So he flew off and fetched another acorn and dropped it in, and tried to flirt his eye to the hole quick enough to see what become of it, but he was too late. He held his eye there as much as a minute; then he raised up and sighed, and says, "Confound it, I don't seem to understand this thing, no way; however, I'll tackle her again." He fetched another acorn, and done his level best to see what become of it, but he couldn't. He says, "Well, I never struck no such a hole as this, before; I'm of the opinion it's a totally new kind of a hole." Then he begun to get mad. He held in for a spell, walking up and down the comb of the roof and shaking his head and muttering to himself; but his feelings got the upper hand of him, presently, and he broke loose and cussed himself black in the face. I never see a bird take on so about a little thing. When he got through he walks to the hole and looks in again for half a minute; then he says, "Well, you're a long hole, and a deep hole, and a mighty singular hole altogether—but I've started in to fill you, and I'm d—d if I don't fill you, if it takes a hundred years!"

'And with that, away he went. You never see a bird work so since you was born. He laid into his work like a nigger, and the way he hove acorns into that hole for about two hours and a half was one of the most exciting and astonishing spectacles I ever struck. He never stopped to take a look any more—he just hove 'em in and went for more. Well at last he could hardly flop his wings, he was so tuckered out. He comes a-drooping down, once more, sweating like an ice-pitcher, drops his acorn in and says, "Now I guess I've got the bulge on you by this time!" So he bent down for a look. If you'll believe me, when his head come up again he was just pale with rage. He says, "I've shovelled acorns enough in there to keep the family thirty years, and if I can see a sign of one of 'em I wish I may land in a museum with a belly full of sawdust in two minutes!"

'He just had strength enough to crawl up on to the comb and lean his back agin the chimbly, and then he collected his impressions and begun to free his mind. I see in a second that what I had mistook for profanity in the mines was only just the rudiments, as you may say.

'Another jay was going by, and heard him doing his devotions, and stops to inquire what was up. The sufferer told him the whole circumstance, and says, "Now yonder's the hole, and if you don't believe me, go and look for yourself." So this fellow went and looked, and comes back and says, "How many did you say you put in there?" "Not any less than two tons," says the sufferer. The other jay went and looked again. He couldn't seem to make it out, so he raised a yell, and three more jays come. They all examined the hole, they all made the sufferer tell it over again, then they all discussed it, and got off as many leather-headed opinions about it as an average crowd of humans could have done.

'They called in more jays; then more and more, till pretty soon this whole region 'peared to have a blue flush about it. There must have been five thousand of them; and such another jawing and disputing and ripping and cussing, you never heard. Every jay in the whole lot put his eye to the hole and delivered a more chuckle-headed opinion about the mystery than the jay that went there before him. They examined the house all over, too. The door was standing half open, and at last one old jay happened to go and light on it and look in. Of course that knocked the mystery galley-west in a second. There lay the acorns, scattered all over the floor. He flopped his wings and raised a whoop. "Come here!" he says, "Come here, everybody; hang'd if this fool hasn't been trying to fill up a house with acorns!" They all came a-swooping down like a blue cloud, and as each fellow lit on the door and took a glance, the whole absurdity of the contract that that first jay had tackled hit him home and he fell over backwards suffocating with laughter, and the next jay took his place and done the same.

'Well, sir, they roosted around here on the house-top and the trees for an hour, and guffawed over that thing like human beings. It ain't any use to tell me a blue-jay hasn't got a sense of humour, because I know better. And memory, too. They brought jays here from all over the United States to look down that hole, every summer for three years. Other birds too. And they could all see the point, except an owl that come from Nova Scotia to visit the Yo Semite, and he took this thing in on his way back. He said he couldn't see anything funny in it. But then he was a good deal disappointed about Yo Semite, too.'

36

PUNCH, BROTHERS, PUNCH!

Mark Twain

Will the reader please to cast his eye over the following lines, and see if he can discover anything harmful in them?

Conductor, when you receive a fare,
Punch in the presence of the passenjare!
A blue trip slip for an eight-cent fare,
A buff trip slip for a six-cent fare,

A pink trip slip for a three-cent fare,
Punch in the presence of the passenjare!

CHORUS

Punch, brothers! punch with care!
Punch in the presence of the passenjare!

I came across these jingling rhymes in a newspaper, a little while ago, and read them a couple of times. They took instant and entire possession of me. All through breakfast they went waltzing through my brain; and when, at last, I rolled up my napkin, I could not tell whether I had eaten anything or not. I had carefully laid out my day's work the day before—thrilling tragedy in the novel which I am writing. I went to my den to begin my deed of blood. I took up my pen, but all I could get it to say was, 'Punch in the presence of the passenjare.' I fought hard for an hour, but it was useless. My head kept humming, 'A blue trip slip for an eight-cent fare, a buff trip slip for a six-cent fare,' and so on and so on, without peace or respite. The day's work was ruined—I could see that plainly enough. I gave up and drifted down-town, and presently discovered that my feet were keeping time to that relentless jingle. When I could stand it no longer I altered my step. But it did no good; those rhymes accommodated themselves to the new step and went on harassing me just as before. I returned home, and suffered all the afternoon; suffered all through an unconscious and unrefreshing dinner; suffered, and cried, and jingled all through the evening; went to bed and rolled, tossed, and jingled right along, the same as ever; got up at midnight frantic, and tried to read; but there was nothing visible upon the whirling page except 'Punch! punch in the presence of the passenjare.' By sunrise I was out of my mind, and everybody marvelled and was distressed at the idiotic burden of my ravings—'Punch! oh, punch! punch in the presence of the passenjare!'

Two days later, on Saturday morning, I arose, a tottering wreck, and went forth to fulfil an engagement with a valued friend, the Rev. Mr———, to walk to the Talcott Tower, ten miles distant. He stared at me, but asked no questions. We started. Mr———talked, talked, talked as is his wont. I said nothing; I heard nothing. At the end of a mile, Mr———said 'Mark, are you sick? I never saw a man look so haggard and worn and absent-minded. Say something, do!'

Drearily, without enthusiasm, I said: 'Punch brothers, punch with care! Punch in the presence of the passenjare!'

My friend eyed me blankly, looked perplexed, they said:

'I do not think I get your drift, Mark. Then does not seem to be any relevancy in what you have said, certainly nothing sad; and yet—maybe it was the way you said the words—I never heard anything that sounded so pathetic. What is—'

But I heard no more. I was already far away with my pitiless, heartbreaking 'blue trip slip for an eight-cent fare, buff trip slip for a six-cent fare, pink trip slip for a three-cent fare; punch in the presence of the passenjare.' I do not know what occurred during the other nine miles. However, all of a sudden Mr———laid his hand on my shoulder and shouted:

'Oh, wake up! wake up! wake up! Don't sleep all day! Here we are at the Tower, man! I have talked myself deaf and dumb and blind, and never got a response. Just look at this magnificent autumn landscape! Look at it! look at it! Feast your eye on it! You have travelled; you have seen boaster landscapes elsewhere. Come, now, deliver an honest opinion. What do you say to this?'

I sighed wearily; and murmured:—

'A buff trip slip for a six-cent fare, a pink trip slip for a three-cent fare, punch in the presence of the passenjare.'

Rev. Mr———stood there, very grave, full of concern, apparently, and looked long at me; then he said:

'Mark, there is something about this that I cannot understand. Those are about the same words you said before; there does not seem to be anything in them, and yet they nearly break my heart when you say them. Punch in the—how is it they go?'

I began at the beginning and repeated all the lines.

My friend's face lighted with interest. He said:—

'Why, what a captivating jingle it is! It is almost music. It flows along so nicely. I have nearly caught the rhymes myself. Say them over just once more, and then I'll have them, sure.'

I said them over. Then Mr———said them. He made one little mistake, which I corrected. The next time and the next he got them right. Now a great burden seemed to tumble from my shoulders. That torturing jingle departed out of my brain, and a grateful sense of rest and peace descended upon me. I was light-hearted enough to sing; and I did sing for half an hour, straight along, as we went jogging homeward. Then my freed tongue found blessed speech again, and the pent talk of many a weary hour began to gush and flow. It flowed on and on, joyously, jubilantly, until the fountain was empty and dry. As I wrung my friend's hand at parting, I said:—

'Haven't we had a royal good time! But now I remember, you haven't said a word for two hours. Come, come, out with something!'

The Rev. Mr———turned a lacklustre eye upon me, drew a deep sigh, and said, without animation, without apparent consciousness:

'Punch, brothers, punch with care! Punch in the presence of the passenjare!'

A pang shot through me as I said to myself, 'Poor fellow, poor fellow! he has got it, now.'

I did not see Mr———for two or three days after that. Then, on Tuesday evening, he staggered into my presence and sank dejectedly into a seat. He was pale, worn; he was a wreck. He lifted his faded eyes to my face and said:—

'Ah, Mark, it was a ruinous investment that I made in those heartless rhymes. They have ridden me like a nightmare, day and night, hour after hour, to this very moment. Since I saw you I have suffered the torments of the lost. Saturday evening I had a sudden call, by telegraph, and took the night train for Boston. The occasion was the death of a valued old friend who had requested that I should preach his funeral sermon. I took my seat in the cars and set myself to framing the discourse. But I never got beyond the opening paragraph; for then the train started and the car-wheels began their "clack, clack-clack-clack-clack! clack-clack!—clack-clack-clack!" and right away those odious rhymes fitted themselves to that accompaniment. For an hour I sat there and set a syllable of those rhymes to every separate and distinct clack the car-wheels made. Why, I was as fagged out, then, as if I had been chopping wood all day. My skull was splitting with headache. It seemed to me that I must go mad if I sat there any longer; so I undressed and went to bed. I stretched myself out in my berth, and—well, you know what the result was. The thing went right along, just the same. "Clack-clack clack, a blue trip slip, clack-clack-clack, for an eight-cent fare; clack-clack-clack, a buff trip slip, clack clack-clack, for a six-cent fare, and so on, and so on, and so on punch in the presence of the passenjare!" Sleep? Not a single wink! I was almost a lunatic when I got to Boston. Don't ask me about the funeral. I did the best I could, but every solemn individual sentence was meshed and tangled and woven in and out with "Punch, brothers, punch with care, punch in the presence of the passenjare." And the most distressing thing was that my delivery dropped into the undulating rhythm of those pulsing rhymes, and I could actually catch absentminded people nodding time to the swing of it with their stupid heads. And, Mark, you may believe it or not, but before I got through the entire assemblage were placidly bobbing their heads in solemn unison, mourners, undertaker, and all. The moment I had finished, I fled to the anteroom in a state bordering on frenzy. Of course it would be my luck to find a sorrowing and aged maiden aunt of the deceased there, who had arrived from Springfield too late to get into the church. She began to sob, and said:—

"'Oh, oh, he is gone, he is gone, and I didn't see him before he died!'"

"'Yes!' I said, 'he is gone, he is gone, he is gone—oh, will this suffering never cease!'"

"'You loved him, then! Oh, you too loved him!'"

"'Loved him! Loved who?'"

"'Why, my poor George! my poor nephew!'"

"'Oh—him! Yes—oh, yes, yes. Certainly—certainly. Punch—punch—oh, this misery will kill me!'"

"'Bless you! bless you, sir, for these sweet words! I, too, suffer in this dear loss. Were you present during his last moments?'"

"'Yes. I—whose last moments?'"

"'His. The dear departed's.'"

"'Yes! Oh, yes—yes—yes! I suppose so, I think so, I don't know! Oh, certainly—I was there I was there!'"

"'Oh, what a privilege! what a precious privilege! And his last words—oh, tell me, tell me his last words! What did he say?'"

"'He said—he said—oh, my head, my head, my head! He said—he said—he never said anything but Punch, punch, punch in the presence of the passenjare! Oh, leave me, madam! In the name of all that is generous, leave me to my madness, my misery, my despair!—a buff trip slip for a six-cent fare, a pink trip slip for a three-cent fare—endu—rance can no fur—ther go!—PUNCH in the presence of the passenjare!'"

My friend's hopeless eyes rested upon mine a pregnant minute, and then he said impressively:—

'Mark, you do not say anything. You do not offer me any hope. But, ah me, it is just as well—it is just as well. You could not do me any good. The time has long gone by when words could comfort me. Something tells me that my tongue is doomed to wag forever to the jigger of that remorseless jingle. There—there it is coming on me again: a blue trip slip for an eight-cent fare, a buff trip slip for a—'

Thus murmuring faint and fainter, my friend sank into a peaceful trance and forgot his sufferings in a blessed respite.

How did I finally save him from an asylum? I took him to a neighbouring university and made him discharge the burden of his persecuting rhymes into the eager ears of the poor, unthinking students. How is it with them, now? The result is too sad to tell. Why did I write this article? It was for a worthy, even a noble, purpose. It was to warn you, reader, if you should came across those merciless rhymes, to avoid them—avoid them as you would a pestilence.

37

THE STORY OF THE BAD LITTLE BOY

Mark Twain

Once there was a bad little boy whose name was Jim—though, if you will notice, you will find that bad little boys are nearly always called James in your Sunday-school books. It was strange, but still it was true, that this one was called Jim.

He didn't have any sick mother, either—a sick mother who was pious and had the consumption, and would be glad to lie down in the grave and be at rest but for the strong love she bore her boy, and the anxiety she felt that the world might be harsh and cold toward him when she was gone. Most bad boys in the Sunday books are named James, and have sick mothers, who teach them to say, 'Now, I lay me down,' etc., and sing them to sleep with sweet, plaintive voices, and then kiss them good night, and kneel down by the bedside and weep. But it was different with this fellow. He was named Jim, and there wasn't anything the matter with his mother—no consumption, nor anything of that kind. She was rather stout than otherwise, and she was not pious; moreover, she was not anxious on Jim's account. She said if he were to break his neck it wouldn't be much loss. She always spanked Jim to sleep, and she never kissed him good night; on the contrary, she boxed his ears when she was ready to leave him.

Once this little bad boy stole the key of the pantry, and slipped in there and helped himself to some jam, and filled up the vessel with tar, so that his mother would never know the difference; but all at once a terrible feeling didn't come over him, and something didn't seem to whisper to him, 'Is it right to disobey my mother? Isn't it sinful to do this? Where do bad little boys go who gobble up their good kind mother's jam?' and then he didn't kneel down all alone and promise never to be wicked any more, and rise up with a light, happy heart, and go and tell his mother all about it, and beg her forgiveness, and be blessed by her with tears of pride and thankfulness in her eyes. No; that is the way with all other bad boys in the books; but it happened otherwise with this Jim, strangely enough. He ate that jam, and said it was bully, in his sinful, vulgar way; and he put in the tar, and said that was bully also, and laughed, and observed 'that the old woman would get up and snort' when she found it out; and when she did find it out, he denied knowing anything about it, and she whipped him severely, and he did the crying himself. Everything about this boy was curious—everything turned out differently with him from the way it does to the bad Jameses in the books.

Once he climbed up in Farmer Acorn's apple tree to steal apples, and the limb didn't break, and he didn't fall and break his arm, and get torn by the farmer's great dog, and then languish on a sickbed for weeks, and repent and become good. Oh, no; he stole as many apples as he wanted and came down all right; and he was all ready for the dog, too, and knocked him endways with a brick when he came to tear him. It was very strange—nothing like it ever happened in those mild little books with marbled backs, and with pictures in them of men with swallow-tailed coats and bell-crowned hats, and pantaloons that are short in the legs, and women with the waists of their dresses under their arms, and no hoops on. Nothing like it in any of the Sunday-school books.

Once he stole the teacher's penknife, and, when he was afraid it would be found out and he would get whipped, he slipped it into George Wilson's cap poor Widow Wilson's son, the moral boy, the good little boy of the village, who always obeyed his mother, and never told an untruth, and was fond of his lessons, and infatuated with Sunday-school. And when the knife dropped from the cap, and poor George hung his head and blushed, as if in conscious guilt, and the grieved teacher charged the theft upon him, and was just in the very act of bringing the switch down upon his trembling shoulders, a white-haired, improbable justice of the peace did not suddenly appear in their midst, and strike an attitude and say, 'Spare this noble boy—there stands the cowering culprit! I was passing the school door at recess, and, unseen myself, I saw the theft committed!' And then Jim didn't get whaled, and the venerable justice didn't read the tearful school a homily, and take George by the hand and say such boy deserved to be exalted, and then tell him come and make his home with him, and sweep out the office, and make fires, and run errands, and chop wood, and study law, and help his wife do household labours, and have all the balance of the time to play and get forty cents a month, and be happy. No it would have happened that way in the books, but didn't happen that way to Jim. No meddling old clam of a justice dropped in to make trouble, and so the model boy George got thrashed, and Jim was glad of it because, you know, Jim hated moral boys. Jim said he was 'down on them milksops.' Such was the coarse language of this bad, neglected boy.

But the strangest thing that ever happened to Jim was the

time he went boating on Sunday, and didn't get drowned, and that other time that he got caught out in the storm when he was fishing on Sunday and didn't get struck by lightning. Why, you might look, and look, all through the Sunday-school books from now till next Christmas, and you would never come across anything like this. Oh, no; you would find that all the bad boys who go boating on Sunday invariably get drowned; and all the bad boys who get caught out in storms when they are fishing on Sunday infallibly get struck by lightning. Boats with bad boys in them always upset on Sunday, and it always storms when bad boys go fishing on the Sabbath. How this Jim ever escaped is a mystery to me.

This Jim bore a charmed life—that must have been the way of it. Nothing could hurt him. He even gave the elephant in the menagerie a plug of tobacco, and the elephant didn't knock the top of his head off with his trunk. He browsed around the cupboard after essence-of peppermint, and didn't make a mistake and drink aqua fortis. He stole his father's gun and went hunting on the Sabbath, and didn't shoot three or four of his fingers off. He struck his little sister on the temple with his fist when he was angry, and she didn't linger in pain through long summer days, and die with sweet words of forgiveness upon her lips that redoubled the anguish of his breaking heart. No; she got over it. He ran off and went to sea at last, and didn't come back and find himself sad and alone in the world, his loved ones sleeping in the quiet churchyard, and the vine-embowered home of his boyhood tumbled down and gone to decay. Ah, no; he came home as drunk as a piper, and got into the station-house the first thing.

And he grew up and married, and raised a large family, and brained them all with an axe one night, and got wealthy by all manner of cheating and rascality; and now he is the infernalest wickedest scoundrel in his native village, and is universally respected, and belongs to the legislature.

So you see there never was a bad James in the Sunday-school books that had such a streak of luck as this sinful Jim with the charmed life.

38

THE STORY OF THE GOOD LITTLE BOY

Mark Twain

Once there was a good little boy by the name of Jacob Blivens. He always obeyed his parents, no matter how absurd and unreasonable their demands were; and he always learned his book, and never was late at Sabbath-school. He would not play hookey, even when his sober judgment told him it was the most profitable thing he could do. None of the other boys could ever make that boy out, he acted so strangely. He wouldn't lie, no matter how convenient it was. He just said it was wrong to lie, and that was sufficient for him. And he was so honest that he was simply ridiculous. The curious ways that that Jacob had, surpassed everything. He wouldn't play marbles on Sunday, he wouldn't rob birds' nests, he wouldn't give hot pennies to organ-grinders' monkeys; he didn't seem to take any interest in any kind of rational amusement. So the other boys used to try to reason it out and come to an understanding of him, but they couldn't arrive at any satisfactory conclusion. As I said before, they could only figure out a sort of vague idea that he was 'afflicted,' and so they took him under their protection, and never allowed any harm to come to him.

This good little boy read all the Sunday-school books; they were his greatest delight. This was the whole secret of it. He believed in the gold little boys they put in the Sunday-school book; he had every confidence in them. He longed to come across one of them alive once; but he never did. They all died before his time, maybe. Whenever he read about a particularly good one he turned over quickly to the end to see what became of him, because he wanted to travel thousands of miles and gaze on him; but it wasn't any use; that good little boy always died in the last chapter, and there was a picture of the funeral, with all his relations and the Sunday-school children standing around the grave in pantaloons that were too short, and bonnets that were too large, and everybody crying into handkerchiefs that had as much as a yard and a half of stuff in them. He was always headed off in this way. He never could see one of those good little boys on account of his always dying in the last chapter.

Jacob had a noble ambition to be put in a Sunday school book. He wanted to be put in, with pictures representing him gloriously declining to lie to his mother, and her weeping for joy about it; and pictures representing him standing on the doorstep giving a penny to a poor beggar-woman with six children, and telling her to spend it freely, but not to be extravagant, because extravagance is a sin; and pictures of him magnanimously refusing to tell on the bad boy who always lay in wait for him around the corner as he came from school, and welted him over the head with a lath, and then chased him home, saying, 'Hi! hi!' as he proceeded. That was the ambition of young Jacob Blivens. He wished to be put in a Sunday-school book. It made him feel a little uncomfortable sometimes when he reflected that the good little boys always died. He loved to live, you know, and this was the most unpleasant feature about being a Sunday-school-book boy. He knew it was not healthy to be good. He knew it was more fatal than consumption to be so supernaturally good as the boys in the books were he knew that none of them had ever been able to stand it long, and it pained him to think that if they put him in a book he wouldn't ever see it, or even if they did get the book out before he died it wouldn't be popular without any picture of his funeral in the back part of it. It couldn't be much of a Sunday-school book that couldn't tell about the advice he gave to the community when he was dying. So at last, of course, he had to make up his mind to do the best he could under the circumstances—to live right, and hang on as long as he could and have his dying speech all ready when his time came.

But somehow nothing ever went right with the good little boy; nothing ever turned out with him the way it turned out with the good little boys in the books. They always had a good time, and the bad boys had the broken legs; but in his case there was a screw loose somewhere, and it all happened just the other way. When he found Jim Blake stealing apples, and went under the tree to read to him about the bad little boy who fell out of a neighbour's apple tree and broke his arm, Jim fell out of the tree, too, but he fell on him and broke his arm, and Jim wasn't hurt at all. Jacob couldn't understand that. There wasn't anything in the books like it.

And once, when some bad boys pushed a blind man over in the mud, and Jacob ran to help him up and receive his blessing, the blind man did not give him any blessing at all, but whacked him over the head with his stick and said he would like to catch him shoving him again, and then pretending to help him up. This was not in accordance with any of the books. Jacob looked them all over to see.

One thing that Jacob wanted to do was to find a lame dog that hadn't any place to stay, and was hungry and persecuted, and bring him home and pet him and have that dog's imperishable gratitude. And at last he found one and was happy; and he brought him home and fed him, but when he was going to pet him the dog flew at him and tore all the clothes off him except those that were in front, and made a spectacle of him that was astonishing. He examined authorities, but he could not understand the matter. It was of the same breed of dogs that was in the books, but it acted very differently. Whatever this boy did he got into trouble. The very things the boys in the books got rewarded for turned out to be about the most unprofitable things he could invest in.

Once, when he was on his way to Sunday-school, he saw some bad boys starting off pleasuring in a sailboat. He was filled with consternation, because he knew from his reading that boys who went sailing on Sunday invariably got drowned. So he ran out on a raft to warn them, but a log turned with him and slid him into the river. A man got him out pretty soon, and the doctor pumped the water out of him, and gave him a fresh start with his bellows, but he caught cold and lay sick abed nine weeks. But the most unaccountable thing about it was that the bad boys in the boat had a good time all day, and then reached home alive and well in the most surprising manner. Jacob Blivens said there was nothing like these things in the books. He was perfectly dumfounded.

When he got well he was a little discouraged, but he resolved to keep on trying anyhow. He knew that so far his experiences wouldn't do to go in a book, but he hadn't yet reached the allotted term of life for good little boys, and he hoped to be able to make a record yet if he could hold on till his time was fully up. If everything else failed he had his dying speech to fall back on.

He examined his authorities, and found that it was now

time for him to go to sea as a cabin-boy. He called on a ship-captain and made his application, and when the captain asked for his recommendations he proudly drew out a tract and pointed to the word, 'To Jacob Blivens, from his affectionate teacher.' But the captain was a coarse, vulgar man, and he said, 'Oh, that be blowed! that wasn't any proof that he knew how to wash dishes or handle a slush-bucket, and he guessed he didn't want him.' This was altogether the most extraordinary thing that ever happened to Jacob in all his life. A compliment from a teacher, on a tract, had never failed to move the tenderest emotions of ship-captains, and open the way to all offices of honour and profit in their gift—it never had in any book that ever he had read. He could hardly believe his senses.

This boy always had a hard time of it. Nothing ever came out according to the authorities with him. At last, one day, when he was around hunting up bad little boys to admonish, he found a lot of them in the old iron-foundry fixing up a little joke on fourteen or fifteen dogs, which they had tied together in long procession, and were going to ornament with empty nitroglycerin cans made fast to their tails. Jacob's heart was touched. He sat down on one of those cans (for he never minded grease when duty was before him), and he took hold of the foremost dog by the collar, and turned his reproving eye upon wicked Tom Jones. But just at that moment Alderman McWelter, full of wrath, stepped in. All the bad boys ran away, but Jacob Blivens rose in conscious innocence and began one of those stately little Sunday-school-book speeches which always commence with 'Oh, sir!' in dead opposition to the fact that no boy, good or bad, ever starts a remark with 'Oh, sir.' But the alderman never waited to hear the rest. He took Jacob Blivens by the ear and turned him around, and hit him a whack in the rear with the flat of his hand; and in an instant that good little boy shot out through the roof and soared away toward the sun with the fragments of those fifteen dogs stringing after him like the tail of a kite. And there wasn't a sign of that alderman or that old iron-foundry left on the face of the earth; and, as for young Jacob Blivens, he never got a chance to make his last dying speech after all his trouble fixing it up, unless he made it to the birds; because, although the bulk of him came down all right in a tree-top in an adjoining county, the rest of him was apportioned around among four townships, and so they had to hold five inquests on him to find out whether he was dead or not, and how it occurred. You never saw a boy scattered so.—[This glycerin catastrophe is borrowed from a floating newspaper item, whose author's name I would give if I knew it.—M. T.]

Thus perished the good little boy who did the best he could, but didn't come out according to the books. Every boy who ever did as he did prospered except him. His case is truly remarkable. It will probably never be accounted for.

39

TEDDY MARTIN'S BRIEF

William Mackay

Teddy Martin occupied chambers in Lime Court, Temple. His rooms were situated on the first floor, and from his front window the visitor could command an uninterrupted view of the sundial over the way, upon which was inscribed one of those useful moral legends which in earlier times our rude forefathers were accustomed to carve upon such slabs as marked the flight of time. Those who trod the well-worn flags of Lime Court would sometimes hear the tinkling of a piano welling out over the geraniums in those front windows, and sometimes the piano would tinkle an accompaniment to snatches of opera-bouffe sung by a showy but somewhat unsympathetic female voice. Barristers' clerks passing beneath and hearing this harmony would wink knowingly at each other, and interchange opinions regarding the Martin *ménage*.

All the world knows of Martin's celebrated 'Crystal Ale' at nine shillings the nine-gallon cask. Teddy Martin was the son of the maker of that famous brew. It will be, therefore, inferred that the young man was not quite so dependent on the support of solicitors as other members of his Inn. Indeed, his allowance was so large as to make him the envy of many brilliant but impecunious members of the Junior Bar, who hated him for his prosperity, and grudged him the briefs which at long intervals were confided to his care.

Like many other young gentlemen of taste and fortune, Teddy Martin was a persistent supporter of the British Drama. He was quite catholic in his tastes. Irving was not too dull for him; nor was the Gaiety too fast. If, indeed, the truth must be told, he preferred those theatres at which burlesque entertainment formed the staple fare; and even found amusement in the festive society of those vestals whose agreeable mission it is to keep burning the sacred lamp of burlesque. He formed acquaintance with the ladies of the chorus. A member of the Junior Bar, he cultivated the society of members of the Junior Stage.

It was the voice of one of these sirens which woke the echoes in Lime Court after the shadows had fallen and the lamp had been lit in the court below, and which scandalized Mr Solon, Q.C., struggling with a brief of several hundred folios in the chambers beneath.

Martin has never inquired into my domestic secrets, and I have no wish to inquire into Martin's. Topsy Varden, it is true, left the stage shortly after she had become acquainted with Mr Martin; had appeared in his chambers, and had taken possession of his piano. I have met her there, but know no more than the porter whether she resided in Lime Court *en permanence* or whether she only visited Mr Martin, for whom she seemed to have a great partiality. Perhaps she came early in the morning and returned late at night to her mother in Camden Town.

At that time I was writing dramatic notices for the *Slough of Despond*—a Society organ—and was, when I visited Teddy's chambers, the subject of a vast amount of agreeable wheedling on the part of Miss Varden, who assured me that she never would be happy off the stage—*that* she wouldn't; that she knew of my influence with Jones of the Royal Bandbox, and with Robinson of the Royal Potentates' Theatres, and that if I didn't get her a 'shop' at one of the houses in question I was a wretch—*that* I was. In fact, she talked of nothing else; didn't appear to know anything that was going on in the world, and never read any newspaper except the *Mummers' Mouthpiece*.

One morning I called on Teddy Martin, and found him at breakfast. Topsy had arrived very early that morning, apparently, for she was at breakfast with her admirer, and had done him the compliment to come in a white morning gown, with wonderful arrangements in lace at the throat and wrists. I found the ingenuous Martin in high glee over a brief for the prosecution in a case in which he was to appear that day at the Old Bailey.

'Come with me, my boy,' he exclaimed; 'it's a great case. And if only my learned leader *would* absent himself, I'd give them a taste of my quality.'

I had nothing better to do, and consented.

'Take *me* too,' said Miss Topsy, with an admirable affectation of piteous imploring. It was bad enough for Topsy to visit at his chambers, but he was not likely to run the risk of flaunting her gay presence in the temple of justice herself. He put her off with a kind word, adding:

'But you'll be here when we return; we'll all go to dinner at Verrey's, have a box at the theatre, and enjoy ourselves amazingly, eh? And you'll come with us, old fellow, won't you?'

Again I consented. We took leave of the fair young creature, and when we got to the bottom of the court, heard strains of 'The Blue Alsatian Mountains' trilling over the flower-boxes on the window-sill.

'Capital girl that,' said Teddy, pressing my arm; 'good as gold—all heart, and that sort of thing.'

'Of course,' I answered. The expression of one's real sentiments under such circumstances is not only extremely ill-bred, but it will most assuredly serve to fan the flame in your friend's heart, and gain for yourself his everlasting distrust. So I said 'Of course,' and we tramped through Fleet Street, up Ludgate Hill, and turned into the Old Bailey, closely followed by Teddy's little clerk bearing Teddy's blue bag, with his initials beautifully worked in white silk on the outside.

The case in which Teddy was concerned lasted all day. But besides opening it in a somewhat abashed and hesitating way, and thereafter cross-examining an utterly unimportant witness, I could not see that Teddy had much more to do with the case than myself, who had been accommodated with a seat in the row of benches apportioned to the bar, situated just behind my friend. All the real work was performed by Mr Rowland, Q.C., who prosecuted for the Treasury; and to his skill, resource and mastery of details, it appeared to me, the conviction of the prisoner was entirely attributable. I merely mention this because I subsequently heard Teddy take to himself all the credit of having secured the verdict on that memorable occasion.

After the unfortunate man in the dock had been sentenced and removed to the seclusion of his cell, Teddy packed up his papers, stuffed them into his bag, and leaving that receptacle to be removed by his clerk, accompanied me back to Lime Court. The piano was still going, and the voice of the siren gave forth the brisk chorus of a bouffe drinking-song.

Topsy Varden must have visited her home with her mother in Camden Town during our absence in Court, for she had abandoned the white breakfast gown of the morning, and was arrayed in a costly dinner dress, so arranged as to exhibit a great amount of her arms and chest. As Teddy saluted her it was evident that his admiration was sincere. Her reciprocal expression was that of an actress—hollow, insincere, worthless.

'I've had such a win, Topsy!'

'Have you been bettin'? Am I on?' were the rapid questions of this child of art.

'You little silly! I mean at the Old Bailey. I've got my man convicted. He's to be hanged by the neck until death by strangulation ensues.'

'La!' exclaimed Topsy. She would have been much more interested if the win had been on the turf. She, however, thought it well to add, 'What did he do?'

'Shot a bobby—desperate character—think he'd have shot *me* if he'd had a chance. Funny defence that,' he said, turning to me.

The defence had been that his brain had been turned—that he had been a respectable working man until a dearly beloved sister of his had left him and 'gone wrong.' He had been 'queer' ever since, said some of the witnesses. But that was surely no reason why he should go about the streets shooting policemen. So the jury did its duty and the judge did *his*—with a black cap on his head.

As this explanation of the defence was given, I noticed that Topsy's expressionless face grew pale, and her bosom rose and fell quickly above her dress. Her voice was thick as she asked,—

'And—who—was—he? What—was—his—name?'

My friend replied briefly,—

'Jabez Omrod.'

Topsy sprang towards him with flashing eyes, as though to clutch his throat; but before she could accomplish her object, she fell back, and in falling moaned almost inarticulately,—

'You have killed my brother!'

∞

Since that day Teddy has never held a brief, nor does he appear anxious to hold one. His interest in the minor ornaments of the drama has considerably abated. I know not what has become of the ill-fated Topsy. Perhaps she has returned for good to her mother in Camden Town.

40

BLUEBEARD'S CUPBOARD

William Mackay

Mr Augustus Lincoln was the manager of the Theatre Royal, Sheppey Island. He was an actor of the old school, and illustrated with great success the charnel house department of dramatic literature. Regarded simply from an artistic point of view, the performances given at the Theatre Royal may be described as fine and even formidable representations, but commercially considered they could scarcely be regarded as triumphs. The Sheppey Islanders were, at the time of which we are writing, people of a low and degraded taste, and showed a grovelling preference for the entertainments given at the music-halls. The permission to indulge in beer and tobacco, which is accorded in Caves of Harmony, may have had something to do with this preference; but it must be admitted that the Islanders considered 'Hamlet,' 'The Stranger,' and 'The Iron Chest,' a trifle gloomy, even when illuminated by the genius of Mr Augustus Lincoln. Indeed, had it not been for an accident, this enterprising lessee and manager would have been obliged, long before the incidents about to be related, to shut up his theatre and appear in a highly popular *rôle* on the stage of the Bankruptcy Court.

Mr Lincoln's accident was the Amateur. That most

industrious and most sanguine of mortals, having hawked his comedies, melodramas, and romantic plays to all the London managers with all the customary want of success, determined that Something must be Done. If caterers in the West End, blind to their own interests, and careless of the intellectual elevation of their patrons, refused to give him a show, as the bald phraseology of the stage has it, the amateur, with fine philanthropic feeling, determined to give himself a show. Now the Theatre Royal, Sheppey Island, was very often closed, and on such occasions, when he could raise a sufficient sum to pay for the advertisement, the circumstance was duly announced in the *Era*. It was through the medium of that highly diverting miscellany that Lincoln and the Amateur were brought together. And from the moment that introduction was effected, Lincoln never knew what it was to have the brokers in the house, an incident which, up to that time, was of not unfrequent occurrence.

The manager was an enthusiast in his way, and threw his whole heart and soul into playing the leading characters in the amateur comedies, melodramas and romantic plays which he placed on his stage. And the ambitious authors who resorted to this means of publicity, were as a rule, so extremely pleased with the histrionic efforts of Mr Lincoln, that in addition to the sum agreed upon for the representation, most of the mute inglorious ones would insist on making a little present to the conscientious manager-actor. But Mr Lincoln was as proud as an Elliston, and carried himself with as much dignity. So that whenever the token of the Amateur's gratitude was offered in the shape of money, the offended manager would draw himself grandly up and say, 'Sir, I cannot accept a gift of money; though should you like to present me with a new hat, I shall not say you nay.' The Amateur usually took the hint, and in a few days a band-box containing a hat, was duly delivered at the stage door of the Theatre Royal. Yet strange to say, no Sheppey Islander had ever seen Mr Lincoln in a new hat. Indeed, they had never seen him except in a very old one, which by a judicious use of oil and a silk handkerchief, showed bravely enough when cocked on the side of Mr Lincoln's head.

It is, of course, easy to guess the reason of this. The Amateur donors never thought of consulting their benefactor as to the size of his head, or as to the peculiar shape which he most affected. And so it happened, that not one of the head-dresses sent to him was of any practical benefit. For if it happened to be anything like a fit, it was sure to be of a shape to which Mr Lincoln would not condescend. He had not, however, discarded them, but had placed them carefully in a cupboard in his bedroom, which cupboard he always kept carefully locked, carrying the key of it on his bunch. At rare intervals he would exhibit his collection to some old crony—just as a collector would show his pictures, or a connoisseur his cellar. Connected with each hat was a memory. The entire assortment was a sort of history of the Theatre Royal, Sheppey Island, and as he pointed out the trophies he would couple with each the name of the amateur drama, the triumphant success of which it was intended to commemorate. Thus he would point to a tall beaver, with preposterous brim, such as comic artists place on the head of John Bull, and say,—'That is my Queen of Circassia's hat;' or he would exhibit a light gossamer of most undoubtedly dandaical proportions, saying,—'That is my Murdered Monk's hat;'—so on through the collection. There was a 'Prodigal Son's' hat, and an 'Act on the Square' hat. The hat of the 'Pilgrim Fathers—a Nautical Drama,' and the hat of 'The Little Pig that Paid the Rent; an Irish Tragedy.'

Mr Lincoln was more proud of his hats than of any other

circumstance connected with his theatrical career—save one, and that was, that Mr Gladstone had seen him play Hamlet and had expressed himself entirely satisfied with the performance.

In an evil moment, and at the mature age of fifty-two, Mr Augustus Lincoln fell in love, and as often happens with the intellectually great, he fell in love with the very last person in the world whom he ought to have sought. Milly Brassey was a pert, pink-cheeked, saucy-eyed beauty, who played chambermaid parts in his company. The Amateurs thought very much of Milly, and as she was not proud in the matter of receiving presents, it may be taken for granted that the sealskin jacket and diamond rings came from the gifted creatures whose works she had helped to illustrate. Off the stage she was a giddy, giggling little woman, always ready for a flirtation, and was madly loved by the *jeune premier*, and the low comedian of the company. Indeed, it is a matter of notoriety that a hostile meeting would have taken place between these jealous lovers had it not transpired that Milly was about to be led to the altar by the manager himself. So instead of meeting in Greenwich Park over the murderous muzzles of revolvers, they met in the 'Goat and Compasses' over two glasses of cold gin.

Lincoln's wedding was a very quiet affair. After all, no such very great change was to take place in the life of the bride. She was already a member of Lincoln's company. She had now become a member of his household as well. Milly was a clever little actress, and if she did not really love her husband, she made that devoted man think that she did. His faith in her was unlimited, and although others thought that she flirted alternately with Philip Beresford, the jeune premier, and with Alf. Wild, the low comedian, Lincoln with a firm belief in his wife's honesty and a still firmer belief in his own charms, saw nothing whatever. He was perfectly contented, and the amateurs, increasing in perseverance and impatience, brought him month after month new dramas for illustration, and new hats in token of esteem.

All might have gone well had it not been for the hats. Everybody in Lincoln's company wanted a hat. Neither a jeune premier, nor a low comedian, can afford an unstinted indulgence in hats on two pounds a week, even when that modest stipend is regularly paid. Actors usually carry large ulster-cloaks that cover a multitude of sins. But a bad hat or a bad boot is always *en évidence*. To say that Milly was gifted with curiosity is simply to say that Milly was a woman. That she soon began to question her husband as to the contents of the locked cupboard, therefore goes without saying. But although Lincoln would have trusted her with almost any other secret, he was reticent concerning this. He had a sort of prescience that the volatile Milly might turn his collection into ridicule, and merely observing in answer to his wife's queries that it was 'Bluebeard's Cupboard,' refused to be further cross-examined on the subject. Milly promised not to annoy him any more in the matter, and religiously kept her promise; only when he was out she tried every key in the house on the lock that kept her from a delightful mystery, and at last she found one that fitted, and opening 'Bluebeard's Cupboard' found it full,—not of heads without hats, but of hats without heads. So full was the cupboard of these samples of the hatter's art, that she selected two, feeling confident, that from so large a bag, a brace would never be missed. These she secreted, and when her husband returned (he had gone to meet an Amateur, who was big with a tragedy called 'The Paralytic'), she met him with a kiss, and they were quite happy till it was time to go to the theatre.

A week afterwards another Amateur wanted to see Mr Lincoln. On this occasion the appointment was made at a Club in Adelphi Terrace. The interview was a short one, and Mr Lincoln was able to bend his steps eastward some two hours before the time he had mentioned to Milly. He had to make a call in Greenwich, and in the Main Street of that highly-depressing village, he happened to look over the blind in a pastry cook's window. He stopped suddenly, and shouted in a tone of the utmost consternation, 'My "Murdered Monk's" hat!' And then after a pause, 'My "Prodigal Son's" hat.' He looked again, and saw that the hats covered the empty heads of Philip Beresford and Alf. Wild, between whom sat his wife devouring open tarts, and laughing consumedly at her own jokes. He entered stealthily, and soon heard enough to show that he, her husband, was the subject of her witticisms. He strode up to them, and smashed the hats over the heads of the wearers, calling them varlets and minions. The Amateur of Adelphi Terrace had been good. So he was enabled to put his hand in his waistcoat pocket, and withdraw six sovereigns. Handing two to each, he said solemnly, 'In lieu of a week's notice. Begone!' and then on his wife making a gesture of remonstrance, he said, in louder tones, 'D'ye hear. All of ye. Begone!' They went. And he has never seen any of them since.

41

THE DEVIL'S PLAYTHINGS

William Mackay

On the first day of April in the year of our Lord one thousand eight hundred and seventy-five the following advertisement appeared in the *Times* newspaper.

> 'Housemaid and Companion.—Wanted immediately a smart active young woman, who thoroughly understands her business: a small house, and only one in family: washing given out: must have first-class references; good wages given; send copies of discharges to Mrs G., Lambird Cottage, Thornton Heath.'

The 'Mrs G.' who advertised in these terms was a widow lady, named Gillison, and among those who applied for the situation was Susan Copeland, of the village of Stockbury in the county of Kent. How a copy of the *Times* happened to arrive in Stockbury, does not appear upon the evidence. But in all probability it had been sent to the Vicar, and the wife of that worthy clergyman, who had an insatiable thirst for the knowledge that is to be obtained from advertisements, came upon this 'Want' of Mrs Gillison, and brought it before the notice of Susan Copeland. Susan was the model villager, the prize-girl of Stockbury, and having served brilliantly as an under nurse to the Vicar's family, she was now anxious, as the saying goes, 'to better herself.' Susan was a tall brown-eyed girl. She affected great simplicity in her dress, wore her hair brushed flat down on her forehead, and in a general way looked more like a Puritan maiden than is customary with the daughters of Kentish farmers. Susan was eighteen years of age, and was engaged to Thomas Ash. As Susan Copeland was the model girl of Stockbury, it was only right that she should become engaged to the model young man. And that young man was Tom. He had secured all the prizes in the Boys' department, while she had been sedulously engaged in acquiring all the honours from the Girls'. Indeed, these two swooped down upon the prize list, and by reason of their superior attainments and conspicuous virtue swept off all before them.

Satisfied with the Vicar's report, Mrs Gillison of Thornton Heath engaged Susan in the real and somewhat unusual capacity of 'Housemaid and Companion' at a yearly salary of £20, which to a Stockbury girl appeared a tolerable fortune. And it was arranged that Thomas Ash should take his betrothed to London, and deliver her safely at the house of Mrs Gillison. There was much sorrow in the village of Stockbury, when Susan took her departure for the great metropolis, and her boxes contained many tokens of the affectionate esteem in which she was held by her contemporaries. All thoughts of rivalry were now lost in a universal sentiment of sorrow. It was felt that in losing Miss Copeland, Stockbury was robbed of much of its moral lustre. It is not necessary to enumerate the presents which her friends forced upon her. Most of them had taken the shape of literature, and ranged from the 'Dairyman's Daughter' to the hymnal of the inimitable Watts; from 'Baxter's Saints' Rest' presented by the Vicar to a highly coloured history of Jack and the Beanstalk, the gift of a small brother. So beloved, respected, and lamented,

Susan left her native village proudly escorted by the man who hereafter was to lead her to the altar.

Mrs Gillison, when she had duly inspected, cross-examined, and examined-in-chief her new 'housemaid and companion,' professed herself entirely satisfied; and Susan, who had a fine literary taste of her own, was delighted to find that her duties would be very light and that she would have the coveted leisure in which to improve her mind. Mrs Gillison was an active, smart little woman, who did her own cooking. There was, moreover, a boy kept on the premises to carry coal, clean boots, and perform other menial offices. Indeed, Susan's duties were, in the first place, to keep clean the few rooms, of which Lambird Cottage consisted, and to afford to Mrs Gillison that companionship which is found desirable by widow ladies of a certain age. Mrs Gillison was not a lady of much education—her husband had been a pork butcher in the Walworth Road—and it was part of Susan's duty to read to her in the evening the entertaining fictions which she purchased when she took her walks abroad. The old lady was omniverous, but chiefly relished the stirring fictions compiled by the Penny Dreadful authors, and at times had appetite for such boy's literature as dealt with pirates or robbers, or the wild Indians of the West. Dickens she rated 'a low feller,' but she revelled in Ouida, and was particularly partial to the earlier fictions of Bulwer Lytton. Susan Copeland's excursions into the field of fiction had hitherto gone no further than 'Ministering Children,' and other books with a religious purpose. Her mind, therefore, became greatly expanded while reading for her mistress, and she became possessed of many views of life, which were to her at once strange and stimulating.

When Susan had been three months with the widow of the pork butcher her mistress handed her five golden sovereigns, that being the amount of wages then due, and Susan went out to the contiguous village of Croydon to purchase a new bonnet. She had never before purchased a head-dress so fashionable. Her tastes, however, had improved since she left the little village of Stockbury, and she wanted a bonnet which would suit the new style of doing her hair; for, with the consent of her mistress, she no longer wore her hair brushed flat down on the forehead like a Puritan, but adopted the fashionable 'fringe' just then, to the eternal shame of English womanhood, coming into vogue. A 'housemaid and companion' is a more privileged person than a housemaid, or a companion, and when Susan returned from Croydon with her purchase she walked into Mrs Gillison's sitting-room without knocking at the door. Mrs Gillison was sitting at the table and started when her servant entered—started, then grew pale, then grew red, and then looked down with a shamefaced expression, more like that of a peccant school-girl than that of a grown woman. On the table before her lay a pack of cards with their faces exposed. Mrs Gillison had, in fact, been discovered in the act of playing 'Patience.' It would be ridiculous to assert that the mere act of engaging in this very monotonous and even foolish pursuit is wicked in itself, and should occasion a blush on the cheek of matured innocence. But Susan Copeland had been brought up to consider cards the devil's plaything, and Mrs Gillison had often heard her express her opinions on the subject, when she happened upon an allusion to the card-table in any of the novels which she read. Indeed, so great was the confusion of the widow at being discovered in the midst of an occupation which that model Sunday scholar regarded with honest and hearty aversion that not only did she blush, she added to her sin by uttering a deliberate falsehood.

'I—I—was only tellin' my fortune,' she said in an apologetic tone.

But in the countenance of her maid she saw pictured neither aversion nor reproach, but only awakened interest and active curiosity. She took up a King and an Ace, regarded them carefully, and then said slowly,—

'And so these are real cards?'

Much relieved her mistress answered,—

'Of course. There ain't much harm in 'em, is there?'

'Not to *look* at,' replied the cautious handmaiden. 'But I suppose the wickedness is in playing with them.'

'Not a bit. There never was a better man than my husband, and me an' him played cribbage every night of our lives.'

Susan never took her eyes off the King and Ace which she still held. She was fascinated. She had even forgotten about her new bonnet. She said in a dreamy, half-conscious sort of way,—

'I believe it must be in the playing the wickedness is. I would like to see what it is. Will you show me—so that I may avoid it?'

Never in her life did Mrs Gillison comply more willingly with a request.

'Of course, my dear, of course. Sit down opposite me there. Pick 'em all up. That's right. Now hand 'em to me. This is the way we shuffle. D'ye see? And that's the way we cut. There's no harm in that, is there? Now run an' fetch the cribbage board off my chest of drawers. It's a long board with ivory in it, an' a lot of little holes at the side. Run along.'

In another half hour Susan had begun to master the intricacies of the game, and was pegging away with an ardour which astonished even Mrs Gillison, who was delighted at this new departure. The last words she said to herself as she turned into bed were,—

'What a treasure that girl is to be sure!'

Strange to relate the following evening found Mrs Gillison

and Susan Copeland sitting at the same table with the same cribbage board between them, evincing the same determined interest in the game. Susan had quite made up her mind that she had not yet arrived at the sinful phase of card playing.

'I suppose,' she ventured on this occasion, 'that the sin of it is when you play for money.'

'I don't see no sin in playin' for money. Me an' my husband always played sixpence a game.'

'Suppose—suppose,' said Susan, doubtfully, 'that we try—just to see.'

Mrs Gillison was delighted. She was at heart as determined a gambler as ever punted at Monaco. She had now discovered in her Paragon the only virtue in which she had considered her wanting. So they continued their game—only playing for sixpences. When Mrs Gillison retired *that* night her last observation was,—

"Ow that gurl do improve in her card playin' to be sure.'

And indeed Mrs Gillison did not do her protégée more than justice. She did improve with rapid strides. The same faculty which enabled her to take away the village school prizes from all comers, now gave her the power of acquiring the mysteries of the pack. In time she began to consider cribbage a somewhat slow amusement, and her mistress, nothing loath, undertook to open up for her the beauties of écarté. This Susan considered an altogether more agreeable pastime. And after she had played it a week her mistress on going to bed made *this* remark,—

'The way that gurl turns up the King is astonishin'.'

It was astonishing. In fact, Susan turned the King up with such success that at the end of twelve months her mistress owed her five hundred pounds which she could not pay. Then it was that Susan discovered the sinfulness of cards. It consisted in playing and not paying. She told her mistress so, and considered that she was only doing her duty as a religious and well brought-up young woman in warning that abandoned person of the danger of giving way to habits of dishonesty. This little monetary difficulty occasioned unpleasantness between mistress and maid. Relations between them became strained. Mrs Gillison was—to use her own expression—dying for a game of cards, and Susan Copeland refused to play except for ready money. Eventually it became so apparent that the unscrupulous old woman either would not or could not pay what she had lost, that Susan in the defence of her just rights was obliged to call in her legal adviser.

Thomas Ash, still true to his Susan, and pining at a separation so lengthened, had obtained a situation in the London police, and although he had not succeeded in getting put upon the Thornton Heath district he felt that he was near his sweetheart, and could occasionally have an interview with her when off duty. One evening Susan told her mistress that her friend had called, and the old lady, now looking worn and faded, followed her maid to the kitchen, where, to her great surprise and terror, she beheld a policeman of formidable size and severe aspect. She burst out crying and begged Susan to spare her—not to arrest her and she would pay all—she would indeed. Thomas Ash reassured the lady, informing her that he was present in his private capacity to advise, not in his public capacity to arrest. He was present to assist, not to alarm. The advice which he gave was simple and direct. He advised her to sell her house and furniture, and so settle Susan's demand. The defaulting gambler at first refused, but Thomas Ash put the heinousness of her crime in such a very strong light that she at last consented, and Lambird Cottage with its contents became the property of strangers.

Ash left the police and took a beer house called the 'Spotted Cow,' and in due course married Susan. They are greatly respected by their customers, and have shown unexampled kindness to the wretched woman, who tried to rob the gentle Susan. They have, for a consideration paid quarterly, given Mrs Gillison a home, and she endeavours to prove her gratitude by doing all the kitchen work, mending the socks of the only child, and preparing the linen, for another which is daily expected. Sometimes Susan will lend her six pennies of an evening with which to play cribbage, and they play quite happily till the Paragon has won the pennies all back again.

42

LOVE AND A DIARY

William Mackay

You will find recorded in a hundred places the history of the flirt, who, carrying her affectation of coldness too far, is misunderstood at last by her lover. He, devoted man, leaves her presence to wander about the world, while she atones for her indiscretion by a life-long repentance. This capricious maiden figures in comedy, tragedy, and farce. She is the heroine of innumerable novels, and her folly and fidelity form the theme of at least one popular song. In this Tale she figures once again; and the only excuse for presenting her is that she appears in connection with a circumstance or coincidence so strange as to appear incredible. It is nevertheless absolutely true.

Those who have followed the red deer on Exmoor need not be told that Dulverton is a hunting centre, situated on the border of Somerset. Such readers will recall, not unpleasantly, the morning bustle in the yard of the 'Lion' when there has been a meet in the neighbourhood. The rubbing down of nags, the excitement of grooms, the greetings of red-coated sportsmen. Among those who most enthusiastically supported the Devon and Somerset Stag hounds at the date of this story's commencement were Squire Arbery and his daughter Kate. She was an excellent horsewoman, and understood the long, precipitous coombes, and knew how to take the deceptive moor-bog, which showed as solid ground to the uninitiated, and was generally in at the death, when the stag, with glassy eye, outstretched tongue and quivering flank, fell beneath the fangs of the pack.

Kate Arbery had performed in such scenes, times without number, and had invariably succeeded in exciting the admiration of the field. The admiration of one unfortunate wight had developed into a passion. His name was Chilcott. The Chilcotts were hunting men from all time, and Henry Chilcott valued his accomplishments because he believed they would give him favour in the eyes of Miss Arbery. Henry was young and enthusiastic. His brother Arthur, who was two years his senior, regarded the infatuation of Henry as one of the heaviest misfortunes which could have befallen him.

'Take my word for it, Harry, she has no heart,' he would say to him at times.

But the other replied lightly that he couldn't see how such an anatomical omission was possible, and fell more and more hopelessly in love every day. These people belonged to the same sphere, and opportunities for the interchange of sentiment were frequent. Upon Henry Chilcott the effect of such interchanges of sentiment with Kate Arbery varied. Sometimes he would return to his home elated, beaming, and hilarious. At other times he would come back down-hearted, misanthropic, and despairing. And his brother, interpreting the symptoms, knew that Kate had given him high reasons for hope, or that she had treated him with studied coldness and hauteur. Harry's nature was a singularly simple and unsuspecting one. He attributed her varying moods to anything but the right cause. But after a year of assiduous attention and of much love-making of the kind when no word of love has been spoken, Harry Chilcott determined to know the worst.

There had been a meet at Anstey Barrows, and after a long and exciting chase the stag was killed at the Water's-meet on the Lynn. But few of those who saw the stag break were in at the death. Among those few were Kate Arbery and her admirer. After they had witnessed the agreeable spectacle of disembowelling 'the stag of ten,' an operation completed with great nicety and despatch by the huntsmen, they rode together slowly in the direction of home—for their horses were by no means so fresh as when they streamed away towards the water from Anstey Barrows. Then he spoke. And she, full of high spirits and the keen sense of enjoyment born of sport, at first bantered her gallant, and then snubbed him. She was simply borne away by a fine flow of animal spirits. He accepted her answers seriously and in silence. He had received his sentence, and he had no right to question the wisdom of the judge. Though she might, he thought, have been less cruelly severe in her manner of awarding it.

The grey shades of evening were closing in by the time they reached her father's gates. As they were flung open, Kate saw that Harry held his horse in.

'You'll come up to the house, will you not?' she said.

He answered sorrowfully,—

'No, I wish to say good-bye.'

'Oh! good-bye, then.'

'But I mean,' he said, 'shake hands with me. For it is good-bye for ever.'

Had he been a close observer of human nature he would have seen that Kate reddened and then turned white. She recovered herself in a moment, however. He approached her. She held out her hand. He bent over it and said 'Good-bye.' She felt a hot tear fall that seemed to burn through her glove. But she only said with supreme airiness of manner, 'Good-bye,' and galloped up through the avenue of chestnuts.

Harry was as good as his word. He took the portion of goods that fell to him, and went into a far country. And now Miss Arbery began to evince an interest in Arthur Chilcott, which she had never before exhibited. She made all sorts of excuses for seeing that gentleman, and at last she did what she might have done before, confessed her love for Harry, and commanded his brother to bring him back to her. Ladies do occasionally make preposterous demands of this sort, imagining that it is the duty of Society at large, to repair the evil of their own making. But Arthur was cynical. He professed himself unable to reconcile Kate's expressions with Kate's actions.

'I will prove to you that I love him. You are his brother. You shall see my diary. You shall read my confessions. And then you will bring him back, will you not?' she pleaded.

To a woman in her present state of mind, Arthur Chilcott knew that he might as well say 'Yes' as anything else. Besides which 'yes' is more easily said than any other word in the language. So he said it; and received, with many injunctions as to strict secrecy, the precious diary. It was folded up in brown paper. He put it into his pocket; took leave of Miss Arbery and the Squire, and went home.

Arthur Chilcott, though capable of advising well when consulted about the affairs of others, was not triumphantly discreet in the conduct of his own. And soon after the departure of his brother, he became very badly afflicted with the mania for that species of gambling, which goes by the name of speculation. He dabbled in all sorts and conditions of stocks, and in the course of a couple of years, had muddled away his whole fortune. Chilcott Manor, with the fine grounds attached, had to be brought to the hammer. The pictures, books, plate, and wines were duly entered in the unsympathetic pages of the auctioneer, and Arthur came up to London, to live in chambers, heartily wishing that he had never indulged in any sport more hazardous than hunting the red-deer of Exmoor.

Harry Chilcott, after many wanderings in foreign lands, during the course of which he had never forwarded an address, or any indication of the course of his aimless adventures, arrived in London. He was tolerably well cured of his passion—or fancied that he was, which is perhaps not exactly the same thing. Happening to pass through Holborn one day, he stopped at the second-hand bookshop of Mr Whalley, and began turning over the volumes that lay higgledy-piggledy in a deal box bearing the intimation, 'All these at fourpence.' Of course this intimation did not mean that the whole boxful would be sold for that ridiculously inadequate sum, but that each volume could be purchased for a simple groat. The box contained a miscellaneous and somewhat battered assortment of literary works. There was an odd volume of Swift's 'Letters to Stella;' a 'Euclid' minus the title page; volume the fourth of Rollin's 'Ancient History;' three or four numbers of 'Blackwood;' a 'Book of Common Prayer' with one clasp, an incomplete copy of 'The Whole Duty of Man' and—

And! what is this?

Harry Chilcott took up a little book of manuscript. His hand trembled as he opened it and gazed at the handwriting. He turned eagerly to the flyleaf. One word was written there—

'Kate.'

It was enough. He ran into the shop, deposited fourpence, and rushed with his prize to the Charing Cross Hotel, at which establishment, probably for economical reasons, he was staying. He locked himself into his room, and as he read page after page, uttered that scrap of autobiographical intelligence, which at some time or other most of the sons of Adam have felt impelled to repeat—'What a fool I have been!' Against the dates of an entire twelve months were entries in which Kate Arbery confessed her affection; entries in which she admitted regret that she should have teased her lover; entries in which she vowed that she would never marry mortal man unless Harry Chilcott asked her to be his.

Finally he turned to the date of the day following that upon which he had bidden her 'good-bye for ever.' And he read thus,—

'(Date.) I have not slept all night thinking of my darling. How could I have been so cruel? He is so patient—so kind. But he did not *mean* "good-bye." It cannot be. I *must* see him. You will come back to me, Harry, I *know* you will. I could cry my eyes out with vexation.'

And so on.

The infatuated man shut the book, and absolutely shouted with exultation,—

'Yes! Kate, I have got your message, and I fly to your arms.'

Before carrying into effect this resolution he purchased garments more suitable to the accepted lover than the rough, and, indeed, eccentric clothes which he had picked up on his travels. Then he wrote to his brother Arthur, believing that unhappy speculator still to be in the neighbourhood of Dulverton, and the following evening he and his portmanteau were delivered safe and sound at the door of the 'Lion.' There was great commotion in the principal room of that famous inn. Indeed, a high carousal was being carried on, and loud songs and louder laughter filled the establishment. Harry was in high spirits himself, and would have joined the hilarious farmers had it not been that the waiter, who conducted him to his room, informed him that the roysterers downstairs were celebrating the marriage of Miss Kate Arbery to Parson Snowe, a ceremony which had been performed that morning in the parish church.

For about an hour the disappointed lover sat silent. Then he took the Diary and wrote in it, 'A wedding present for Parson Snowe.' He wrapped the volume up, addressed it to the reverend bridegroom, and trudged to the post-office with it. Arrived there, however, his better nature triumphed. He went back to the 'Lion,' and undoing the packet turned once more to the page in which Kate commanded him to come back. He reverently kissed the entry. Then he thrust Kate's Diary into the flames, and silently watched it burn away to white ashes.

43

MISS BRILL

Katherine Mansfield

Although it was so brilliantly fine—the blue sky powdered with gold and great spots of light like white wine splashed over the Jardins Publiques—Miss Brill was glad that she had decided on her fur. The air was motionless, but when you opened your mouth there was just a faint chill, like a chill from a glass of iced water before you sip, and now and again a leaf came drifting—from nowhere, from the sky. Miss Brill put up her hand and touched her fur. Dear little thing! It was nice to feel it again. She had taken it out of its box that afternoon, shaken out the moth-powder, given it a good brush, and rubbed the life back into the dim little eyes. 'What has been happening to me?' said the sad little eyes. Oh, how sweet it was to see them snap at her again from the red eiderdown!... But the nose, which was of some black composition, wasn't at all firm. It must have had a knock, somehow. Never mind—a little dab of black sealing-wax when the time came—when it was absolutely necessary.... Little rogue! Yes, she really felt like that about it. Little rogue biting its tail just by her left ear. She could have taken it off and laid it on her lap and stroked it. She felt a tingling in her hands and arms, but that came from walking, she supposed. And when she breathed, something light and sad—

no, not sad, exactly—something gentle seemed to move in her bosom.

There were a number of people out this afternoon, far more than last Sunday. And the band sounded louder and gayer. That was because the Season had begun. For although the band played all the year round on Sundays, out of season it was never the same. It was like someone playing with only the family to listen; it didn't care how it played if there weren't any strangers present. Wasn't the conductor wearing a new coat, too? She was sure it was new. He scraped with his foot and flapped his arms like a rooster about to crow, and the bandsmen sitting in the green rotunda blew out their cheeks and glared at the music. Now there came a little 'flutey' bit—very pretty!—a little chain of bright drops. She was sure it would be repeated. It was; she lifted her head and smiled.

Only two people shared her 'special' seat: a fine old man in a velvet coat, his hands clasped over a huge carved walking-stick, and a big old woman, sitting upright, with a roll of knitting on her embroidered apron. They did not speak. This was disappointing, for Miss Brill always looked forward to the conversation. She had become really quite expert, she thought, at listening as though she didn't listen, at sitting in other people's lives just for a minute while they talked round her.

She glanced, sideways, at the old couple. Perhaps they would go soon. Last Sunday, too, hadn't been as interesting as usual. An Englishman and his wife, he wearing a dreadful Panama hat and she button boots. And she'd gone on the whole time about how she ought to wear spectacles; she knew she needed them; but that it was no good getting any; they'd be sure to break and they'd never keep on. And he'd been so patient. He'd suggested everything—gold rims, the kind that curved round your ears, little pads inside the bridge. No, nothing would please her.

'They'll always be sliding down my nose!' Miss Brill had wanted to shake her.

The old people sat on the bench, still as statues. Never mind, there was always the crowd to watch. To and fro, in front of the flower-beds and the band rotunda, the couples and groups paraded, stopped to talk, to greet, to buy a handful of flowers from the old beggar who had his tray fixed to the railings. Little children ran among them, swooping and laughing; little boys with big white silk bows under their chins, little girls, little French dolls, dressed up in velvet and lace. And sometimes a tiny staggerer came suddenly rocking into the open from under the trees, stopped, stared, as suddenly sat down 'flop,' until its small high-stepping mother, like a young hen, rushed scolding to its rescue. Other people sat on the benches and green chairs, but they were nearly always the same, Sunday after Sunday, and—Miss Brill had often noticed—there was something funny about nearly all of them. They were odd, silent, nearly all old, and from the way they stared they looked as though they'd just come from dark little rooms or even—even cupboards!

Behind the rotunda the slender trees with yellow leaves down drooping, and through them just a line of sea, and beyond the blue sky with gold-veined clouds.

Tum-tum-tum tiddle-um! tiddle-um! tum tiddley-um tum ta! blew the band.

Two young girls in red came by and two young soldiers in blue met them, and they laughed and paired and went off arm-in-arm. Two peasant women with funny straw hats passed, gravely, leading beautiful smoke-coloured donkeys. A cold, pale nun hurried by. A beautiful woman came along and dropped her bunch of violets, and a little boy ran after to hand them to her, and she took them and threw them away as if they'd been poisoned. Dear me! Miss Brill didn't know whether to admire that or not! And now an ermine toque and a gentleman in grey met just in front of her. He was tall, stiff, dignified, and she was wearing the ermine toque she'd bought when her hair was yellow. Now everything, her hair, her face, even her eyes, was the same colour as the shabby ermine, and her hand, in its cleaned glove, lifted to dab her lips, was a tiny yellowish paw. Oh, she was so pleased to see him—delighted! She rather thought they were going to meet that afternoon. She described where she'd been—everywhere, here, there, along by the sea. The day was so charming—didn't he agree? And wouldn't he, perhaps?... But he shook his head, lighted a cigarette, slowly breathed a great deep puff into her face, and even while she was still talking and laughing, flicked the match away and walked on. The ermine toque was alone; she smiled more brightly than ever. But even the band seemed to know what she was feeling and played more softly, played tenderly, and the drum beat, 'The Brute! The Brute!' over and over. What would she do? What was going to happen now? But as Miss Brill wondered, the ermine toque turned, raised her hand as though she'd seen someone else, much nicer, just over there, and pattered away. And the band changed again and played more quickly, more gayly than ever, and the old couple on Miss Brill's seat got up and marched away, and such a funny old man with long whiskers hobbled along in time to the music and was nearly knocked over by four girls walking abreast.

Oh, how fascinating it was! How she enjoyed it! How she loved sitting here, watching it all! It was like a play. It was exactly like a play. Who could believe the sky at the back wasn't painted? But it wasn't till a little brown dog trotted on solemn and then slowly trotted off, like a little 'theatre' dog, a little dog that had been drugged, that Miss Brill discovered what it was that made it so exciting. They were all on the stage. They weren't only the audience, not only looking on; they were acting. Even she had a part and came every Sunday. No doubt somebody would have noticed if she hadn't been there; she was part of the performance after all. How strange she'd never thought of it like that before! And yet it explained why she made such a point of starting from home at just the same time each week—so as not to be late for the performance—and it also explained why she had quite a queer, shy feeling at telling her English pupils how she spent her Sunday afternoons. No wonder! Miss Brill nearly laughed out loud. She was on the stage. She thought of the old invalid gentleman to whom she read the newspaper four afternoons a week while he slept in the garden. She had got quite used to the frail head on the cotton pillow, the hollowed eyes, the open mouth and the high pinched nose. If he'd been dead she mightn't have noticed for weeks; she wouldn't have minded. But suddenly he knew he was having the paper read to him by an actress! 'An actress!' The old head lifted; two points of light quivered in the old eyes. 'An actress—are ye?' And Miss Brill smoothed the newspaper as though it were the manuscript of her part and said gently; 'Yes, I have been an actress for a long time.'

The band had been having a rest. Now they started again. And what they played was warm, sunny, yet there was just a faint chill—a something, what was it?—not sadness—no, not sadness—a something that made you want to sing. The tune lifted, lifted, the light shone; and it seemed to Miss Brill that in another moment all of them, all the whole company, would begin singing. The young ones, the laughing ones who were moving together, they would begin, and the men's voices, very resolute and brave, would join them. And then she too, she too, and the others on the benches—they would come in with a kind of accompaniment—something low, that scarcely rose or fell, something so beautiful—moving.... And Miss Brill's eyes filled with tears and she looked smiling at all the other members of the company. Yes, we understand, we understand, she thought—though what they understood she didn't know.

Just at that moment a boy and girl came and sat down where the old couple had been. They were beautifully dressed; they were in love. The hero and heroine, of course, just arrived from his father's yacht. And still soundlessly singing, still with that trembling smile, Miss Brill prepared to listen.

'No, not now,' said the girl. 'Not here, I can't.'

'But why? Because of that stupid old thing at the end there?' asked the boy. 'Why does she come here at all—who wants her? Why doesn't she keep her silly old mug at home?'

'It's her fu-fur which is so funny,' giggled the girl. 'It's exactly like a fried whiting.'

'Ah, be off with you!' said the boy in an angry whisper. Then: 'Tell me, *ma petite chère*—'

'No, not here,' said the girl. 'Not *yet*.'

∞

On her way home she usually bought a slice of honey-cake at the baker's. It was her Sunday treat. Sometimes there was an almond in her slice, sometimes not. It made a great difference. If there was an almond it was like carrying home a tiny present—a surprise—something that might very well not have been there. She hurried on the almond Sundays and struck the match for the kettle in quite a dashing way.

But to-day she passed the baker's by, climbed the stairs, went into the little dark room—her room like a cupboard—and sat down on the red eiderdown. She sat there for a long time. The box that the fur came out of was on the bed. She unclasped the necklet quickly; quickly, without looking, laid it inside. But when she put the lid on she thought she heard something crying.

44

THE DISTRICT DOCTOR

Ivan Turgenev

One day in autumn on my way back from a remote part of the country I caught cold and fell ill. Fortunately the fever attacked me in the district town at the inn; I sent for the doctor. In half-an-hour the district doctor appeared, a thin, dark-haired man of middle height. He prescribed me the usual sudorific, ordered a mustard-plaster to be put on, very deftly slid a five-ruble note up his sleeve, coughing drily and looking away as he did so, and then was getting up to go home, but somehow fell into talk and remained. I was exhausted with feverishness; I foresaw a sleepless night, and was glad of a little chat with a pleasant companion. Tea was served. My doctor began to converse freely. He was a sensible fellow, and expressed himself with vigour and some humour. Queer things happen in the world: you may live a long while with some people, and be on friendly terms with them, and never once speak openly with them from your soul; with others you have scarcely time to get acquainted, and all at once you are pouring out to him—or he to you—all your secrets, as though you were at confession. I don't know how I gained the confidence of my new friend—anyway, with nothing to lead up to it, he told me a rather curious incident; and here I will report his tale for the information of the indulgent reader. I will try to tell it in the doctor's own words.

'You don't happen to know,' he began in a weak and quavering voice (the common result of the use of unmixed Berezov snuff); 'you don't happen to know the judge here, Mylov, Pavel Lukich?... You don't know him?... Well, it's all the same.' (He cleared his throat and rubbed his eyes.) 'Well, you see, the thing happened, to tell you exactly without mistake, in Lent, at the very time of the thaws. I was sitting at his house—our judge's, you know—playing preference. Our judge is a good fellow, and fond of playing preference. Suddenly' (the doctor made frequent use of this word, suddenly) 'they tell me, "There's a servant asking for you." I say, "What does he want?" They say, "He has brought a note—it must be from a patient." "Give me the note," I say. So it is from a patient—well and good—you understand—it's our bread and butter... But this is how it was: a lady, a widow, writes to me; she says, "My daughter is dying. Come, for God's sake!" she says, "and the horses have been sent for you."... Well, that's all right. But she was twenty miles from the town, and it was midnight out of doors, and the roads in such a state, my word! And as she was poor herself, one could not expect more than two silver rubles, and even that problematic; and perhaps it might only be a matter of a roll of linen and a sack of oatmeal in payment. However, duty, you know, before everything: a fellow-creature may be dying. I hand over my cards at once to Kalliopin, the member of the provincial commission, and return home. I look; a wretched little trap was standing at the steps, with peasant's horses, fat—too fat—and their coat as shaggy as felt; and the coachman sitting with his cap off out of respect. Well, I think to myself, "It's clear, my friend, these patients aren't rolling in riches."... You smile; but I tell you, a poor man like me has to take everything into consideration... If the coachman sits like a prince, and doesn't touch his cap, and even sneers at you behind his beard, and flicks his whip—then you may bet on six rubles. But this case, I saw, had a very different air. However, I think there's no help for it; duty before everything. I snatch up the most necessary drugs, and set off. Will you believe it? I only just managed to get there at all. The road was infernal: streams, snow, watercourses, and the dyke had suddenly burst there—that was the worst of it! However, I arrived at last. It was a little thatched house. There was a light in the windows; that meant they expected me. I was met by an old lady, very venerable, in a cap. "Save her!" she says; "she is dying." I say, "Pray don't distress yourself—where is the invalid?" "Come this way." I see a clean little room, a lamp in the corner; on the bed a girl of twenty, unconscious. She was in a burning heat, and breathing heavily—it was fever. There were two other girls, her sisters, scared and in tears. "Yesterday," they tell me, "she was perfectly well and had a good appetite; this morning she complained of her head, and this evening, suddenly, you see, like this." I say again: "Pray don't be uneasy." It's a doctor's duty, you know—and I went up to her and bled her, told them to put on a mustard-plaster, and prescribed a mixture. Meantime I looked at her; I looked at her, you know—there, by God! I had never seen such a face!—she was a beauty, in a word! I felt quite shaken with pity. Such lovely features; such eyes!... But, thank God! she became easier; she fell into a perspiration, seemed to come to her senses, looked round, smiled, and passed her hand over her face... Her sisters bent over her. They ask, "How are you?" "All right," she says, and turns away. I looked at her; she had fallen asleep. "Well," I say, "now the patient should be left alone." So we all went out on tiptoe; only a maid remained, in case she was wanted. In the parlour there was a samovar standing on the table, and a bottle of rum; in our profession one can't get on without it. They gave me tea; asked me to stop the night... I consented: where could I go, indeed, at that time of night? The old lady kept groaning. "What is it?" I say; "she will live; don't worry yourself; you had better take a little rest yourself; it is about two o'clock." "But will you send to wake me if anything happens?" "Yes, yes." The old lady went away, and the girls too went to their own room; they made up a bed for me in the parlour. Well, I went to bed—but I could not get to sleep, for a wonder! for in reality I was very tired. I could not get my patient out of my head. At last I could not put up with it any longer; I got up suddenly; I think to myself, "I will go and see how the patient is getting on." Her bedroom was next to the parlour. Well, I got up, and gently opened the door—how my heart beat! I looked in: the servant was asleep, her mouth wide open, and even snoring, the wretch! but the patient lay with her face towards me and her arms flung wide apart, poor girl! I went up to her...when suddenly she opened her eyes and stared at me! "Who is it? who is it?" I was in confusion. "Don't be alarmed, madam," I say; "I am the doctor; I have come to see how you feel." "You the doctor?" "Yes, the doctor; your mother sent for me from the town; we have bled you, madam; now pray go to sleep, and in a day or two, please God! we will set you on your feet again." "Ah, yes, yes, doctor, don't let me die...please, please." "Why do you talk like that? God bless you!" She is in a fever again, I think to myself; I felt her pulse; yes, she was feverish. She looked at me, and then took me by the hand. "I will tell you why I don't want to die: I will tell you... Now we are alone; and only, please don't you...not to any one... Listen..." I bent down; she moved her lips quite to my ear; she touched my cheek with her hair—I confess my head went round—and began to whisper... I could make out nothing of it... Ah, she was delirious!... She whispered and whispered, but so quickly, and as if it were not in Russian; at last she finished, and shivering dropped her head on the pillow, and threatened me with her finger: "Remember, doctor, to no one." I calmed her somehow, gave her something to drink, waked the servant, and went away.'

At this point the doctor again took snuff with exasperated energy, and for a moment seemed stupefied by its effects.

'However,' he continued, 'the next day, contrary to my expectations, the patient was no better. I thought and thought, and suddenly decided to remain there, even though my other patients were expecting me... And you know one can't afford to disregard that; one's practice suffers if one does. But, in the first place, the patient was really in danger; and secondly, to tell the truth, I felt strongly drawn to her. Besides, I liked the whole family. Though they were really badly off, they were singularly, I may say, cultivated people... Their father had been a learned man, an author; he died, of course, in poverty, but he had managed before he died to give his children an excellent education; he left a lot of books too. Either because I looked after the invalid very carefully, or for some other reason; anyway, I can venture to say all the household loved me as if I were one of the family... Meantime the roads were in a worse state than ever; all communications, so to say, were cut off completely; even medicine could with difficulty be got from the town... The sick girl was not getting better... Day after day, and day after day...but...here...' (The doctor made a brief pause.) 'I declare I don't know how to tell you.'... (He again took snuff, coughed, and swallowed a little tea.) 'I will tell you without beating about the bush. My patient...how should I say?... Well she had fallen in love with me...or, no, it was not that she was in love...however...really, how should one say?' (The doctor looked down and grew red.) 'No,' he went on quickly, 'in love, indeed! A man should not overestimate himself. She was an educated girl, clever and well-read, and I had even forgotten my Latin, one may say, completely. As to appearance' (the doctor looked himself over with a smile) 'I am nothing to boast of there either. But God Almighty did not make me a fool; I don't take black for white; I know a thing or two; I could see very clearly, for instance that Aleksandra Andreyevna—that was her name—did not feel love for me, but had a friendly, so to say, inclination—a respect or something for me. Though she herself perhaps mistook this sentiment, anyway this was her attitude; you may form your own judgment of it. But,' added the doctor, who had brought out all these disconnected sentences without taking breath, and with obvious embarrassment, 'I seem to be wandering rather—you won't understand anything like this... There, with your leave, I will relate it all in order.'

He drank off a glass of tea, and began in a calmer voice.

'Well, then. My patient kept getting worse and worse. You are not a doctor, my good sir; you cannot understand what passes in a poor fellow's heart, especially at first, when he begins to suspect that the disease is getting the upper hand of him. What becomes of his belief in himself? You suddenly grow so timid; it's indescribable. You fancy then that you have forgotten everything you knew, and that the patient has no faith in you, and that other people begin to notice how distracted you are, and tell you the symptoms with reluctance; that they are looking at you suspiciously, whispering... Ah! it's horrid! There must be a remedy, you think, for this disease, if one could find it. Isn't this it? You try—no, that's not it! You don't allow the medicine the necessary time to do good... You clutch at one thing, then at another. Sometimes you take up a book of medical prescriptions—here it is, you think! Sometimes, by Jove, you pick one out by chance, thinking to leave it to fate... But meantime a fellow-creature's dying, and another doctor would have saved him. "We must have a consultation," you say; "I will not take the responsibility on myself." And what a fool you look at such times! Well, in time you learn to bear it; it's nothing to you. A man has died—but it's not your fault; you treated him by the rules. But what's still more torture to you is to see blind faith in you, and to feel yourself that you are not able to be of use. Well, it was just this blind faith that the whole of Aleksandra Andreyevna's family had in me; they had forgotten to think that their daughter was in danger. I, too, on my side assure them that it's nothing, but meantime my heart sinks into my boots. To add to our troubles, the roads were in such a state that the coachman was gone for whole days together to get medicine. And I never left the patient's room; I could not tear myself away; I tell her amusing stories, you know, and play cards with her. I watch by her side at night. The old mother thanks me with tears in her eyes; but I think to myself, "I don't deserve your gratitude." I frankly confess to you—there is no object in concealing it now—I was in love with my patient. And Aleksandra Andreyevna had grown fond of me; she would not sometimes let any one be in her room but me. She began to talk to me, to ask me questions; where I had studied, how I lived, who are my people, whom I go to see. I feel that she ought not to talk; but to forbid her to—to forbid her resolutely, you know—I could not. Sometimes I held my head in my hands, and asked myself, "What are you doing, villain?"... And she would take my hand and hold it, give me a long, long look, and turn away, sigh, and say, "How good you are!" Her hands were so feverish, her eyes so large and languid... "Yes," she says, "you are a good, kind man; you are not like our neighbours...

No, you are not like that... Why did I not know you till now!" "Aleksandra Andreyevna, calm yourself," I say... "I feel, believe me, I don't know how I have gained...but there, calm yourself... All will be right; you will be well again." And meanwhile I must tell you,' continued the doctor, bending forward and raising his eyebrows, 'that they associated very little with the neighbours, because the smaller people were not on their level, and pride hindered them from being friendly with the rich. I tell you, they were an exceptionally cultivated family; so you know it was gratifying for me. She would only take her medicine from my hands...she would lift herself up, poor girl, with my aid, take it, and gaze at me... My heart felt as if it were bursting. And meanwhile she was growing worse and worse, worse and worse, all the time; she will die, I think to myself; she must die. Believe me, I would sooner have gone to the grave myself; and here were her mother and sisters watching me, looking into my eyes...and their faith in me was wearing away. "Well? how is she?" "Oh, all right, all right!" All right, indeed! My mind was failing me. Well, I was sitting one night alone again by my patient. The maid was sitting there too, and snoring away in full swing; I can't find fault with the poor girl, though; she was worn out too. Aleksandra Andreyevna had felt very unwell all the evening; she was very feverish. Until midnight she kept tossing about; at last she seemed to fall asleep; at least, she lay still without stirring. The lamp was burning in the corner before the holy image. I sat there, you know, with my head bent; I even dozed a little. Suddenly it seemed as though some one touched me in the side; I turned round... Good God! Aleksandra Andreyevna was gazing with intent eyes at me...her lips parted, her cheeks seemed burning. "What is it?" "Doctor, shall I die?" "Merciful Heavens!" "No, doctor, no; please don't tell me I shall live...don't say so...If you knew... Listen! for God's sake don't conceal my real position," and her breath came so fast. "If I can know for certain that I must die...then I will tell you all—all!" "Aleksandra Andreyevna, I beg!" "Listen; I have not been asleep at all... I have been looking at you a long while... For God's sake!... I believe in you; you are a good man, an honest man; I entreat you by all that is sacred in the world— tell me the truth! If you knew how important it is for me... Doctor, for God's sake tell me... Am I in danger?" "What can I tell you, Aleksandra Andreyevna, pray?" "For God's sake, I beseech you!" "I can't disguise from you," I say, "Aleksandra Andreyevna; you are certainly in danger; but God is merciful." "I shall die, I shall die." And it seemed as though she were pleased; her face grew so bright; I was alarmed. "Don't be afraid, don't be afraid! I am not frightened of death at all." She suddenly sat up and leaned on her elbow. "Now...yes, now I can tell you that I thank you with my whole heart...that you are kind and good—that I love you!" I stare at her, like one possessed; it was terrible for me, you know. "Do you hear, I love you!" "Aleksandra Andreyevna, how have I deserved—" "No, no, you don't—you don't understand me."... And suddenly she stretched out her arms, and taking my head in her hands, she kissed it... Believe me, I almost screamed aloud... I threw myself on my knees, and buried my head in the pillow. She did not speak; her fingers trembled in my hair; I listen; she is weeping. I began to soothe her, to assure her... I really don't know what I did say to her. "You will wake up the girl," I say to her; "Aleksandra Andreyevna, I thank you...believe me...calm yourself." "Enough, enough!" she persisted; "never mind all of them; let them wake, then; let them come in—it does not matter; I am dying, you see... And what do you fear? why are you afraid? Lift up your head... Or, perhaps, you don't love me; perhaps I am wrong... In that case, forgive me." "Aleksandra Andreyevna, what are you saying!... I love you, Aleksandra Andreyevna." She looked straight into my eyes, and opened her arms wide. "Then take me in your arms." I tell you frankly, I don't know how it was I did not go mad that night. I feel that my patient is killing herself; I see that she is not fully herself; I understand, too, that if she did not consider herself on the point of death, she would never have thought of me; and, indeed, say what you will, it's hard to die at twenty without having known love; this was what was torturing her; this was why, in despair, she caught at me—do you understand now? But she held me in her arms, and would not let me go. "Have pity on me, Aleksandra Andreyevna, and have pity on yourself," I say. "Why," she says; "what is there to think of? You know I must die." ... This she repeated incessantly... "If I knew that I should return to life, and be a proper young lady again, I should be ashamed...of course, ashamed...but why now?" "But who has said you will die?" "Oh, no, leave off! you will not deceive me; you don't know how to lie—look at your face."... "You shall live, Aleksandra Andreyevna; I will cure you; we will ask your mother's blessing...we will be united—we will be happy." "No, no, I have your word; I must die...you have promised me... you have told me."... It was cruel for me—cruel for many reasons. And see what trifling things can do sometimes; it seems nothing at all, but it's painful. It occurred to her to ask me, what is my name; not my surname, but my first name. I must needs be so unlucky as to be called Trifon. Yes, indeed; Trifon Ivanich. Every one in the house called me doctor. However, there's no help for it. I say, "Trifon, madam." She frowned, shook her head, and muttered something in French—ah, something unpleasant, of course!—and then she laughed—disagreeably too. Well, I spent the whole night with her in this way. Before morning I went away, feeling as though I were mad. When I went again into her room it was daytime, after morning tea. Good God! I could scarcely recognize her; people are laid in their grave looking better than that. I swear to you, on my honour, I don't understand—I absolutely don't understand—now, how I lived through that experience. Three days and nights my patient still lingered on. And what nights! What things she said to me! And on the last night—only imagine to yourself—I was sitting near her, and kept praying to God for one thing only: "Take her," I said, "quickly, and me with her." Suddenly the old mother comes unexpectedly into the room. I had already the evening before told her—the mother—there was little hope, and it would be well to send for a priest. When the sick girl saw her mother she said: "It's very well you have come; look at us, we love one another—we have given each other our word." "What does she say, doctor? what does she say?" I turned livid. "She is wandering," I say; "the fever." But she: "Hush, hush; you told me something quite different just now, and have taken my ring. Why do you pretend? My mother is good—she will forgive—she will understand—and I am dying... I have no need to tell lies; give me your hand." I jumped up and ran out of the room. The old lady, of course, guessed how it was.

'I will not, however, weary you any longer, and to me too, of course, it's painful to recall all this. My patient passed away the next day. God rest her soul!' the doctor added, speaking quickly and with a sigh. 'Before her death she asked her family to go out and leave me alone with her.'

'"Forgive me," she said; "I am perhaps to blame towards you...my illness...but believe me, I have loved no one more than you...do not forget me...keep my ring."'

The doctor turned away; I took his hand.

'Ah!' he said, 'let us talk of something else, or would you

care to play preference for a small stake? It is not for people like me to give way to exalted emotions. There's only one thing for me to think of; how to keep the children from crying and the wife from scolding. Since then, you know, I have had time to enter into lawful wedlock, as they say... Oh...I took a merchant's daughter—seven thousand for her dowry. Her name's Akulina; it goes well with Trifon. She is an ill-tempered woman, I must tell you, but luckily she's asleep all day... Well, shall it be preference?'

We sat down to preference for halfpenny points. Trifon Ivanich won two rubles and a half from me, and went home late, well pleased with his success.

45

HOW A MUZHIK FED TWO OFFICIALS

M.Y. Saltykov

Once upon a time there were two Officials. They were both empty-headed, and so they found themselves one day suddenly transported to an uninhabited isle, as if on a magic carpet.

They had passed their whole life in a Government Department, where records were kept; had been born there, bred there, grown old there, and consequently hadn't the least understanding for anything outside of the Department; and the only words they knew were: 'With assurances of the highest esteem, I am your humble servant.'

But the Department was abolished, and as the services of the two Officials were no longer needed, they were given their freedom. So the retired Officials migrated to Podyacheskaya Street in St Petersburg. Each had his own home, his own cook and his pension.

Waking up on the uninhabited isle, they found themselves lying under the same cover. At first, of course, they couldn't understand what had happened to them, and they spoke as if nothing extraordinary had taken place.

'What a peculiar dream I had last night, your Excellency,' said the one Official. 'It seemed to me as if I were on an uninhabited isle.'

Scarcely had he uttered the words, when he jumped to his feet. The other Official also jumped up.

'Good Lord, what does this mean! Where are we?' they cried out in astonishment.

They felt each other to make sure that they were no longer dreaming, and finally convinced themselves of the sad reality.

Before them stretched the ocean, and behind them was a little spot of earth, beyond which the ocean stretched again. They began to cry—the first time since their Department had been shut down.

They looked at each other, and each noticed that the other was clad in nothing but his night shirt with his order hanging about his neck.

'We really should be having our coffee now,' observed the one Official. Then he bethought himself again of the strange situation he was in and a second time fell to weeping.

'What are we going to do now?' he sobbed. 'Even supposing we were to draw up a report, what good would that do?'

'You know what, your Excellency,' replied the other Official, 'you go to the east and I will go to the west. Toward evening we will come back here again and, perhaps, we shall have found something.'

They started to ascertain which was the east and which was the west. They recalled that the head of their Department had once said to them, 'If you want to know where the east is, then turn your face to the north, and the east will be on your right.' But when they tried to find out which was the north, they turned to the right and to the left and looked around on all sides. Having spent their whole life in the Department of Records, their efforts were all in vain.

'To my mind, your Excellency, the best thing to do would be for you to go to the right and me to go to the left,' said one Official, who had served not only in the Department of Records, but had also been teacher of handwriting in the School for Reserves, and so was a little bit cleverer.

So said, so done. The one Official went to the right. He came upon trees, bearing all sorts of fruits. Gladly would he have plucked an apple, but they all hung so high that he would have been obliged to climb up. He tried to climb up in vain. All he succeeded in doing was tearing his night shirt. Then he struck upon a brook. It was swarming with fish.

'Wouldn't it be wonderful if we had all this fish in Podyacheskaya Street!' he thought, and his mouth watered. Then he entered woods and found partridges, grouse and hares.

'Good Lord, what an abundance of food!' he cried. His hunger was going up tremendously.

But he had to return to the appointed spot with empty hands. He found the other Official waiting for him.

'Well, Your Excellency, how went it? Did you find anything?'

'Nothing but an old number of the *Moscow Gazette*, not another thing.'

The Officials lay down to sleep again, but their empty stomachs gave them no rest. They were partly robbed of their sleep by the thought of who was now enjoying their pension, and partly by the recollection of the fruit, fishes, partridges, grouse and hares that they had seen during the day.

'The human pabulum in its original form flies, swims and grows on trees. Who would have thought it your Excellency?' said the one Official.

'To be sure,' rejoined the other Official. 'I, too, must admit that I had imagined that our breakfast rolls, came into the world just as they appear on the table.'

'From which it is to be deduced that if we want to eat a pheasant, we must catch it first, kill it, pull its feathers and roast it. But how's that to be done?'

'Yes, how's that to be done?' repeated the other Official.

They turned silent and tried again to fall asleep, but their hunger scared sleep away. Before their eyes swarmed flocks of pheasants and ducks, herds of porklings, and they were all so juicy, done so tenderly and garnished so deliciously with olives, capers and pickles.

'I believe I could devour my own boots now,' said the one Official.

'Gloves, are not bad either, especially if they have been born quite mellow,' said the other Official.

The two Officials stared at each other fixedly. In their glances gleamed an evil-boding fire, their teeth chattered and a dull groaning issued from their breasts. Slowly they crept upon each other and suddenly they burst into a fearful frenzy. There was a yelling and groaning, the rags flew about, and the Official who had been teacher of handwriting bit off his colleague's order and swallowed it. However, the sight of blood brought them both back to their senses.

'God help us!' they cried at the same time. 'We certainly don't mean to eat each other up. How could we have come to such a pass as this? What evil genius is making sport of us?'

'We must, by all means, entertain each other to pass the time away, otherwise there will be murder and death,' said the one Official.

'You begin,' said the other.

'Can you explain why it is that the sun first rises and then sets? Why isn't it the reverse?'

'Aren't you a funny man, your Excellency? You get up first, then you go to your office and work there, and at night you lie down to sleep.'

'But why can't one assume the opposite, that is, that one goes to bed, sees all sorts of dream figures, and then gets up?'

'Well, yes, certainly. But when I was still an Official, I always thought this way: "Now it is dawn, then it will be day, then will come supper, and finally will come the time to go to bed."'

The word 'supper' recalled that incident in the day's doings, and the thought of it made both Officials melancholy, so that the conversation came to a halt.

'A doctor once told me that human beings can sustain themselves for a long time on their own juices,' the one Official began again.

'What does that mean?'

'It is quite simple. You see, one's own juices generate other juices, and these in their turn still other juices, and so it goes on until finally all the juices are consumed.'

'And then what happens?'

'Then food has to be taken into the system again.'

'The devil!'

No matter what topic the Officials chose, the conversation invariably reverted to the subject of eating; which only increased their appetite more and more. So they decided to give up talking altogether, and, recollecting the *Moscow Gazette* that the one of them had found, they picked it up and began to read eagerly.

BANQUET GIVEN BY THE MAYOR

'The table was set for one hundred persons. The magnificence of it exceeded all expectations. The remotest provinces were represented at this feast of the gods by the costliest gifts. The golden sturgeon from Sheksna and the silver pheasant from the Caucasian woods held a rendezvous with strawberries so seldom to be had in our latitude in winter…'

'The devil! For God's sake, stop reading, your Excellency. Couldn't you find something else to read about?' cried the other Official in sheer desperation. He snatched the paper from his colleague's hands, and started to read something else.

'Our correspondent in Tula informs us that yesterday a sturgeon was found in the Upa (an event which even the oldest inhabitants cannot recall, and all the more remarkable since they recognized the former police captain in this sturgeon). This was made the occasion for giving a banquet in the club. The prime cause of the banquet was served in a large wooden platter garnished with vinegar pickles. A bunch of parsley stuck out of its mouth. Doctor P——who acted as toast-master saw to it that everybody present got a piece of the sturgeon. The sauces to go with it were unusually varied and delicate—'

'Permit me, your Excellency, it seems to me you are not so careful either in the selection of reading matter,' interrupted the first Official, who secured the *Gazette* again and started to read:

'One of the oldest inhabitants of Viatka has discovered a new and highly original recipe for fish soup. A live cod-fish (*lota vulgaris*) is taken and beaten with a rod until its liver swells up with anger…'

The Officials' heads drooped. Whatever their eyes fell upon had something to do with eating. Even their own thoughts were fatal. No matter how much they tried to keep their minds off beefsteak and the like, it was all in vain; their fancy returned invariably, with irresistible force, back to that for which they were so painfully yearning.

Suddenly an inspiration came to the Official who had once taught handwriting.

'I have it!' he cried delightedly. 'What do you say to this, your Excellency? What do you say to our finding a *muzhik*?'

'A muzhik, your Excellency? What sort of a muzhik?'

'Why a plain ordinary muzhik. A muzhik like all other muzhiks. He would get the breakfast rolls for us right away, and he could also catch partridges and fish for us.'

'Hm, a muzhik. But where are we to fetch one from, if there is no muzhik here?'

'Why shouldn't there be a muzhik here? There are muzhiks everywhere. All one has to do is hunt for them. There certainly must be a muzhik hiding here somewhere so as to get out of working.'

This thought so cheered the Officials that they instantly jumped up to go in search of a muzhik.

For a long while they wandered about on the island without the desired result, until finally a concentrated smell of black bread and old sheep skin assailed their nostrils and guided them in the right direction. There under a tree was a colossal muzhik lying fast asleep with his hands under his head. It was clear that to escape his duty to work he had impudently withdrawn to this island. The indignation of the Officials knew no bounds.

'What, lying asleep here, you lazy-bones you!' they raged at him. 'It is nothing to you that there are two Officials here who are fairly perishing of hunger. Up, forward, march, work.'

The Muzhik rose and looked at the two severe gentlemen standing in front of him. His first thought was to make his escape, but the Officials held him fast.

He had to submit to his fate. He had to work.

First he climbed up on a tree and plucked several dozen of the finest apples for the Officials. He kept a rotten one for himself. Then he turned up the earth and dug out some potatoes. Next he started a fire with two bits of wood that he rubbed against each other. Out of his own hair he made a snare and caught partridges. Over the fire, by this time burning brightly, he cooked so many kinds of food that the question arose in the Officials' minds whether they shouldn't give some to this idler.

Beholding the efforts of the Muzhik, they rejoiced in their hearts. They had already forgotten how the day before they had nearly been perishing of hunger, and all they thought of now was: 'What a good thing it is to be an Official. Nothing bad can ever happen to an Official.'

'Are you satisfied, gentlemen?' the lazy Muzhik asked.

'Yes, we appreciate your industry,' replied the Officials.

'Then you will permit me to rest a little?'

'Go take a little rest, but first make a good strong cord.'

The Muzhik gathered wild hemp stalks, laid them in water, beat them and broke them, and toward evening a good stout cord was ready. The Officials took the cord and bound the Muzhik to a tree, so that he should not run away. Then they laid themselves to sleep.

Thus day after day passed, and the Muzhik became so skilful that he could actually cook soup for the Officials in his bare hands. The Officials had become round and well-fed and happy. It rejoiced them that here they needn't spend any money and that in the meanwhile their pensions were accumulating in St Petersburg.

'What is your opinion, your Excellency,' one said to the other after breakfast one day, 'is the Story of the Tower of Babel true? Don't you think it is simply an allegory?'

'By no means, your Excellency, I think it was something that really happened. What other explanation is there for the existence of so many different languages on earth?'

'Then the Flood must really have taken place, too?'

'Certainly, else how would you explain the existence of Antediluvian animals? Besides, the *Moscow Gazette* says—'

They made search for the old number of the *Moscow Gazette*, seated themselves in the shade, and read the whole sheet from beginning to end. They read of festivities in Moscow, Tula, Penza and Riazan, and strangely enough felt no discomfort at the description of the delicacies served.

There is no saying how long this life might have lasted. Finally, however, it began to bore the Officials. They often thought of their cooks in St Petersburg, and even shed a few tears in secret.

'I wonder how it looks in Podyacheskaya Street now, your Excellency,' one of them said to the other.

'Oh, don't remind me of it, your Excellency. I am pining away with homesickness.'

'It is very nice here. There is really no fault to be found with this place, but the lamb longs for its mother sheep. And it is a pity, too, for the beautiful uniforms.'

'Yes, indeed, a uniform of the fourth class is no joke. The gold embroidery alone is enough to make one dizzy.'

Now they began to importune the Muzhik to find some way of getting them back to Podyacheskaya Street, and strange to say, the Muzhik even knew where Podyacheskaya Street was. He had once drunk beer and mead there, and as the saying goes, everything had run down his beard, alas, but nothing into his mouth. The Officials rejoiced and said: 'We are Officials from Podyacheskaya Street.'

'And I am one of those men—do you remember?—who sit on a scaffolding hung by ropes from the roofs and paint the outside walls. I am one of those who crawl about on the roofs like flies. That is what I am,' replied the Muzhik.

The Muzhik now pondered long and heavily on how to give great pleasure to his Officials, who had been so gracious to him, the lazy-bones, and had not scorned his work. And he actually succeeded in constructing a ship. It was not really a ship, but still it was a vessel that would carry them across the ocean close to Podyacheskaya Street.

'Now, take care, you dog, that you don't drown us,' said the Officials, when they saw the raft rising and falling on the waves.

'Don't be afraid. We muzhiks are used to this,' said the Muzhik, making all the preparations for the journey. He gathered swan's-down and made a couch for his two Officials, then he crossed himself and rowed off from shore.

How frightened the Officials were on the way, how sea-sick they were during the storms, how they scolded the coarse Muzhik for his idleness, can neither be told nor described. The Muzhik, however, just kept rowing on and fed his Officials on herring. At last, they caught sight of dear old Mother Neva. Soon they were in the glorious Catherine Canal, and then, oh joy! they struck the grand Podyacheskaya Street. When the cooks saw their Officials so well-fed, round and so happy, they rejoiced immensely. The Officials drank coffee and rolls, then put on their uniforms and drove to the Pension Bureau. How much money they collected there is another thing that can neither be told nor described. Nor was the Muzhik forgotten. The Officials sent a glass of whiskey out to him and five kopeks.

Now, Muzhik, rejoice.

46

THE SERVANT

S.T. Semyonov

I

Gerasim returned to Moscow just at a time when it was hardest to find work, a short while before Christmas, when a man sticks even to a poor job in the expectation of a present. For three weeks the peasant lad had been going about in vain seeking a position.

He stayed with relatives and friends from his village, and although he had not yet suffered great want, it disheartened him that he, a strong young man, should go without work.

Gerasim had lived in Moscow from early boyhood. When still a mere child, he had gone to work in a brewery as bottle-washer, and later as a lower servant in a house. In the last two years he had been in a merchant's employ, and would still have held that position, had he not been summoned back to his village for military duty. However, he had not been drafted. It seemed dull to him in the village, he was not used to the country life, so he decided he would rather count the stones in Moscow than stay there.

Every minute it was getting to be more and more irksome

for him to be tramping the streets in idleness. Not a stone did he leave unturned in his efforts to secure any sort of work. He plagued all of his acquaintances, he even held up people on the street and asked them if they knew of a situation—all in vain.

Finally Gerasim could no longer bear being a burden on his people. Some of them were annoyed by his coming to them; and others had suffered unpleasantness from their masters on his account. He was altogether at a loss what to do. Sometimes he would go a whole day without eating.

II

One day Gerasim betook himself to a friend from his village, who lived at the extreme outer edge of Moscow, near Sokolnik. The man was coachman to a merchant by the name of Sharov, in whose service he had been for many years. He had ingratiated himself with his master, so that Sharov trusted him absolutely and gave every sign of holding him in high favour. It was the man's glib tongue, chiefly, that had gained him his master's confidence. He told on all the servants, and Sharov valued him for it.

Gerasim approached and greeted him. The coachman gave his guest a proper reception, served him with tea and something to eat, and asked him how he was doing.

'Very badly, Yegor Danilych,' said Gerasim. 'I've been without a job for weeks.'

'Didn't you ask your old employer to take you back?'

'I did.'

'He wouldn't take you again?'

'The position was filled already.'

'That's it. That's the way you young fellows are. You serve your employers so-so, and when you leave your jobs, you usually have muddied up the way back to them. You ought to serve your masters so that they will think a lot of you, and when you come again, they will not refuse you, but rather dismiss the man who has taken your place.'

'How can a man do that? In these days there aren't any employers like that, and we aren't exactly angels, either.'

'What's the use of wasting words? I just want to tell you about myself. If for some reason or other I should ever have to leave this place and go home, not only would Mr Sharov, if I came back, take me on again without a word, but he would be glad to, too.'

Gerasim sat there downcast. He saw his friend was boasting, and it occurred to him to gratify him.

'I know it,' he said. 'But it's hard to find men like you, Yegor Danilych. If you were a poor worker, your master would not have kept you twelve years.'

Yegor smiled. He liked the praise.

'That's it,' he said. 'If you were to live and serve as I do, you wouldn't be out of work for months and months.'

Gerasim made no reply.

Yegor was summoned to his master.

'Wait a moment,' he said to Gerasim. 'I'll be right back.'

'Very well.'

III

Yegor came back and reported that inside of half an hour he would have to have the horses harnessed, ready to drive his master to town. He lighted his pipe and took several turns in the room. Then he came to a halt in front of Gerasim.

'Listen, my boy,' he said, 'if you want, I'll ask my master to take you as a servant here.'

'Does he need a man?'

'We have one, but he's not much good. He's getting old, and it's very hard for him to do the work. It's lucky for us that the neighbourhood isn't a lively one and the police don't make a fuss about things being kept just so, else the old man couldn't manage to keep the place clean enough for them.'

'Oh, if you can, then please do say a word for me, Yegor Danilych. I'll pray for you all my life. I can't stand being without work any longer.'

'All right, I'll speak for you. Come again tomorrow, and in the meantime take this ten-kopek piece. It may come in handy.'

'Thanks, Yegor Danilych. Then you will try for me? Please do me the favour.'

'All right. I'll try for you.'

Gerasim left, and Yegor harnessed up his horses. Then he put on his coachman's habit, and drove up to the front door. Mr Sharov stepped out of the house, seated himself in the sleigh, and the horses galloped off. He attended to his business in town and returned home. Yegor, observing that his master was in a good humour, said to him:

'Yegor Fiodorych, I have a favour to ask of you.'

'What is it?'

'There's a young man from my village here, a good boy. He's without a job.'

'Well?'

'Wouldn't you take him?'

'What do I want him for?'

'Use him as man of all work round the place.'

'How about Polikarpych?'

'What good is he? It's about time you dismissed him.'

'That wouldn't be fair. He has been with me so many years. I can't let him go just so, without any cause.'

'Supposing he *has* worked for you for years. He didn't work for nothing. He got paid for it. He's certainly saved up a few dollars for his old age.'

'Saved up! How could he? From what? He's not alone in the world. He has a wife to support, and she has to eat and drink also.'

'His wife earns money, too, at day's work as charwoman.'

'A lot she could have made! Enough for *kvas*.'

'Why should you care about Polikarpych and his wife? To tell you the truth, he's a very poor servant. Why should you throw your money away on him? He never shovels the snow away on time, or does anything right. And when it comes his turn to be night watchman, he slips away at least ten times a night. It's too cold for him. You'll see, some day, because of him, you will have trouble with the police. The quarterly inspector will descend on us, and it won't be so agreeable for you to be responsible for Polikarpych.'

'Still, it's pretty rough. He's been with me fifteen years. And to treat him that way in his old age—it would be a sin.'

'A sin! Why, what harm would you be doing him? He won't starve. He'll go to the almshouse. It will be better for him, too, to be quiet in his old age.'

Sharov reflected.

'All right,' he said finally. 'Bring your friend here. I'll see what I can do.'

'Do take him, sir. I'm so sorry for him. He's a good boy, and he's been without work for such a long time. I know he'll do his work well and serve you faithfully. On account of having to report for military duty, he lost his last position. If it hadn't been for that, his master would never have let him go.'

IV

The next evening Gerasim came again and asked:

'Well, could you do anything for me?'

'Something, I believe. First let's have some tea. Then we'll go see my master.'

Even tea had no allurements for Gerasim. He was eager for a decision; but under the compulsion of politeness to his host, he gulped down two glasses of tea, and then they betook themselves to Sharov.

Sharov asked Gerasim where he had lived before and what work he could do. Then he told him he was prepared to engage him as man of all work, and he should come back the next day ready to take the place.

Gerasim was fairly stunned by the great stroke of fortune. So overwhelming was his joy that his legs would scarcely carry him. He went to the coachman's room, and Yegor said to him:

'Well, my lad, see to it that you do your work right, so that I shan't have to be ashamed of you. You know what masters are like. If you go wrong once, they'll be at you forever after with their fault-finding, and never give you peace.'

'Don't worry about that, Yegor Danilych.'

'Well—well.'

Gerasim took leave, crossing the yard to go out by the gate. Polikarpych's rooms gave on the yard, and a broad beam of light from the window fell across Gerasim's way. He was curious to get a glimpse of his future home, but the panes were all frosted over, and it was impossible to peep through. However, he could hear what the people inside were saying.

'What will we do now?' was said in a woman's voice.

'I don't know, I don't know,' a man, undoubtedly Polikarpych, replied. 'Go begging, I suppose.'

'That's all we can do. There's nothing else left,' said the woman. 'Oh, we poor people, what a miserable life we lead. We work and work from early morning till late at night, day after day, and when we get old, then it's, "Away with you!"'

'What can we do? Our master is not one of us. It wouldn't be worth the while to say much to him about it. He cares only for his own advantage.'

'All the masters are so mean. They don't think of any one but themselves. It doesn't occur to them that we work for them honestly and faithfully for years, and use up our best strength in their service. They're afraid to keep us a year longer, even though we've got all the strength we need to do their work. If we weren't strong enough, we'd go of our own accord.'

'The master's not so much to blame as his coachman. Yegor Danilych wants to get a good position for his friend.'

'Yes, he's a serpent. He knows how to wag his tongue. You wait, you foul-mouthed beast, I'll get even with you. I'll go straight to the master and tell him how the fellow deceives him, how he steals the hay and fodder. I'll put it down in writing, and he can convince himself how the fellow lies about us all.'

'Don't, old woman. Don't sin.'

'Sin? Isn't what I said all true? I know to a dot what I'm saying, and I mean to tell it straight out to the master. He should see with his own eyes. Why not? What can we do now anyhow? Where shall we go? He's ruined us, ruined us.'

The old woman burst out sobbing.

Gerasim heard all that, and it stabbed him like a dagger. He realized what misfortune he would be bringing the old people, and it made him sick at heart. He stood there a long while, saddened, lost in thought, then he turned and went back into the coachman's room.

'Ah, you forgot something?'

'No, Yegor Danilych.' Gerasim stammered out, 'I've come—listen—I want to thank you ever and ever so much—for the way you received me—and—and all the trouble you took for me—but—I can't take the place.'

'What! What does that mean?'

'Nothing. I don't want the place. I will look for another one for myself.'

Yegor flew into a rage.

'Did you mean to make a fool of me, did you, you idiot? You come here so meek—"Try for me, do try for me"—and then you refuse to take the place. You rascal, you have disgraced me!'

Gerasim found nothing to say in reply. He reddened, and lowered his eyes. Yegor turned his back scornfully and said nothing more.

Then Gerasim quietly picked up his cap and left the coachman's room. He crossed the yard rapidly, went out by the gate, and hurried off down the street. He felt happy and lighthearted.

47

AN OMINOUS BABY

Stephen Crane

A baby was wandering in a strange country. He was a tattered child with a frowsled wealth of yellow hair. His dress, of a checked stuff, was soiled, and showed the marks of many conflicts, like the chain-shirt of a warrior. His sun-tanned knees shone above wrinkled stockings, which he pulled up occasionally with an impatient movement when they entangled his feet. From a gaping shoe there appeared an array of tiny toes.

He was toddling along an avenue between rows of stolid brown houses. He went slowly, with a look of absorbed interest on his small flushed face. His blue eyes stared curiously. Carriages went with a musical rumble over the smooth asphalt. A man with a chrysanthemum was going up steps. Two nursery maids chatted as they walked slowly, while their charges hobnobbed amiably between perambulators. A truck wagon roared thunderously in the distance.

The child from the poor district made his way along the brown street filled with dull grey shadows. High up, near the roofs, glancing sun-rays changed cornices to blazing gold and silvered the fronts of windows. The wandering baby stopped and stared at the two children laughing and playing in their carriages among the heaps of rugs and cushions. He braced his legs apart in an attitude of earnest attention. His lower jaw fell, and disclosed his small, even teeth. As they moved on, he followed the carriages with awe in his face as if contemplating a pageant. Once one of the babies, with twittering laughter, shook a gorgeous rattle at him. He smiled jovially in return.

Finally a nursery maid ceased conversation and, turning, made a gesture of annoyance.

'Go 'way, little boy,' she said to him. 'Go 'way. You're all dirty.'

He gazed at her with infant tranquillity for a moment, and then went slowly off dragging behind him a bit of rope he had acquired in another street. He continued to investigate the new scenes. The people and houses struck him with interest as would flowers and trees. Passengers had to avoid the small, absorbed figure in the middle of the sidewalk. They glanced at the intent baby face covered with scratches and dust as with scars and with powder smoke.

After a time, the wanderer discovered upon the pavement a pretty child in fine clothes playing with a toy. It was a tiny fire-engine, painted brilliantly in crimson and gold. The wheels rattled as its small owner dragged it uproariously about by means of a string. The babe with his bit of rope trailing behind him paused and regarded the child and the toy. For a long while he remained motionless, save for his eyes, which followed all movements of the glittering thing. The owner paid no attention to the spectator, but continued his joyous imitations of phases of the career of a fire-engine. His gleeful baby laugh rang against the calm fronts of the houses. After a little the wandering baby began quietly to sidle nearer. His bit of rope, now forgotten, dropped at his feet. He removed his eyes from the toy and glanced expectantly at the other child.

'Say,' he breathed softly.

The owner of the toy was running down the walk at top speed. His tongue was clanging like a bell and his legs were galloping. He did not look around at the coaxing call from the small tattered figure on the curb.

The wandering baby approached still nearer, and presently spoke again.

'Say,' he murmured, 'le' me play wif it?'

The other child interrupted some shrill tootings. He bended his head and spoke disdainfully over his shoulder.

'No,' he said.

The wanderer retreated to the curb. He failed to notice the bit of rope, once treasured. His eyes followed as before the winding course of the engine, and his tender mouth twitched.

'Say,' he ventured at last, 'is dat yours?'

'Yes,' said the other, tilting his round chin. He drew his property suddenly behind him as if it were menaced. 'Yes,' he repeated, 'it's mine.'

'Well, le' me play wif it?' said the wandering baby, with a trembling note of desire in his voice.

'No,' cried the pretty child with determined lips. 'It's mine. My ma-ma buyed it.'

'Well, tan't I play wif it?' His voice was a sob. He stretched forth little covetous hands.

'No,' the pretty child continued to repeat. 'No, it's mine.'

'Well, I want to play wif it,' wailed the other. A sudden fierce frown mantled his baby face. He clenched his fat hands and advanced with a formidable gesture. He looked some wee battler in a war.

'It's mine! It's mine,' cried the pretty child, his voice in the treble of outraged rights.

'I want it,' roared the wanderer.

'It's mine! It's mine!'

'I want it!'

'It's mine!'

The pretty child retreated to the fence, and there paused at bay. He protected his property with outstretched arms. The small vandal made a charge. There was a short scuffle at the fence. Each grasped the string to the toy and tugged. Their faces were wrinkled with baby rage, the verge of tears. Finally, the child in tatters gave a supreme tug and wrenched the string from the other's hands. He set off rapidly down the street, bearing the toy in his arms. He was weeping with the air of a wronged one who has at last succeeded in achieving his rights. The other baby was squalling lustily. He seemed quite helpless. He rung his chubby hands and railed.

After the small barbarian had got some distance away, he paused and regarded his booty. His little form curved with pride. A soft, gleeful smile loomed through the storm of tears. With great care he prepared the toy for travelling. He stopped a moment on a corner and gazed at the pretty child, whose small figure was quivering with sobs. As the latter began to show signs of beginning pursuit, the little vandal turned and vanished down a dark side street as into a cavern.

48

A GREAT MISTAKE

Stephen Crane

An Italian kept a fruit-stand on a corner where he had good aim at the people who came down from the elevated station, and at those who went along two thronged streets. He sat most of the day in a backless chair that was placed strategically.

There was a babe living hard by, up five flights of stairs, who regarded this Italian as a tremendous being. The babe had investigated this fruit-stand. It had thrilled him as few things he had met with in his travels had thrilled him. The sweets of the world had laid there in dazzling rows, tumbled in luxurious heaps. When he gazed at this Italian seated amid such splendid treasures, his lower lip hung low and his eyes, raised to the vendor's face, were filled with deep respect, worship, as if he saw omnipotence.

The babe came often to this corner. He hovered about the stand and watched each detail of the business. He was fascinated by the tranquillity of the vendor, the majesty of power and possession. At times he was so engrossed in his contemplation that people, hurrying, had to use care to avoid bumping him down.

He had never ventured very near to the stand. It was his

habit to hang warily about the curb. Even there he resembled a babe who looks unbidden at a feast of gods.

One day, however, as the baby was thus staring, the vendor arose, and going along the front of the stand, began to polish oranges with a red pocket handkerchief. The breathless spectator moved across the side walk until his small face almost touched the vendor's sleeve. His fingers were gripped in a fold of his dress.

At last, the Italian finished with the oranges and returned to his chair. He drew a newspaper printed in his language from behind a bunch of bananas. He settled himself in a comfortable position, and began to glare savagely at the print. The babe was left face to face with the massed joys of the world. For a time he was a simple worshipper at this golden shrine. Then tumultuous desires began to shake him. His dreams were of conquest. His lips moved. Presently into his head there came a little plan. He sidled nearer, throwing swift and cunning glances at the Italian. He strove to maintain his conventional manner, but the whole plot was written upon his countenance.

At last he had come near enough to touch the fruit. From the tattered skirt came slowly his small dirty hand. His eyes were still fixed upon the vendor. His features were set, save for the under lip, which had a faint fluttering movement. The hand went forward.

Elevated trains thundered to the station and the stairway poured people upon the sidewalks. There was a deep sea roar from feet and wheels going ceaselessly. None seemed to perceive the babe engaged in a great venture.

The Italian turned his paper. Sudden panic smote the babe. His hand dropped, and he gave vent to a cry of dismay. He remained for a moment staring at the vendor. There was evidently a great debate in his mind. His infant intellect had defined this Italian. The latter was undoubtedly a man who would eat babes that provoked him. And the alarm in the babe when this monarch had turned his newspaper brought vividly before him the consequences if he were detected. But at this moment the vendor gave a blissful grunt, and tilting his chair against a wall, closed his eyes. His paper dropped unheeded.

The babe ceased his scrutiny and again raised his hand. It was moved with supreme caution toward the fruit. The fingers were bent, claw-like, in the manner of great heart-shaking greed. Once he stopped and chattered convulsively, because the vendor moved in his sleep. The babe, with his eyes still upon the Italian, again put forth his hand, and the rapacious fingers closed over a round bulb.

And it was written that the Italian should at this moment open his eyes. He glared at the babe a fierce question. Thereupon the babe thrust the round bulb behind him, and with a face expressive of the deepest guilt, began a wild but elaborate series of gestures declaring his innocence. The Italian howled. He sprang to his feet, and with three steps overtook the babe. He whirled him fiercely, and took from the little fingers a lemon.

49

AN ELOQUENCE OF GRIEF

Stephen Crane

The windows were high and saintly, of the shape that is found in churches. From time to time a policeman at the door spoke sharply to some incoming person. 'Take your hat off!' He displayed in his voice the horror of a priest when the sanctity of a chapel is defied or forgotten. The courtroom was crowded with people who sloped back comfortably in their chairs, regarding with undeviating glances the procession and its attendant and guardian policemen that moved slowly inside the spear-topped railing. All persons connected with a case went close to the magistrate's desk before a word was spoken in the matter, and then their voices were toned to the ordinary talking strength. The crowd in the courtroom could not hear a sentence; they could merely see shifting figures, men that gestured quietly, women that sometimes raised an eager eloquent arm. They could not always see the judge, although they were able to estimate his location by the tall stands surmounted by white globes that were at either hand of him. And so those who had come for curiosity's sweet sake wore an air of being in wait for a cry of anguish, some loud painful protestation that would bring the proper thrill to their jaded, world-weary nerves—wires that refused to vibrate for ordinary affairs.

Inside the railing the court officers shuffled the various groups with speed and skill; and behind the desk the magistrate patiently toiled his way through mazes of wonderful testimony.

In a corner of this space, devoted to those who had business before the judge, an officer in plain clothes stood with a girl that wept constantly. None seemed to notice the girl, and there was no reason why she should be noticed, if the curious in the body of the courtroom were not interested in the devastation which tears bring upon some complexions. Her tears seemed to burn like acid, and they left fierce pink marks on her face. Occasionally the girl looked across the room, where two well-dressed young women and a man stood waiting with the serenity of people who are not concerned as to the interior fittings of a jail.

The business of the court progressed, and presently the girl, the officer, and the well-dressed contingent stood before the judge. Thereupon two lawyers engaged in some preliminary fire-wheels, which were endured generally in silence. The girl, it appeared, was accused of stealing fifty dollars' worth of silk clothing from the room of one of the well-dressed women. She had been a servant in the house.

In a clear way, and with none of the ferocity that an accuser often exhibits in a police-court, calmly and moderately, the two young women gave their testimony. Behind them stood their escort, always mute. His part, evidently, was to furnish the dignity, and he furnished it heavily, almost massively.

When they had finished, the girl told her part. She had full, almost Afric, lips, and they had turned quite white. The lawyer for the others asked some questions, which he did—be it said, in passing—with the air of a man throwing flower-pots at a stone house.

It was a short case and soon finished. At the end of it the

judge said that, considering the evidence, he would have to commit the girl for trial. Instantly the quick-eyed court officer began to clear the way for the next case. The well-dressed women and their escort turned one way and the girl turned another, toward a door with an austere arch leading into a stone-paved passage. Then it was that a great cry rang through the courtroom, the cry of this girl who believed that she was lost.

The loungers, many of them, underwent a spasmodic movement as if they had been knived. The court officers rallied quickly. The girl fell back opportunely for the arms of one of them, and her wild heels clicked twice on the floor. 'I am innocent! Oh, I am innocent!'

People pity those who need none, and the guilty sob alone; but innocent or guilty, this girl's scream described such a profound depth of woe—it was so graphic of grief, that it slit with a dagger's sweep the curtain of common-place, and disclosed the gloom-shrouded spectre that sat in the young girl's heart so plainly, in so universal a tone of the mind, that a man heard expressed some far-off midnight terror of his own thought.

The cries died away down the stone-paved passage. A patrol-man leaned one arm composedly on the railing, and down below him stood an aged, almost toothless wanderer, tottering and grinning.

'Plase, yer honer,' said the old man as the time arrived for him to speak, 'if ye'll lave me go this time, I've niver been dhrunk befoor, sir.'

A court officer lifted his hand to hide a smile.

50

A DETAIL

Stephen Crane

The tiny old lady in the black dress and curious little black bonnet had at first seemed alarmed at the sound made by her feet upon the stone pavements. But later she forgot about it, for she suddenly came into the tempest of the Sixth Avenue shopping district, where from the streams of people and vehicles went up a roar like that from headlong mountain torrents.

She seemed then like a chip that catches, recoils, turns and wheels, a reluctant thing in the clutch of the impetuous river. She hesitated, faltered, debated with herself. Frequently she seemed about to address people; then of a sudden she would evidently lose her courage. Meanwhile the torrent jostled her, swung her this and that way.

At last, however, she saw two young women gazing in at a shop-window. They were well-dressed girls; they wore gowns with enormous sleeves that made them look like full-rigged ships with all sails set. They seemed to have plenty of time; they leisurely scanned the goods in the window. Other people had made the tiny old woman much afraid because obviously they were speeding to keep such tremendously important engagements. She went close to the girls and peered in at the same window. She watched them furtively for a time. Then finally she said—

'Excuse me!'

The girls looked down at this old face with its two large eyes turned towards them.

'Excuse me, can you tell me where I can get any work?'

For an instant the two girls stared. Then they seemed about to exchange a smile, but, at the last moment, they checked it. The tiny old lady's eyes were upon them. She was quaintly serious, silently expectant. She made one marvel that in that face the wrinkles showed no trace of experience, knowledge; they were simply little, soft, innocent creases. As for her glance, it had the trustfulness of ignorance and the candour of babyhood.

'I want to get something to do, because I need the money,' she continued since, in their astonishment, they had not replied to her first question. 'Of course I'm not strong and I couldn't do very much, but I can sew well; and in a house where there was a good many men folks, I could do all the mending. Do you know any place where they would like me to come?'

The young women did then exchange a smile, but it was a subtle tender smile, the edge of personal grief.

'Well, no, *madame*,' hesitatingly said one of them at last; 'I don't think I know any one.'

A shade passed over the tiny old lady's face, a shadow of the wing of disappointment.

'Don't you?' she said, with a little struggle to be brave, in her voice.

Then the girl hastily continued—'But if you will give me your address, I may find some one, and if I do, I will surely let you know of it.'

The tiny old lady dictated her address, bending over to

watch the girl write on a visiting card with a little silver pencil. Then she said—

'I thank you very much.' She bowed to them, smiling, and went on down the avenue.

As for the two girls, they walked to the curb and watched this aged figure, small and frail, in its black gown and curious black bonnet. At last, the crowd, the innumerable wagons, intermingling and changing with uproar and riot, suddenly engulfed it.